SCOTTISH SEA STORIES

SCOTTISH SEA STORIES

SELECTED AND EDITED
by
Glen Murray

POLYGON
EDINBURGH

Published by
Polygon
22 George Square
Edinburgh EH8 9LF

Editorial arrangement and Preface
© Glen Murray 1996.

Reprinted 1998

Other material
© as acknowledged on pages 247–248.

Set in Garamond by Headway Ltd, Glasgow
Printed in Great Britain by Biddles Ltd, Guildford.

ISBN 0 7486 6208 1
A CIP record for this title is available.

The publisher acknowledges subsidy from

THE SCOTTISH ARTS COUNCIL

towards the publication of this volume.

CONTENTS

PREFACE

Apart from a short land border the sea delineates Scotland by a coastline so irregular and so deeply indented that its length is very great for such a small country. Hundreds of islands surround that coast, and great fingers of sea lochs reach inland so far that it is impossible to be in Scotland and be more than fifty miles from the sea. Where the land is inhospitable and the terrain inaccessible the sea has always offered a livelihood, a way to travel and a source of mystery and adventure, insinuating itself into the imagination of the people, ebbing and flowing in their songs and stories.

Traditional tales involving the sea are many and diverse so that those told here in the words of a modern storyteller are the merest tip of a very great iceberg. There may also be written stories from early times whose whereabouts make it impractical to try to track down and whose language make it impractical to reproduce in a book aimed at a general readership. So my selection starts in the eighteenth century with the work of a writer whose name is not generally closely associated with the sea but whose early career gave him a wealth of experience of seafaring life and provided the material for a substantial (and some would argue the most interesting) part of his first novel. *Roderick Random* captures not only the vicissitudes but the sounds and smells of life in the wooden navy, vigorously establishing a tradition of sea writing in both Scottish and English literature.

There are other 'adventure' stories in this selection, but I have tried to represent something of the diversity of Scottish experience of the sea. So the droll humour of Para Handy, the bustle of the Glasgow shipyards, the tough crofting life of the Western Isles and the people who routinely cross the 'narrow seas' of Orkney mingle with some swashbuckling from Michael Scott and David W. Bone's stirring windjammer voyage.

At the end of the day the selection is personal and idiosyncratic. Needless to say, there is more good Scottish sea writing omitted than included and many aspects of Scots maritime experience are overlooked. A comprehensive anthology with the same title would be a vastly bigger book. Although most of the authors will be familiar, I have selected less well known or less accessible pieces— the sea passages from *Treasure Island* and *The Silver Darlings*, for example, are too well known to be reproduced here. I have also tried not to define 'story' too restrictively.

However defined, I hope the book will not only give pleasure in its own right but might launch the reader on a voyage of discovery (or rediscovery) of the often apparently sunken treasure of Scottish sea fiction.

Glen Murray

TRADITIONAL TALES

The Kelpie of Corryvreckan

Many years ago, Beltane Eve rejoicings were going on at Moy, not far from Loch Buie in Mull. When the bonfires were blazing, and the dancing and revelry were at a height, there appeared a young and handsome stranger, mounted on a white steed, who seized the loveliest of the village maidens, swung her into the saddle before him, and galloped with her over mountain and moor to the dark sea-shore.

He then dismounted and asked the maiden if she would be his, *a so suas a chaoidh* (for evermore). Bewildered by this tempestuous wooing and weary after travelling the rocky road on horseback, the girl asked if he was taking her to some dwelling across the sea or if he had a ship waiting for her, as she would fain rest. To this he replied:

I have no dwelling beyond the sea,
I have no good ship waiting for thee.
Thou shalt sleep with me on a couch of foam
And the depths of the sea shall be thy home.

Only then did she realise that she had been carried off by none other than the dreaded Kelpie of Corryvreckan, who could assume man's form at will. She turned her eyes on the horse and saw that its saddle was of seaweed, its bridle of pearl, and its bit of coral. Its mane was like the froth of the waves and, as she gazed, it plunged into the billows and became one with the foam of the sea. Its erstwhile rider then seized her in his arms and bore her with him into the green depths. The maiden's shrieks were heard above the loud roaring of the blast as they sank

Down to the rocks where the serpents creep
Twice five hundred fathoms deep.

Next morning, a fisherman saw her corpse floating near the shore and recognised her by her lily-white skin and golden hair. She was buried under a rock on the shore with the dirge of the waves for her requiem. Every year, on Beltane Eve, it is said that the Kelpie gallops across the green on his sea-horse, swift as the wind, with the mournful ghost of a maiden held fast on the saddle before him.

A John o' Groats seal legend

Some years ago, there lived near John o' Groats' house in a small cottage by the shore, a man who made his living by catching seals and selling their skins.

He laughed at the idea that it was unlucky to kill seals and said that they were most worth killing of all animals, for their skins were so large that he got a good deal of money for them.

One day a stranger, mounted on a gigantic horse, rode up to his croft. He called to the seal catcher to come out, saying that his master desired to do business with him. The seal catcher was delighted, and climbed up behind the dark horseman. He soon began to gasp for breath, so fast did they go.

The cold winter's wind that was before them, they overtook her, and the cold winter's wind that was behind them, she did not overtake them. And stop nor stay of that full race did they make none until they came to the brink of the sea. There, on the edge of a precipice, the horseman pulled up his steed and said, 'We have almost reached my master's dwelling.' As he spoke he went to the edge of the cliff and looked down. The seal catcher did the same, and saw nothing but the lonely sea and the grey sky. 'Where is your master?' he asked. For answer, the stranger clasped him in his arms and leapt with him over the precipice. As they passed through the cool darkness of the ocean depths, the seal catcher found that he could breathe quite easily. He felt neither pain nor discomfort; but only an increasing sense of wonder.

At last they came to the bottom of the sea. There were hundreds of seals, young and old, stretched out on the sandy floor of the ocean and, on looking round, the seal catcher saw that his guide had turned into a seal also. He led him to where an old grey seal lay, moaning with pain. Nearby lay a blood-stained knife, which he recognised as his own. Then he remembered that some hours before he had stabbed a seal which had plunged into the sea with the knife in its back.

'This is my master,' said his guide, pointing to the wounded seal. 'It was your hand that wounded him, and your hand alone can heal him.'

Bitterly ashamed of what he had done, the seal catcher bound up the wound to the best of his ability and the old seal rose up strong and well again. The guide said that he would take the seal catcher home again if he would promise never again to hunt seals. This he promised gladly.

The guide changed into the shape of a man once more and, taking the seal catcher by the hand, rose with him through the waves. The horse was waiting on the top of the cliff and they mounted it once more and galloped like the wind until they reached the seal catcher's cottage.

The seal catcher dismounted and the stranger handed him a bag of gold, then, reminding him of his promise, wheeled his horse round and passed swiftly out of sight.

The seal catcher kept his word and never again hunted seals. He prospered and lived happily ever after.

The Mermaid and the Lord of Colonsay

Many years ago, there lived on the island of Colonsay a young chieftain renowned for his prowess in battle. He was betrothed to a beautiful lady whom he loved dearly, and their wedding day had been fixed, when a messenger came across the sea from the King of Scotland asking the Lord of Colonsay to help him to drive off a horde of fierce invaders threatening to take his kingdom.

The chieftain ordered his ship to be made ready and went to bid farewell to his lady. She gave him a ruby ring, telling him to wear it always for her sake. 'As long as my heart is yours,' she said, the jewel will glow with blood-red fire.' He then set off for the wars.

On reaching the mainland he fought with the King against his enemies and overcame them. Once more he set sail for his native isle.

The sea was calm and the rowers strong and when daylight had faded and the moon was casting its silvery gleams over the water the boat was within sight of the island. Full of joy at the prospect of meeting his lady so soon, the young chieftain could not sleep, but paced the deck, looking out across the waves to the land ahead.

Suddenly he saw, reclining on the crest of a wave, a most beautiful maiden, with golden hair reaching to her waist and great blue eyes. Thinking that she must have fallen overboard from some other ship, he called to the crew to cease rowing. But they either would not, or could not, obey him and the boat sped swiftly on. The Lord of Colonsay remembered all he had heard of the merfolk who dwelt in the caves of the ocean, and a shudder crept over him at the thought that he was looking at one of their number. His affection was fixed on the lady he had left on Colonsay and he had no desire to be tempted by a mermaid's siren wiles. He drew back, but as the boat swept past the sea-maiden stretched out a white hand and seizing the unfortunate man round the waist, dived down with him into the depths of the sea.

The boatmen, who had seen nothing of this, soon missed their master and came to the conclusion that he had fallen overboard. They carried back this sad news to the people of Colonsay. They mourned him as dead, but his lady held to the belief that he would one day return alive and well.

Meanwhile, the young chieftain had been carried down through the ocean by his captor. Green and purple distances were above him and green and purple distances below. He saw the sea-monsters heaving past, the hulks of wrecked ships and the bones of drowned mariners; and, further down, where gloom gave way to gloom, vast livid tangles of seaweed that coiled and writhed like living things. At last she brought him to a wonderful region at the bottom of the sea, where the floor was sandy yellow and the roof was the dark blue ocean. Here there were hundreds of caves, all opening out of each other, the sand was covered with pink coral and mother-of-pearl and, half-buried in it, there were jewels and cups and plates of gold and silver that had been taken from the holds of wrecked treasure-ships.

Here the sea-maiden tried by all her wiles to persuade the chieftain to stay, leaning over him so that he could feel the softness of her yellow hair and gaze into the depths of her blue eyes. She spoke to him, and her voice was low and honey-sweet. But he spurned all her advances and, springing to his feet, demanded to be taken back at once to the land above the sea.

'Think better of it,' cried the mermaid. 'If you will not stay with me willingly, I shall place you in a cave, the entrance to which is barred by the sea, and there you shall remain for ever and your lady will waste her life waiting for your return. Think better of it, and give me your love.'

'Never,' replied the young chieftain, declaring that he would rather die than be false.

As he spoke the pink coral, the yellow sand and the treasure-trove vanished from sight and he saw in front of him only a black gaping hole across which the waves dashed, barring any exit. The mermaid plunged through the hole into the sea, lashing the water to fury with her tail.

The chieftain was left alone to mourn his fate and to sigh for his island home and his lady. He often looked at the ruby ring on his finger and saw that it still glowed brightly, and he knew by that that his lady had remained faithful to him. The sight of the blood-red stone always gave him renewed courage.

One day the mermaid swam into the cave, looking more beautiful than ever, with a jewelled comb holding back her golden hair. She spoke gently to him and promised to let him go if he would grant her one favour. When he asked her what she wanted, she replied, 'your ruby ring.'

She had, of course, no intention of letting him go if he gave it to her, but knew that once she had it in her possession she could find a way to send it to the lady as proof of her lover's death. Then, she reasoned, the lady would wed someone else and the knight, believing that she had been unfaithful, would lose all interest in her and be content to dwell for ever under the sea.

But the chieftain saw a chance of escape if he promised to grant her request. He said that he would gladly give her the ring if she would do him a favour in return.

'Carry me once more to the surface of the sea,' he said, 'and let me look for the last time on my beloved island. Then I will give you the ring.'

She bore him upwards through the water to where the stars looked down on Colonsay, then held out her hand for the ring. The chieftain slipped from her grasp and gave a mighty spring on to a ledge of smooth rock that ran out from the shore.

Mad with rage and disappointment at having been outwitted by a mortal, the mermaid dived from sight beneath the waves. The people of Colonsay believe to this day that, when they sail over the spot where she disappeared, they can hear the wild lament which she sighs for ever under the sea for the chieftain she loved and lost.

A PRESS-GANGED SURGEON

I saw no resource but the army or navy, between which I hesitated so long that I found myself reduced to a starving condition. My spirit began to accommodate itself to my beggarly fate, and I became so mean as to go down towards Wapping with an intention to inquire for an old schoolfellow who, I understood, had got command of a small coasting vessel, then in the river, and implore his assistance. But my destiny prevented this abject piece of behaviour; for, as I crossed Tower-wharf, a squat, tawny fellow, with a hanger by his side and a cudgel in his hand, came up to me, calling, 'Yo, ho! Brother, you must come along with me.' As I did not like his appearance, instead of answering his salutation, I quickened my pace, in hope of ridding myself of his company; upon which he whistled aloud and immediately another sailor appeared before me, who laid hold of me by the collar and began to drag me along. Not being of a humour to relish such treatment, I disengaged myself of the assailant, and with one blow of my cudgel, laid him motionless on the ground. Perceiving myself surrounded in a trice by ten or a dozen more, I exerted myself with such dexterity and success that some of my opponents were fain to attack me with drawn cutlasses. After an obstinate engagement, in which I received a large wound on my head, and another on my left cheek, I was disarmed, taken prisoner, and carried on board a pressing tender, where, after being pinioned like a malefactor, I was thrust down into the hold among a parcel of the most miserable wretches, the sight of whom well-nigh distracted me.

As the commanding officer had not humanity enough to order my wounds dressed, and I could not use my own hands, I desired one of my fellow-captives, who was unfettered, to take a handkerchief out of my pocket and tie it round my head to stop the bleeding. He pulled out my handkerchief, 'tis true; but instead of applying it to the use for which I designed it, went to the grating of the hatchway and, with astonishing composure, sold it before my face, to a bum-boat woman then on board, for a quart of gin with which he treated my companions, regardless of my circumstances and entreaties.

I complained bitterly of this robbery to the midshipman on deck, telling him at the same time that unless my hurts were dressed I should bleed to death. But compassion was a weakness of which no man could justly accuse this person who, squirting a mouthful of dissolved tobacco upon me through the gratings, told me I was a mutinous dog, and that I might die and be damned. Finding there was no other remedy, I appealed to patience and laid up this usage in my memory, to be recalled at a fitter season. In the meantime, loss of blood, vexation and want of food contributed, with the noisome stench of the place, to throw me into a swoon, out of which I was recovered by a tweak of the nose, administered by the tar who stood sentinel over us, who at the same time regaled me with a draught of flip, and comforted me with the hopes of being put on board the *Thunder* next day, where I should be freed of my handcuffs and cured of my wounds by the doctor. I no sooner heard him name the *Thunder* than I asked if he had belonged to that ship long. He giving me to understand that he had belonged to her five years, I inquired if he knew Lieutenant Bowling?

'Know Lieutenant Bowling?' said he, 'Odds my life! And that I do! And a good seaman he is, as ever stepped upon forecastle, and a brave fellow as ever cracked biscuit; none of your Guinea pigs, nor your fresh-water, wishy-washy, fair-weather fowls. Many a taut gale of wind has honest Tom Bowling and I weathered together. Here's his health with all my heart, wherever he is, aloft or alow, in heaven or in hell, all's one for that, he need not be ashamed to show himself.'

I was so much affected with this eulogium that I could not refrain from telling him that I was Lieutenant Bowling's kinsman, in consequence of which connection he expressed an inclination to serve me and, when he was relieved, brought some cold boiled beef on a platter, and biscuit, on which we supped plentifully, and afterwards drank another can of flip together.

Next day, along with the other pressed men, I was put aboard the *Thunder*, lying at the Nore. When we came alongside, the mate who guarded us thither ordered my handcuffs to be taken off, that I might get on board the easier. This circumstance being observed by some of the company, who had stood upon the gang-boards to see us enter, one of them called to Jack Rattlin, who was busied in doing this friendly office for me, 'Hey, Jack, what Newgate galley have you boarded in the river as you came along? Have we not thieves enow among us already?' Another, observing my wounds, which remained exposed to the air, told me that my seams were uncaulked and that I must be new payed. A third, seeing my hair clotted together with blood, as it were, into distinct cords, took notice that my bows were manned with red ropes instead of my side. A fourth asked me if I could not keep my yards square without iron braces? And, in short, a thousand witticisms of the same nature were passed upon me before I could get up the ship's side.

After we had been all entered upon the ship's books, I inquired of one of my shipmates where the surgeon was, that I might have my wounds dressed, and had actually got as far as the middle deck (for our ship carried eighty guns) in my way to the cock-pit when I was met by the same midshipman who had used me so barbarously in the tender. He, seeing me free from my chains, asked, with an insolent air, who had released me.

To this question I foolishly answered, with a countenance that too plainly declared the state of my thoughts, 'Whoever did it, I am persuaded did not consult you in the affair.'

I had no sooner uttered these words than he cried, 'Damn you, you saucy son of a bitch. I'll teach you to talk so to your officer.'

So saying, he bestowed on me several severe stripes with a supple-jack he had in his hand and, going to the commanding officer, made such a report of me that I was immediately put in irons by the master-at-arms and a sentinel placed over me.

Honest Rattlin, as soon as he heard of my condition, came to me and administered all the consolation he could, and then went to the surgeon in my behalf, who sent one of his mates to dress my wounds. This mate was no other than Thomson, an old friend with whom I had become acquainted at the Navy Office. If I knew him at first sight, it was not easy for him to recognise me, disfigured with blood and dirt, and altered by the misery I had undergone. Unknown as I was to him, he surveyed me with looks of compassion and handled my sores with great tenderness. When he had applied what he thought proper and was about to leave me, I asked him if my misfortunes had disguised me so much that he could not recollect my face. Upon this address, he observed me with great earnestness for some time, and at length protested he could not recollect one feature of my countenance. To keep him no longer in suspense I told him my name, which, when he heard, he embraced me with affection and professed his sorrow in seeing me in such a disagreeable situation.

I made him acquainted with my story, and when he heard how inhumanly I had been used in the tender he left me abruptly, assuring me I should see him again soon. I had scarce time to wonder at his sudden departure when the master-at-arms came to the place of my confinement and bade me follow him to the quarter-deck, where I was examined by the first lieutenant, who commanded the ship in the absence of the captain, touching the treatment I had received in the tender from my friend the midshipman, who was present to confront me.

I recounted the particulars of his behaviour to me, not only in the tender but since my being on board the ship, part of which being proved by the evidence of Jack Rattlin and others, who had no great devotion for my oppressor, I was discharged from confinement to make way for him, who was delivered to the master-at-arms to take his turn in the bilboes. And this was not the only satisfaction I enjoyed. For I was, at the request of the surgeon, exempted from all other duty than that of assisting the mates in making and administering medicines to the sick. This good office I owed to the friendship of Mr Thomson, who had represented me in such a favourable light to the surgeon that he demanded me of the lieutenant to supply the place of his third mate, who was lately dead.

When I had obtained this favour, my friend Thomson carried me down to the cock-pit, which is the place allotted for the habitation of the surgeon's mates, and when he had shown me their berth, as he called it, I was filled with astonishment and horror. We descended by divers ladders to a space as dark as a dungeon, which I understood was immersed several feet under water, being immediately above the hold. I had no sooner approached this dismal gulf than my nose was saluted with an intolerable stench of putrified cheese and rancid butter, that issued from an apartment at the foot of the ladder, resembling a chandler's shop, where, by the faint glimmering of a candle, I could perceive a man with a pale meagre countenance sitting behind a kind of desk, having spectacles on his nose and a pen in his hand.

This, I learned of Mr Thomson, was the ship's steward, who sat there to distribute provision to the several messes and to mark what each received. He therefore presented my name to him and desired I might be entered in his mess. Then, taking a light in his hand, conducted me to the place of his residence, which was a square of about six feet, surrounded with the medicine chest, that of the first mate, his own, and a board by way of a table, fastened to the after powder-room. It was also enclosed with canvas nailed round to the beams of the ship, to screen us from the cold, as well as from the view of the midshipmen and quartermasters, who lodged within the cable-tiers on each side of us.

In this gloomy mansion he entertained me with some cold salt pork, which he brought from a sort of locker fixed above the table and, calling for the boy of the mess, sent for a can of flip to crown the banquet. By this time I began to recover my spirits, which had been exceedingly depressed by the appearance of everything about me, and could no longer refrain from asking the particulars of Mr Thomson's fortune since I had seen him in London.

He told me that, being disappointed in his expectations of borrowing money to gratify the rapacious secretary at the Navy Office, he found himself utterly unable to subsist any longer in town, and had actually offered his services in quality of mate to the surgeon of a merchant's ship bound to Guinea on the slaving trade, when one morning a young fellow, of whom he had some acquaintance, came to his lodgings and informed him that he had seen a warrant made out in his name at the Navy Office for surgeon's second mate of a third rate. This unexpected piece of good news he could scarcely believe to be true, more especially as he had been found qualified at Surgeon's Hall for third mate only. But, that he might not be wanting to himself, he went thither to be assured, and actually found it so. Whereupon, demanding his warrant, it was delivered to him, and the oaths administered immediately. That very afternoon he went to Gravesend in the tilt-boat, from whence he took a place in the tide-coach for Rochester. Next morning he got on board the *Thunder*, for which he was appointed, then lying in the harbour at Chatham, and the same day was mustered by the clerk of the cheque.

And well it was for him that such expedition was used, for, in less than twelve hours after his arrival, another William Thomson came on board, affirming that he was the person for whom the warrant was expedited and that the other was an imposter. My friend was grievously alarmed at this accident, the more so as his namesake had very much the advantage over him both in assurance and dress. However, to acquit himself of the suspicion of imposture, he produced several letters, written from Scotland to him in that name, and recollecting that his indentures were in a box on board, he brought them up and convinced all present that he had not assumed a name which did not belong to him. His competitor, enraged that they should hesitate in doing him justice (for, to be sure, the warrant had been designed for him), behaved with so much indecent heat that the commanding officer, who was the same gentleman I had seen, and the surgeon, were offended at his presumption and, making a point of it with their friends in town, in less than a week got the first confirmed in his station.

'I have been on board ever since' said he, 'and, as this way of life is become familiar to me, have no cause to complain of my situation. The surgeon is a good-natured, indolent man; the first mate, who is now on shore on duty, is, indeed a little proud and choleric, as all Welshmen are, but, in the main, a friendly, honest fellow. The lieutenants I have no concern with, and as for the captain, he is too much of a gentleman to know a surgeon's mate, even by sight.'

After dinner, Thomson led me round the ship, showed me the different parts, described their uses, and, as far as he could, made me acquainted with the particulars of the discipline and economy practised on board. He then demanded of the boatswain an hammock for me, which was slung in a very neat manner by my friend Jack Rattlin, and, as I had no bedclothes, procured credit for me with the purser for a mattress and two blankets.

At seven o'clock in the evening, Morgan, the surgeon's first mate, visited the sick and ordered what was proper for each. I assisted Thomson in making up his prescriptions. When I followed him with the medicines into the sick berth or hospital and observed the situation of the patients, I was much less surprised that people should die on board than that any sick person should recover. Here I saw about fifty miserable distempered wretches, suspended in rows, so huddled one upon another that not more than fourteen inches of space was allotted for each with his bed and bedding, deprived of the light of day as well as of fresh air, breathing nothing but a noisome atmosphere of the morbid streams exhaling from their own excrements and diseased bodies, devoured with vermin hatched in the filth that surrounded them and destitute of every convenience necessary for people in that helpless condition.

I could not comprehend how it was possible for the attendants to come near those who hung on the inside, towards the sides of the ship, in order to assist them, as they seemed barricadoed by those who lay on the outside and entirely out of the reach of all visitation. Much less could I conceive how my friend Thomson would be able to administer clysters, that were ordered for some in that situation. Then I saw him thrust his wig in his pocket, strip himself to his waistcoat in a moment, creep on all fours under the hammocks of the sick and, forcing up his bare pate between two, keep them asunder with one shoulder until he had done his duty.

Eager to learn the service, I desired he would give me leave to perform the next operation of that kind. He consenting, I undressed myself after his example. As I crawled along, the ship happened to roll. This motion alarming me, I laid hold of the first thing that came within my grasp with such violence that I overturned it, and soon found, by the smell that issued upon me, that I had not unlocked a box of the most delicious perfume. It was well for me that my nose was none of the most delicate, else I know not how I might have been affected by this vapour, which diffused itself all over the ship, to the utter discomposure of everybody who tarried on the same deck.

Neither was the consequence of this disgrace confined to my sense of smelling only, for I felt my misfortunes more ways than one. That I might not appear altogether disconcerted in this my first essay, I got up, and pushing my head with great force between two hammocks towards the middle, where the greatest resistance was, I made an opening. But not understanding the knack of dexterously turning my shoulder to maintain my advantage, I had the mortification to find myself stuck up, as it were in a pillory, and the weight of three or four people bearing on each side of my neck so that I was in danger of strangulation.

While I remained in this defenceless posture, one of the sick men, rendered peevish by his distemper, was so enraged at the smell I had occasioned and the rude shock he had received from me in my elevation that, with many bitter reproaches, he seized me by the nose, which he tweaked so unmercifully that I roared with anguish. Thomson, perceiving my condition, ordered one of the waiters to my assistance, who with much difficulty disengaged me from this situation and hindered me from taking revenge on the sick man, whose indisposition would not have screened him from the effects of my indignation.

Having made an end of our ministry for that time, we descended to the cock-pit and I cleaned myself as soon as possible and dressed myself for supper.

Supper being over, Mr Morgan having smoked a couple of pipes and supplied the moisture he expended with as many cans of flip, of which we all partook, a certain yawning began to admonish me that it was high time to repair by sleep the injury I had suffered from want of rest the preceding night, which being perceived by my companions, whose time of repose was now arrived, they proposed we should turn in, or in other words go to bed.

Our hammocks, which hung parallel to one another on the outside of the berth, were immediately unlashed and I beheld my messmates spring with great agility into their respective nests, where they seemed to lie concealed, very much at their ease. But it was some time before I could prevail upon myself to trust my carcass, at such a distance from the ground, in a narrow bag, out of which I imagined I should be apt, on the least motion in my sleep, to tumble down at the hazard of breaking my bones. I suffered myself, however, to be persuaded and, taking a leap to get in, threw myself quite over with such violence that, had I not luckily got hold of Thomson's hammock, I should have pitched upon my head on the other side, and in all likelihood fractured my skull.

After some fruitless efforts I succeeded at last, but the apprehension of the jeopardy in which I believed myself withstood all the attacks of sleep, till towards the morning watch when, in spite of my fears, I was overwhelmed with slumber. I did not long enjoy this comfortable situation, being aroused with a noise so loud and shrill that I thought the drums of my ears were burst by it. This was followed by a dreadful summons, pronounced by a hoarse voice which I could not understand.

While I was debating with myself whether or not I should wake my companion and inquire into the occasion of this disturbance, I was informed by one of the quartermasters, who passed by me with a lantern in his hand, that the noise that alarmed me was occasioned by the boatswain's mates who called up the larboard watch, and that I must lay my account with such intervention every morning at the same hour. Being now more assured of my safety, I addressed myself again to rest, and slept till eight o'clock.

Rising and breakfasting with my comrades on biscuit and brandy, the sick were visited and assisted as before, after which visitation my good friend Thomson explained and performed another piece of duty to which I was a stranger. At a certain hour of the morning the boy of the mess went round all the decks, ringing a small hand-bell and, in rhymes composed for the occasion, invited all those who had sores to repair before the mast, where one of the doctor's mates attended with applications to dress them.

A short while later, Morgan received a message from the surgeon to bring the sick-list to the quarter-deck, for the captain had ordered all the patients thither to be reviewed. This inhuman order shocked us extremely, as we knew it would be impossible to carry some of them on deck without immediate danger of their lives. But as we likewise knew it would be to no purpose for us to remonstrate against it, we repaired to the quarter-deck in a body to see this extraordinary muster, Morgan observing by the way that the captain was going to send to the other world a great many evidences to testify against himself.

When we appeared on deck, the captain bade the doctor, who stood bowing at his right hand, look at these lazy, lubberly sons of bitches, who were good for nothing on board but to eat the King's provisions and encourage idleness in the skulkers. The surgeon grinned approbation and taking the list, began to examine the complaints of each as they could crawl to the place appointed. The first who came under his cognisance was a poor fellow just freed of a fever, which had weakened him so much that he could hardly stand. Mr Mackshane (for that was the doctor's name), having felt his pulse, protested he was as well as any man in the world, and the captain delivered him over to the boatswain's mate with orders that he should receive a round dozen at the gangway immediately for counterfeiting himself sick. Before the discipline could be executed the man dropped down on the deck and had well-nigh perished under the hands of the executioner.

The next patient to be considered laboured under a quartan ague. Being then in his interval of health, he discovered no other symptoms of distemper than a pale meagre countenance and emaciated body, upon which he was declared fit for duty and turned over to the boatswain. Being resolved to disgrace the doctor, he died upon the forecastle next day during his cold fit. The third complained of a pleuritic stitch and spitting of blood, for which Doctor Mackshane prescribed exercise at the pump, to promote expectoration. Whether this was improper for one in this situation or that it was used to excess, I know not, but in less than half an hour he was suffocated with a deluge of blood that issued from his lungs. A fourth, with much difficulty, climbed to the quarter-deck, being loaded with a monstrous ascites or dropsy that invaded his chest so much he could scarce fetch his breath. But his disease being interpreted into fat, occasioned by idleness and excess of eating, he was ordered, with a view to promote perspiration and enlarge his chest, to go aloft immediately. It was in vain for this unwieldy wretch to allege his utter incapacity; the boatswain's driver was committed to whip him up with a cat-o'-nine-tails. The smart of this application made him exert himself so much that he actually arrived at the puttock shrouds, but when the enormous weight of his body had nothing else to support it than his weakened arms, either out of spite or necessity, he quitted his hold and plumped into the sea, where he must have been drowned had not a sailor, who was in a boat alongside, saved his life by keeping him afloat till he was hoisted on board with a tackle.

It would be tedious and disagreeable to describe the fate of every miserable wretch that suffered by the inhumanity and ignorance of the captain and surgeon, who so wantonly sacrificed the lives of their fellow-creatures. Many were brought up in the height of fevers and rendered delirious by the injuries they received in the way. Some gave up the ghost in the presence of their inspectors, and others, who were ordered to their duty, languished a few days at work among their fellows and then departed without any ceremony. On the whole, the number of the sick was reduced to less than a dozen, and the authors of this reduction applauded themselves for the service they had done to their king and country.

We stayed not long at the Downs, but took the benefit of the first easterly wind to go round to Spithead. Having received on board provisions for six months, we sailed from St Helen's in the grand fleet bound for the West Indies on the ever memorable expedition of Carthagena.

It was not without great mortification that I saw myself on the point of being transported to such a distant and unhealthy climate, destitute of every convenience that could render such a voyage supportable and under the dominion of an arbitrary tyrant, whose command was almost intolerable. However, as these complaints were common to a great many on board I resolved to submit patiently to my fate and contrive to make myself as easy as the nature of the case would allow.

We got out of the Channel with a prosperous breeze, which died away leaving us becalmed about fifty leagues to the westward of the Lizard. But this state of inaction did not last long, for next night our main-topsail was split by the wind, which in the morning increased to a hurricane. I was awakened by a most horrible din, occasioned by the play of the gun-carriages upon the deck above, the cracking of cabins, the howling of the wind through the shrouds, the confused noise of the ship's crew, the pipes of the boatswain and his mates, the trumpets of the lieutenants and the clanking of the chain pumps. Morgan, who had never been at sea before, turned out in a great hurry, crying, 'Got have mercy and compassion upon us! I believe we have got upon the confines of Lucifer and the damned!' while poor Thomson lay quaking in his hammock, putting up petitions to Heaven for our safety. I rose and joined the Welshman with whom, after we had fortified ourselves with brandy, I went above. If my sense of hearing was startled before, how must my sight have been appalled in beholding the effects of the storm!

The sea was swelled into billows mountain-high, on the top of which our ship sometimes hung as if it was about to be precipitated to the abyss below! Sometimes we sank between two waves that rose on each side higher than our top-mast head and threatened, by dashing together, to overwhelm us in a moment! Of all our fleet, consisting of a hundred and fifty sail, scarce twelve appeared, and these driving under their bare poles at the mercy of the tempest. At length the mast of one of them gave way and tumbled overboard with a hideous crash! Nor was the prospect in our own ship much more agreeable. A number of officers and sailors ran backward and forward with distraction in their looks, hallooing to one another and undetermined what they should attend to first. Some clung to the yards, endeavouring to unbend the sails that were split into a thousand pieces, flapping in the wind. Others tried to furl those that were yet whole, while the masts, at every pitch, bent and quivered like twigs, as if they would have shivered into innumerable splinters!

While I considered this scene with equal terror and astonishment, one of the main braces broke, by the shock whereof two sailors were flung from the yard's arm into the sea, where they perished, and poor Jack Rattlin was thrown down upon the deck, at the expense of a broken leg. Morgan and I ran immediately to his assistance and found a splinter of his shin bone thrust by the violence of the fall through the skin. As this was a case of too great consequence to be treated without the authority of the doctor, I went down to his cabin to inform him of the accident as well as to bring up dressings, which we always kept ready prepared.

I entered his apartment without any ceremony and, by the glimmering of a lamp, perceived him on his knees before something that very much resembled a crucifix. But this I will not insist upon, that I may not seem too much a slave to common report, which indeed assisted my conjecture on this occasion by representing Dr Mackshane as a member of the church of Rome. Be this as it will, he got up in a sort of confusion, occasioned, I suppose, by his being disturbed in his devotion, and in a trice snatched the subject of my suspicion from my sight.

After making an apology for my intrusion, I acquainted him with the situation of Rattlin, but could by no means prevail upon him to visit him on deck where he lay. He bade me desire the boatswain to order some of the men to carry him down to the cock-pit, and in the meantime, said he, I will direct Thomson to get ready the dressings. When I signified to the boatswain the doctor's desire, he swore a terrible oath, that he could not spare one man from the deck, because he expected the mast would go by the board every minute. This piece of information did not at all contribute to my piece of mind. However, as my friend Rattlin complained very much, with the assistance of Morgan, I supported him to the lower deck, whither Mr Mackshane, after much entreaty, ventured to come, attended by Thomson, with a box of dressings and his own servant, who carried a whole set of capital instruments. He examined the fracture and the wound and concluding from a livid colour extending itself upon the limb that a mortification would ensue, resolved to amputate the leg immediately.

This was a dreadful sentence to the patient who, recruiting himself with a quid of tobacco, pronounced with a woeful countenance, 'What! Is there no remedy doctor? Must I be docked? Can't you splice it?'

'Assuredly, Dr Mackshane,' said the first mate, 'with submission, and deference, and veneration to your superior abilities, and opportunities, and stations, look you, I do apprehend, and conjecture, and aver, that there is no occasion nor necessity to smite off this poor man's leg.'

'God Almighty bless you, dear Welshman!' cried Rattlin. 'May you have fair wind and weather wheresoever you're bound and come to an anchor in the Roads of Heaven at last.'

Mackshane, very much incensed at his mate's differing in opinion from him so openly, answered that he was not bound to give an account of his practice to him and, in a peremptory tone, ordered him to apply the tourniquet. At the sight of this Jack, starting up, cried, 'Avast, avast! Damn my heart if you clap your nippers on me till I know wherefore! Mr Random, won't you lend a hand towards saving my precious limb? Odds heart, if Lieutenant Bowling was here he would not suffer Jack Rattlin's leg to be chopped off like a piece of old junk.'

This pathetic address to me, joined to my inclination to serve my honest friend and the reasons I had to believe there was no danger in delaying the amputation, induced me to declare myself of the first mate's opinion, and affirm that the preternatural colour of the skin was owing to an inflammation occasioned by a contusion and common in all such cases, without any indication of an approaching gangrene. Morgan, who had a great opinion of my skill, manifestly exulted in my fellowship, and asked Thomson's sentiments of the matter in hopes of strengthening our association. But he, being of a meek disposition and either dreading the enmity of the surgeon or speaking the dictates of his own judgement, in a modest manner espoused the opinion of Mackshane, who, by this time, having consulted with himself, determined to act in such a manner as to screen himself from censure and at the same time revenge himself on us for our arrogance in contradicting him. With this in view he asked if we would undertake to cure the leg at our peril, that is, be answerable for the consequence. To this question Morgan replied that 'the lives of his creatures are in the hands of Got alone' and that it would be a great presumption in him to undertake for an event that was in the power of his Maker (no more could the doctor promise to cure all the sick to whom he administered his assistance), but that if the patient would put himself under our direction we would do our endeavour to bring his distemper to a favourable issue to which, at present, we saw no obstruction. I signified my concurrence, and Rattlin was so overjoyed that, shaking us both by the hands, he swore nobody else should touch him and, if he died, his blood should be upon his own head.

Mr Mackshane, flattering himself with the prospect of our miscarriage, went away and left us to manage it as we should think proper. Accordingly, having sawed off part of the splinter that stuck through the skin, we reduced the fracture, dressed the wound, applied the eighteen-tailed bandage and put the leg in a box, *secundum artem*. Everything succeeded according to our wish and we had the satisfaction of not only preserving the poor fellow's leg, but likewise of rendering the doctor contemptible among the ship's company, who had all their eyes on us during the course of this cure, which was completed in six weeks.

SUNDAY 3rd OCTOBER

Joseph reported that the wind was still against us. Dr Johnson said, 'A wind, or not a wind? That is the question'; for he can amuse himself at times with a little play of words, or rather sentences. I remember when he turned his cup at Aberbrotherick, where we drank tea, he muttered, *Claudite jam rivos, pueri*. ('Shut up the streams, my boys.' Virgil). I must again and again apologise to fastidious readers, for recording such minute particulars. They prove the scrupulous fidelity of my *Journal*. Dr Johnson said it was a very exact picture of a portion of his life.

While we were chatting in the indolent style of men who were to stay here all this day at least, we were suddenly roused at being told that the wind was fair, that a little fleet of herring-busses was passing by for Mull, and that Mr Simpson's vessel was about to sail. Hugh McDonald, the skipper, came to us, and was impatient that we should get ready, which we soon did. Dr Johnson, with composure and solemnity, repeated the observation of Epictetus, that, 'as man has the voyage of death before him, whatever may be his employment, he should be ready at the master's call; and an old man should never be far from the shore, lest he should not be able to get himself ready. He rode, and I and the other gentlemen walked, about an English mile to the shore, where the vessel lay. Dr Johnson said he should never forget Skye, and returned thanks for all civilities.

We were carried to the vessel in a small boat which she had, and we set sail very briskly about one o'clock. I was much pleased with the motion for many hours. Dr Johnson grew sick, and retired under cover, as it rained a good deal. I kept above, that I might have fresh air, and finding myself not affected by the motion of the vessel, I exulted in being a stout seaman, while Dr Johnson was quite in a state of annihilation. But I was soon humbled; for after imagining that I could go with ease to America or the East Indies, I became very sick, but kept above board, though it rained hard.

As we had been detained so long in Skye by bad weather, we gave up the scheme that Coll had planned for us of visiting several islands, and contented ourselves with the prospect of seeing Mull, and Icolmkill and Inchkenneth, which lie near to it.

Mr Simpson was sanguine in his hopes for a while, the wind being fair for us. He said he would land us at Icolmkill that night. But when the wind failed, it was resolved we should make for the Sound of Mull and land in the harbour of Tobermory. We kept near the five herring vessels for some time, but afterwards four of them got before us, and one little wherry fell behind us.

When we got in full view of the point of Ardnamurchan, the wind changed and was directly against us getting into the Sound. We were then obliged to tack and get forward in that tedious manner. As we advanced, the storm grew greater, and the sea very rough. Coll then began to talk of making for Eigg, or Canna, or his own island. Our skipper said he would get us into the Sound. Having struggled for this for a good while in vain, he said he would push forward till we were nearer the land of Mull, where we might cast anchor and lie until morning, for although before this there had been a good moon, and I had pretty distinctly seen not only the land of Mull, but up the Sound, and the country of Morvern as at one end of it, the night was now grown very dark.

Our crew consisted of one McDonald, our skipper, and two sailors, one of whom had but one eye; Mr Simpson himself, Coll, and Hugh McDonald his servant, all helped. Simpson said he would willingly go for Coll, if young Coll or his servant would undertake to pilot us to a harbour; but, as the island is low land, it was dangerous to run upon it in the dark. Coll and his servant appeared a little dubious. The scheme of running for Canna seemed to be embraced, but Canna was ten leagues off, all out of our way, and they were afraid to attempt the harbour of Eigg. All these different plans were successively in agitation. The old skipper still tried to make for the land of Mull, but then it was considered that there was no place there where we could anchor in safety.

Much time was lost in striving against the storm. At last it became so rough, and threatened to be so much worse, that Coll and his servant took more courage, and said they would undertake to hit one of the harbours in Coll. 'Then let us run for it in God's name,' said the skipper; and instantly we turned towards it. The little wherry which had fallen behind us had hard work. The master begged that, if we made for Coll, we should put out a light to him. Accordingly one of the sailors waved a glowing peat for some time.

The various difficulties that were started gave me a good deal of apprehension, from which I was relieved when I found we were to run for a harbour before the wind. But my relief was of short duration; for I soon heard that our sails were very bad and were in danger of being torn to pieces, in which case we should be driven upon the rocky shore of Coll. It was very dark and there was a heavy and incessant rain. The sparks of the burning peat flew so much about that I dreaded the vessel might take fire. Then, as Coll was a sportsman and had powder on board, I figured that we might be blown up. Simpson and he appeared a little frightened, which made me more so, and the perpetual talking, or rather shouting, which was carried on in Erse, alarmed me still more. A man is always suspicious of what is being said in an unknown tongue and, if fear be his passion at the time, he grows more afraid.

Our vessel often lay so much on one side that I trembled lest she should be overset and, indeed, they told me afterwards that they had run her sometimes to within an inch of the water, so anxious were they to make what haste they could before the night should be worse. I now saw what I never saw before. A prodigious sea, with immense billows, coming upon a vessel so that it hardly seemed possible to escape. There was something grandly horrible in the sight. I am glad I have seen it once.

Amidst all these terrifying circumstances I endeavoured to compose my mind. It was not easy to do it; for all the stories that I had heard of the dangerous sailing among the Hebrides, which is proverbial, came full upon my recollection. When I thought of those who were dearest to me, and who would suffer severely should I be lost, I upbraided myself as not having a sufficient cause for putting myself in such danger. Piety afforded me comfort, yet I was disturbed by the objections that have been made against a particular providence, and by the arguments of those who maintain that it is in vain to hope that the petitions of an individual, or even of congregations, can have any influence with the Deity, objections which have been often made, and which Dr Hawkesworth has lately revived in his preface to the *Voyages to the South Seas*. But Dr Ogden's excellent doctrine on the efficacy of intercession prevailed.

It was half an hour after eleven before we set ourselves in the course for Coll. As I saw them all busy doing something, I asked Coll, with much earnestness, what I could do. He, with a happy readiness, put into my hand a rope, which was fixed to the top of one of the masts, and told me to hold it until he bade me pull. If I had considered the matter, I might have seen that this could not be of the least service, but his object was to keep me out of the way of those who were busy working the vessel, and at the same time to divert my fear, by employing me and making me think that I was of use. Thus did I stand firm to my post while the wind and rain beat upon me, always expecting a call to pull my rope.

The man with one eye steered; old McDonald and Coll and his servant lay upon the forecastle, looking sharp out for the harbour. It was necessary to carry much 'cloth', as they termed it, that is to say, much sail, in order to keep the vessel off the shore of Coll. This made violent plunging in a rough sea. At last they spied the harbour of Lochiern and Coll cried, 'Thank God, we are safe!' We ran up till we were opposite to it and, soon afterwards, we got into it and cast anchor.

Dr Johnson had all this time been quiet and unconcerned. He had lain down on one of the beds and, having got free from sickness, was satisfied. The truth is, he knew nothing of the danger we were in but, fearless and unconcerned, might have said, in the words which he has chosen for the motto to his *Rambler*, *Quo me cunque rapit tempestas, deferor hospes* ('For as the tempest drives, I shape my way.' Francis). Once, during the doubtful consultations, he asked whither we were going and, upon being told that it was not certain whether to Mull or to Coll, he cried, 'Coll for my money!'

I now went down, with Coll and Mr Simpson, to visit him. He

was lying in philosophick tranquillity, with a greyhound of Coll's at his back keeping him warm. Coll is quite the *Juvenis qui gaudet canibus* ('The lad who likes dogs.' Horace). He had, when we left Talisker, two greyhounds, two terriers, a pointer and a large Newfoundland water-dog. He lost one of his terriers by the road, but still had five dogs with him. I was very ill and desirous to get to shore. When I was told that we could not land that night, as the storm had now increased, I looked so miserably, as Coll afterwards informed me, that what Shakespeare has made the Frenchman say of the English soldiers when scantily dieted, 'Piteous they will look, like drowned mice!' might, I believe, have been well applied to me. There was in the harbour, before us, a Campbelltown vessel, the *Betty*, Kenneth Morison master, taking in kelp, and bound for Ireland. We sent our boat to beg beds for two gentlemen, and that the master would send his boat, which was larger than ours. He accordingly did so, and Coll and I were accommodated in his vessel till the morning.

About eight o'clock we went in the boat to Mr Simpson's vessel and took in Dr Johnson. He was quite well though he had tasted nothing but a dish of tea since Saturday night. On our expressing some surprise at this he said that 'when he lodged in the Temple and had no regular system of life, he had fasted for two days at a time, during which he had gone about visiting, though not at the hours of dinner or supper, that he had drunk tea but eaten no bread, that this was no intentional fasting, but happened just in the course of a literary life.'

A CLIFF RESCUE

The knight and his daughter left the high-road, and following a wandering path among sandy hillocks, partly grown over with furze and the long grass called bent, soon attained the side of the ocean. The tide was by no means so far out as they had computed, but this gave them no alarm. There were seldom ten days in the year when it approached so near the cliffs as not to leave a dry passage. But, nevertheless, at periods of spring-tide, or even when the ordinary flood was accelerated by high winds, this road was altogether covered by sea, and tradition had recorded several fatal accidents on such occasions. Still, such dangers were considered as remote and improbable, and rather served, with other legends, to amuse the hamlet fireside than to prevent anyone from going between Knockwinnock and Monkbarns by the sands.

As Sir Arthur and Miss Wardour paced along, enjoying the pleasant footing afforded by the cool moist hard sand, Miss Wardour could not help observing that the last tide had risen considerably above the usual water-mark. Sir Arthur made the same observation, but without its occurring to either of them to be alarmed at the circumstance. The sun was now resting his huge disk upon the edge of the level ocean, and gilded the accumulation of towering clouds through which he had travelled the livelong day, and which now assembled on all sides, like misfortunes and disasters around a sinking empire and falling monarch. Still, however, his dying splendour gave a sombre magnificence to the massive congregation of vapours, forming out of their unsubstantial gloom the show of pyramids and towers, some touched with gold, some with purple, some with a hue of deep and dark red. The distant sea, stretched beneath this varied and gorgeous canopy, lay almost portentously still, reflecting back the dazzling and level beams of the descending luminary, and the splendid colouring of the clouds amidst which he was setting. Nearer to the beach the tide rippled onward in waves of sparkling silver that, imperceptibly yet rapidly, gained upon the sand.

With a mind employed in admiration of the romantic scene, or perhaps on some more agitating topic, Miss Wardour advanced in silence by her father's side. Following the windings of the beach, they passed one projecting point of headland or rock after another, and now found themselves under a huge and continued extent of the precipices by which that iron-bound coast is in most places defended.

Long projecting reefs of rock, extending under water and only evincing their existence by here and there a peak entirely bare, or by the breakers which foamed over those that were partly covered, rendered Knockwinnock bay dreaded by pilots and shipmasters. The crags which rose between the beach and the mainland, to the height of two or three hundred feet, afforded in their crevices shelter for unnumbered sea-fowl, in situations seemingly secured by their dizzy height from the rapacity of man. Many of these wild tribes, with the instinct which sends them to seek the land before a storm arises, were now winging towards their nests with the shrill and dissonant clang which announces disquietude and fear. The disk of the sun became almost totally obscured ere he had altogether sunk below the horizon, and an early and lurid shade of darkness blotted the serene twilight of a summer evening. The wind began next to arise; but its wild and moaning sound was heard for some time, and its effects became visible on the bosom of the sea, before the gale was felt on shore. The mass of waters, now dark and threatening, began to lift itself in larger ridges, and sink in deeper furrows, forming waves that rose high in foam upon the breakers, or burst upon the beach with a sound resembling distant thunder.

Appalled by this sudden change of weather, Miss Wardour drew close to her father and held his arm fast.

'I wish,' she said at length, but almost in a whisper, as if ashamed to express her increasing apprehensions, 'I wish we had kept the road we intended, or waited at Monkbarns for the carriage.'

Sir Arthur looked round, but did not see, or would not acknowledge, any signs of an immediate storm. They would reach Knockwinnock, he said, long before the tempest began. But the speed with which he walked, and with which Isabella could hardly keep pace, indicated a feeling that some exertion was necessary to accomplish his consolatory prediction.

They were now near the centre of a deep but narrow bay or recess, formed by two projecting capes of high and inaccessible rock, which shot out into the sea like the horns of a crescent; and neither durst communicate the apprehension which each began to entertain, that, from the unusually rapid advance of the tide, they might be deprived of the power of proceeding by doubling the promontory which lay before them, or of retreating by the road which brought them thither.

As they thus pressed forward, longing doubtless to exchange the easy curving line, which the sinuosities of the bay compelled them to adopt, for a straighter and more expeditious path, though less conformable to the line of beauty, Sir Arthur observed a human figure on the beach advancing to meet them.

'Thank God,' he exclaimed, 'we shall get round Halket-head! That person must have passed it.' Thus giving vent to the feeling of hope, though he had suppressed that of apprehension.

'Thank God, indeed!' echoed his daughter, half audibly, half internally, as expressing the gratitude which she strongly felt.

The figure which advanced to meet them made many signs, which the haze of the atmosphere, now disturbed by the wind and by a drizzling rain, prevented them from seeing or comprehending distinctly. Some time before they met, Sir Arthur could recognise the old blue-gowned beggar, Edie Ochiltree. It is said that even the brute creation lay aside their animosities and antipathies when pressed by an instant and common danger. The beach under Halket-head, rapidly diminishing in extent by the encroachments of a spring-tide and a north-west wind, was in like manner a neutral field, where even a justice of the peace and a strolling mendicant might meet upon terms of mutual forbearance.

'Turn back! Turn back!' exclaimed the vagrant. 'Why did ye not turn back when I waved to you?'

'We thought,' replied Sir Arthur, in great agitation, 'we could get round Halket-head.'

'Halket-head! The tide will be running on Halket-head by this time like the Fall of Fyers! It was a' I could do to get round it twenty minutes since - it was coming in three feet abreast. We will maybe get back by Bally-burgh Ness Point yet. The Lord help us! It's our only chance. We can but try.'

'My God, my child!' - 'My father! My dear father!' exclaimed the parent and daughter as, fear lending them strength and speed, they turned to retrace their steps, and endeavoured to double the point, the projection of which formed the southern extremity of the bay.

'I heard ye were here frae the bit callant ye sent to meet your carriage,' said the beggar, as he trudged stoutly on, a step or two behind Miss Wardour, 'and I couldna bide to think o' the dainty young leddy's peril, that has aye been kind to ilka forlorn heart that cam near her. Sae I lookit at the lift and the rin o' the tide, till I settled it that if I could get down in time enough to gie you warning, we wad do weel yet. But I doubt, I doubt, I have been beguiled! For what mortal ee ever saw sic a race as the tide is rinnin' e'en now? See, yonder's the Ratton's Skerry - he aye held his neb abune the water in my day - but he's aneath it now.'

Sir Arthur cast a look in the direction in which the old man pointed. A huge rock, which in general, even in spring tides, displayed a hulk like the keel of a large vessel, was now quite under water, and its place only indicated by the boiling and breaking of the eddying waves which encountered its submarine resistance.

'Mak haste, mak haste, my bonny leddy,' continued the old man, 'mak haste and we may do yet! Take haud o' my arm. An auld and frail arm it's now, but it's been in as sair stress as this is yet. Take haud o' my arm, my winsome leddy! D'ye see yon wee black speck amang the wallowing waves yonder? This morning it was as high as the mast o' a muckle brig. It's sma' eneugh now, but while I see as muckle black about it as the crown o' my hat, I winna believe but we'll get round the Bally-burgh Ness, for a' that's come and gane yet.'

Isabella, in silence, accepted from the old man the assistance which Sir Arthur was less able to afford her. The waves had now encroached so much upon the beach that the firm and smooth footing which they had hitherto had on the sand must be exchanged for a rougher path close to the foot of the precipice, and in some places even raised upon its lower ledges. It would have been utterly impossible for Sir Arthur Wardour, or his daughter, to have found their way along these shelves without the guidance and encouragement of the beggar, who had been there before in high tides, though never, he acknowledged, 'in sae awesome a night as this.'

It was indeed a dreadful evening. The howling of the storm mingled with the shrieks of the sea-fowl, and sounded like the dirge of the three devoted beings who, pent between two of the most magnificent, yet most dreadful objects of nature - a raging tide and an insurmountable precipice - toiled along their painful and dangerous path, often lashed by the spray of some giant billow, which threw itself higher on the beach than those that had preceded it. Each minute did their enemy gain ground perceptibly upon them! Still, however, loth to relinquish the last hopes of life, they bent their eyes on the black rock pointed out by Ochiltree. It was yet distinctly visible among the breakers, and continued to be so, until they came to a turn in their precarious path, where an intervening projection of rock hid it from their sight. Deprived of the beacon on which they had relied, they now experienced the double agony of terror and suspense. They struggled forward, however, but, when they arrived at the point from which they ought to have seen the crag, it was no longer visible. The signal of safety was lost among a thousand white breakers which, dashing upon the point of the promontory, rose in prodigious sheets of snowy foam, as high as the mast of a first-rate man-of-war, against the dark brow of the precipice.

The countenance of the old man fell. Isabella gave a faint shriek and 'God have mercy upon us', which her guide solemnly uttered, was piteously echoed by Sir Arthur.

'My child! My child! To die such a death!'

'My father! My dear father!' his daughter exclaimed, clinging to him, 'and you too, who have lost your own life in endeavouring to save ours!'

'That's not worth counting,' said the old man. 'I hae lived to be weary o' life; and here or yonder, at the back o' a dyke, in a wreath o' snaw, or in the wame o' a wave, what signifies how the auld gaberlunzie dies?'

'Good man,' said Sir Arthur, 'can you think of nothing, of no help? I'll make you rich. I'll give you a farm. I'll...'

'Our riches will soon be equal,' said the beggar, looking out upon the strife of the waters. 'They are sae already. For I hae nae land, and you would give your fair bounds and barony for a square yard of rock that would be dry for twal hours.'

While they exchanged these words, they paused upon the highest ledge of rock to which they could attain. For it seemed that any attempt to move forward could only serve to anticipate their fate. Here, then, they were to await the sure though slow progress of the raging element, something in the situation of the martyrs of the early church who, exposed by heathen tyrants to be slain by wild beasts, were compelled for a time to witness the impatience and rage by which the animals were agitated, while awaiting the signal for undoing their grates and letting them loose upon the victims.

Yet even this fearful pause gave Isabella time to collect the powers of a mind naturally strong and courageous, and which rallied itself at this terrible juncture.

'Must we yield life,' she said, 'without a struggle? Is there no path, however dreadful, by which we could climb the crag, or at least attain some height above the tide, where we could remain till morning or till help comes? They must be aware of our situation, and will raise the country to relieve us.'

Sir Arthur, who heard but scarcely comprehended, his daughter's question, turned, nevertheless, instinctively and eagerly to the old man, as if their lives were in his gift.

Ochiltree paused. 'I was a bauld cragsman,' he said, 'ance in my life, and mony's the kittywake's and lungie's nest hae I harried up amang thae very black rocks. But it's lang, lang syne, and nae mortal could speel them without a rope. And if I had ane, my ee-sight, and my footstep, and my hand-grip, hae a' failed mony a day sinsyne. And then, how could I save *you*? But there was a path here ance, though maybe, if we could see it, ye would rather bide where we are.'

'His name be praised!' he ejaculated suddenly, 'there's ane coming down the crag e'en now!'

Then, exalting his voice, he hilloa'd out to the daring adventurer such instructions as his former practice and the remembrance of local circumstances suddenly forced upon his mind.

'Ye're right! Ye're right! That gate, that gate! Fasten the rope weel round Crummie's Horn, that's the muckle black stane. Cast twa plies round it. That's it, that's it! Now weize yoursell a wee easel-ward. A wee mair yet to that ither stane. We ca'd it the Cat's Lug. There used to be the root o' an aik tree there. That will do! Canny now, lad, canny now. Tak tent and tak time. Lord bless ye, tak time. Vera weel! Now ye maun get to Bessy's Apron, that's the muckle braid flat blue stane. And then, I think, wi' your help and the tow thegither, I'll win at ye, and then we'll be able to get up the young leddy and Sir Arthur.'

The adventurer, following the directions of old Edie, flung him down the end of the rope, which he secured around Miss Wardour, wrapping her previously in his own blue gown, to preserve her as much as possible from injury. Then, availing himself of the rope, which was made fast at the other end, he began to ascend the face of the crag, a most precarious and dizzy undertaking which, however, after one or two perilous escapes, placed him safe on the broad flat stone beside our friend Lovel. Their joint strength was able to raise Isabella to the place of safety which they had attained. Lovel then descended in order to assist Sir Arthur, around whom he adjusted the rope, and again mounting to their place of refuge, with the assistance of old Ochiltree, and such aid as Sir Arthur himself could afford, he raised himself beyond the reach of the billows.

The sense of reprieve from approaching and apparently inevitable death had its usual effect. The father and daughter threw themselves into each other's arms, kissed and wept for joy, although their escape was connected with the prospect of passing a tempestuous night upon a precipitous ledge of rock, which scarce afforded footing for the four shivering beings who now, like the sea-fowl around them, clung there in hopes of some shelter from the devouring element which raged beneath. The spray of the billows, which attained in fearful succession the foot of the precipice, overflowing the beach on which they so lately stood, flew as high as their place of temporary refuge, and the stunning sound with which they dashed against the rocks beneath seemed as if they still demanded the fugitives in accents of thunder as their destined prey. It was a summer night, doubtless, yet the probability was slender that a frame so delicate as that of Miss Wardour should survive till morning the drenching of the spray and the dashing of the rain, which now burst in full violence, accompanied with deep and heavy gusts of wind and added to the constrained and perilous circumstances of their situation.

'The lassie, the puir wee lassie!' said the old man. 'Mony such a night have I weathered at hame and abroad but, God guide us, how can she ever win through it!'

His apprehension was communicated in smothered accents to Lovel. For, with the sort of freemasonry by which bold and ready spirits correspond in moments of danger and become almost instinctively known to each other, they had established a mutual confidence.

'I'll climb up the cliff again,' said Lovel. 'There's daylight enough left to see my footing. I'll climb up and call for more assistance.'

'Do so, do so, for Heaven's sake!' said Sir Arthur eagerly.

'Are ye mad?' said the mendicant. 'Francie o' Fowlsheugh, and he was the best cragsman that ever speel'd heugh (mair by token, he brake his neck upon the Dunbuy of Slaines), wodna hae ventured upon the Halket Head craigs after sundown. It's God's grace, and a great wonder besides, that ye are not in the middle o' that great roaring sea wi' what ye hae done already. I didna think there was the man left alive would hae come down the craigs as ye did. I question an I could hae done it mysell, at this hour and in this weather, in the youngest and yaldest of my strength. But to venture up again! It's a mere and a clear tempting o' Providence.'

'I have no fear,' answered Lovel. 'I marked all the stations perfectly as I came down, and there is still light enough left to see them quite well. I am sure I can do it with perfect safety. Stay here, my good friend, by Sir Arthur and the young lady.'

'Deil be in my feet then,' answered the bedesman sturdily. 'If ye gang, I'll gang too. For between the twa o' us we'll hae mair than wark eneugh to get to the tap o' the heugh.'

'No, no. Stay you here and attend to Miss Wardour. You see Sir Arthur is quite exhausted.'

'Stay yoursell then, and I'll gae,' said the old man. 'Let death spare the green corn and take the ripe.'

'Stay both of you, I charge you,' said Isabella faintly. 'I am well, and can spend the night very well here. I feel quite refreshed.' So saying, her voice failed her. She sank down, and would have fallen from the crag had she not been supported by Lovel and Ochiltree, who placed her in a posture half sitting, half reclining, beside her father who, exhausted by fatigue of body and mind so extreme and unusual, had already sat down on a stone in a sort of stupor.

'It is impossible to leave them,' said Lovel. 'What is to be done? - Hark! Hark! Did I not hear a halloo?'

'The skreigh of a Tammie Norie,' answered Ochiltree. 'I ken the skirl weel.'

'No, by Heaven!' replied Lovel. 'It was a human voice.'

A distant hail was repeated, the sound plainly distinguishable among the various elemental noises, and the clang of the sea mews by which they were surrounded. The mendicant and Lovel exerted their voices in a loud halloo, the former waving Miss Wardour's handkerchief on the end of his staff to make them conspicuous from above. Though the shouts were repeated it was some time before they were in exact reponse to their own, leaving the unfortunate sufferers uncertain whether, in the darkening twilight and increasing storm, they had made the persons, who apparently were traversing the verge of the precipice to bring them assistance, sensible of the place in which they had found refuge. At length their halloo was regularly and distinctly answered, and their courage confirmed, by the assurance that they were within hearing, if not within reach, of friendly assistance.

The shout of human voices from above was soon augmented and the gleam of torches mingled with those lights of evening which still remained amid the darkness of the storm. Some attempt was made to hold communication between the assistants above and the sufferers beneath, who were still clinging to their precarious place of safety, but the howling of the tempest limited their intercourse to cries as inarticulate as those of the winged denizens of the crag, which shrieked in chorus, alarmed by the reiterated sound of human voices where they had seldom been heard.

On the verge of the precipice an anxious group had now assembled. Mr Oldbuck of Monkbarns was the foremost and most earnest, pressing forward with unwonted desperation to the very brink of the crag and extending his head (his hat and wig secured by a handkerchief under his chin) over the dizzy height which made his more timorous assistants tremble.

'Haud a care, haud a care Monkbarns!' cried Caxon, clinging to the skirts of his patron and withholding him from danger as far as strength permitted. 'God's sake, haud a care! Sir Arthur's drowned already, and an ye fa' over the cleugh too there will be but ae wig left in the parish, and that's the minister's.'

'Mind the peak there,' cried Mucklebackit, an old fisherman and smuggler, 'mind the peak. Steenie, Steenie Wilks, bring up the tackle. I'se warrant we'll sune heave them on board, Monkbarns, wad ye but stand out o' the gate.'

'I see them,' said Oldbuck. 'I see them low down on that flat stone. Hilli-hilloa, hilli-ho-a!'

'I see them mysell weel eneugh,' said Mucklebackit. 'They are sitting down yonder like hoodie-crows in a mist. But d'ye think ye'll help them wi' skirling that gate like an auld skart before a flaw o' the weather? Steenie, lad, bring up the mast. Od, I'se hae them up as we used to bouse up the kegs o' gin and brandy lang syne. Get up the pickaxe, make a step for the mast, make the chair fast with the rattlin, haul tight and belay!'

The fishers had brought with them the mast of a boat, and as half the country fellows about had now appeared, either out of zeal or curiosity, it was soon sunk in the ground and sufficiently secured. A yard across the upright mast and a rope stretched along it and reeved through a block at each end formed an extempore crane, which afforded the means of lowering an arm-chair, well secured and fastened, down to the flat shelf on which the sufferers had roosted.

Their joy at hearing the preparations going on for their deliverance was considerably qualified when they beheld the precarious vehicle by means of which they were to be conveyed to upper air. It swung about a yard free of the spot which they occupied, obeying each impulse of the tempest, the empty air all around it, and depending upon the security of a rope which, in the increasing darkness, had dwindled to an almost imperceptible thread. Besides the hazard of committing a human being to the vacant atmosphere in such a slight means of conveyance, there was the fearful danger of the chair and its occupant being dashed, either by the wind or the vibrations of the cord, against the rugged face of the precipice. But to diminish the risk as much as possible, the experienced seaman had let down with the chair another line which, being attached to it and held by the persons beneath, might serve by way of a guy, as Mucklebackit expressed it, to render its descent in some measure steady and regular.

Still, to commit oneself in such a vehicle, through a howling tempest of wind and rain, with a beetling precipice above and a raging abyss below, required that courage which despair alone can inspire. Yet, wild as the sounds and sights of danger were, above, beneath and around, and doubtful and dangerous as the mode of escaping appeared to be, Lovel and the old mendicant agreed, after a moment's consultation and after the former, by a sudden strong pull, had, at his own imminent risk, ascertained the security of the rope, that it would be best to secure Miss Wardour in the chair and trust to the tenderness and care of those above for her being safely craned up to the top of the crag.

'Let my father go first,' exclaimed Isabella. 'For God's sake, my friends, place him first in safety!'

'It cannot be, Miss Wardour,' said Lovel. 'Your life must be first secured. The rope which bears your weight may...'

'I will not listen to a reason so selfish!'

'But ye maun listen to it, my bonnie lassie,' said Ochiltree, 'for a' our lives depend on it. Besides, when ye get on the tap o' the heugh yonder, ye can gie them a round guess o' what's ganging on in this Patmos o' ours; Sir Arthur's far by that, I'm thinking.'

Struck with the truth of this reasoning, she exclaimed, 'True, most true. I am ready and willing to undertake the first risk. What shall I say to our friends above?'

'Just to look that their tackle does not graze on the face o' the crag, and to let the chair down and draw it up hooly and fairly. We will halloo when we are ready.'

With the sedulous attention of a parent to a child, Lovel bound Miss Wardour with his handkerchief, neckcloth and the mendicant's leathern belt to the back and arms of the chair, ascertaining the security of each knot, while Ochiltree kept Sir Arthur quiet.

'What are ye doing wi' my bairn? What are ye doing? She shall not be separated from me. Isabel, stay with me, I command you!'

'Lordsake, Sir Arthur, haud your tongue, and be thankful to God that there's wiser folk than you to manage this job,' cried the beggar, worn out by the unreasonable exclamations of the poor Baronet.

'Farewell, my father!' murmered Isabella. 'Farewell my...my friends!' and shutting her eyes, as Edie's experience recommended, she gave the signal to Lovel, and he to those who were above. She rose, while the chair in which she sat was kept steady by the line which Lovel managed beneath. With a beating heart he watched the flutter of her white dress, until the vehicle was on a level with the brink of the precipice.

'Canny now, lads, canny now!' exclaimed old Mucklebackit, who acted as commodore. 'Swerve the yard a bit. Now. There! There she sits safe on dry land.'

A loud shout announced the successful experiment to her fellow-sufferers beneath, who replied with a ready and cheerful halloo. Monkbarns, in his ecstasy of joy, stripped his greatcoat to wrap up the young lady, and would have pulled off his coat and waistcoat for the same purpose had he not been withheld by the cautious Caxton.

'Haud a care o' us! Your honour will be killed wi' the hoast. Ye'll no' get out o' your night-cowl this fortnight, and that will suit us unco ill. Na, na, there's the chariot down by. Let twa o' the folk carry the young leddy there.'

'You're right,' said Oldbuck, readjusting the sleeves and collar of his coat, 'you're right, Caxon. This is a naughty night to swim in. Miss Wardour, let me convey you to the chariot.'

'Not for worlds till I see my father safe.'

In a few distinct words, evincing how much her resolution had surmounted even the mortal fear of so agitating a hazard, she explained the nature of the situation beneath and the wishes of Lovel and Ochiltree.

'Right, right, that's right too. I should like to see Sir Arthur on dry land myself. But he's safe now, and here a' comes.' For the chair was again lowered and Sir Arthur made fast in it without much consciousness on his own part. 'Here a' comes. Bowse away, my boys! Canny wi' him. A pedigree of a hundred links is hanging on a tenpenny tow. The whole barony of Knockwinnock depends on three plies o' hemp. *Respice finem, respice funem* - look to your end, look to a rope's end. Welcome, welcome, my good old friend to firm land, though I cannot say to warm land or to dry land. A cord for ever against fifty fathom o' water, though not in the sense of the base proverb. A fico for the phrase. Better *sus. per funem*, than *sus. per coll.*'

While Oldbuck ran on in this way, Sir Arthur was safely wrapped in the close embraces of his daughter who, assuming that authority which the circumstances demanded, ordered some of the assistants to convey him to the chariot, promising to follow in a few minutes. She lingered on the cliff, holding an old countryman's arm, to witness probably the safety of those whose dangers she had shared.

'What have we here?' said Oldbuck, as the vehicle once more ascended, 'what patched and weather-beaten matter is this?' Then, as the torches illumed the rough face and grey hairs of old Ochiltree, 'What! Is it thou? Come, old Mocker, I must needs be friends with thee, but who the devil makes up your party besides?'

'Ane that's weel worthy ony twa o' us, Monkbarns. It's the young stranger they ca' Lovel. And he's behaved this blessed night as if he had three lives to rely on, and was willing to waste them a' rather than endanger ither folk's. Ca' hooly, sirs, as ye wad win an auld man's blessing! Mind there's naebody below now to haud the guy. Hae a care o' the Cat's Lug corner. Bide weel aff Crummie's Horn!'

'Have a care indeed,' echoed Oldbuck. 'Take care of him, Mucklebackit.'

'As muckle care as if he were a greybeard o' brandy, and I canna take mair. Yo ho, my hearts! Bowse away with him!'

Lovel did, in fact, run a much greater risk than any of his precursors. His weight was not sufficient to render his ascent steady amid such a storm of wind and he swung like an agitated pendulum at the mortal risk of being dashed against the rocks. But he was young and bold and active, and with assistance of the beggar's stout piked staff, which he had retained by advice of the proprietor, contrived to bear himself from the face of the precipice and the yet more hazardous projecting cliffs which varied its surface. Tossed in empty space, like an idle and unsubstantial feather, with a motion that agitated the brain at once with fear and with dizziness, he retained his alertness of exertion and presence of mind, and it was not until he was safely grounded upon the summit of the cliff that he felt temporary and giddy sickness. As he recovered from a sort of half swoon, he cast his eyes eagerly around. The object which they would most willingly have sought was already in the act of vanishing. Her white garment was just discernible as she followed on the path which her father had taken. She had lingered till she saw the last of their company rescued from danger, and until she had been assured by the hoarse voice of Mucklebackit that 'the callant had come off wi' unbrizzed banes, and that he was but in a kind of dwam.' But Lovel was not aware that she had expressed in his fate even this degree of interest which, though nothing more than was due to a stranger who had assisted her in such a hour of peril, he would have gladly purchased by braving even more imminent danger than he had that evening been exposed to. The beggar she had already commanded to come to Knockwinnock that night. He made an excuse. 'Then tomorrow let me see you.'

The old man promised to obey. Oldbuck thrust something into his hand. Ochiltree looked at it by the torchlight, and returned it.

'Na, na! I never tak gowd. Besides, Monkbarns, ye wad maybe be rueing it the morn.'

Then turning to the group of fishermen and peasants, 'Now, sirs, wha will gie me a supper and some clean pease-strae?'

'I,' 'and I,' 'and I' answered many a ready voice.

'Aweel, since sae it is, and I can only sleep in ae barn at ance, I'll gae down wi' Saunders Mucklebackit. He has aye a soup o' something comfortable about his bigging, and, bairns, I'll maybe live to put ilka and o' ye in mind some ither night that ye hae promised me quarters and my awmous.'

And away he went with the fisherman.

Michael Scott

SAVED FROM PIRATES

It was a very large fleet, nearly three hundred sail of merchant vessels–and a truly noble sight. A line-of-battle ship led and two frigates and three sloops of our class were stationed on the outskirts of the fleet, whipping them in as it were. We made Madeira in fourteen days, looked in, but did not anchor. Superb island, magnificent mountains, white town, and all very fine.

Nothing particular happened for three weeks. One fine evening, (we had by this time progressed into the trades and were within three hundred miles of Barbadoes) the sun had set bright and clear, after a most beautiful day, and we were bowling along right before it, rolling like the very devil. There was no moon and, although the stars sparkled brilliantly, yet it was dark, and as we were the sternmost of the men-of-war, we had the task of whipping in the sluggards. It was my watch on deck. A gun from the Commodore, who showed a number of lights.

'What is that, Mr Kennedy?' said the Captain to the old gunner.

'The Commodore has made the night signal for the sternmost ships to make more sail and close, sir.'

We repeated the signal and stood on, hailing the dullest of the merchantmen in our neighbourhood to make more sail and firing a musket shot now and then over the more distant of them. By and by we saw a large West Indiaman suddenly haul her wind and stand across our bows.

'Forward there!' sung out Mr Splinter, 'stand by to fire a shot from the boat gun at that fellow if he does not bear up. What can he be after? Sergeant Armstrong' to a marine who was standing close by him in the waist. 'get a musket, and fire over him.'

It was done, and the ship immediately bore up on her course again. We now ranged alongside of him on his larboard quarter.

'Ho, the ship, ahoy!'

'Hillo!' was the reply.

'Make more sail, sir, and run into the body of the fleet or I shall fire into you. Why don't you, sir, keep in the wake of the Commodore?' No answer. ' What meant you by hauling your wind just now, sir?'

'Yesh, yesh,' at length responded a voice from the merchantman.

'Something wrong here,' said Mr Splinter. 'Back your maintopsail, sir, and hoist a light at the peak; I shall send a boat on board of you. Boatswain's mate, pipe away the crew of the jolly boat.'

We also hove to and were in the act of lowering down the boat when the officer rattled out, 'Keep all fast with the boat; I can't comprehend that chap's manoeuvres for the soul of me. He has not hove to.'

Once more we were within pistol-shot of him.

'Why don't you heave to, sir?'

All silent.

Presently we could perceive a confusion and noise of struggling on board and angry voices, as if people were trying to force their way up hatchways from below, and a heavy thumping on the deck, and a creaking of the blocks, and rattling of the cordage, while the main-yard was first braced one way and then another, as if two parties were striving for the mastery. At length a voice hailed distinctly.

'We are captured by a...'

A sudden sharp cry, and a splash overboard, told of some fearful deed.

'We are taken by a privateer or pirate,' sung out another voice. This was followed by a heavy crunching blow, as when the spike of a butcher's axe is driven through a bullock's forehead deep into the brain.

By this time all hands had been called and the word had been passed to clear away two of the foremost carronades on the starboard side, and to load them with grape.

'On board there—get below, all of you of the English crew, as I shall fire with grape,' sung out the captain.

The hint was now taken. The ship at length came to the wind. We rounded to under her lee, and an armed boat, with Mr Treenail, myself and sixteen men, with cutlasses, were sent on board.

We jumped on deck and, at the gangway, Mr Treenail stumbled and fell over the body of a dead man, no doubt the one who had hailed last, with his skull cloven to the eyes, and a broken cutlass blade sticking in the gash. We were immediately accosted by the mate, who was lashed down to a ring-bolt close by the bits, with his hands tied at the wrists by sharp cords, so tightly that the blood was spouting from his nails.

'We have been surprised by a privateer schooner, sir. The

Lieutenant of her and twelve men are now in the cabin.'

'Where are the rest of the crew?'

'All secured in the forecastle, except the second mate and boatswain, the men who hailed you just now; the last was knocked on the head and the former was stabbed and thrown overboard.'

We immediately released the men, eighteen in number, and armed them with boarding pikes.

'What vessel is that astern of us?' said Treenail to the mate.

Before he could answer, a shot from the brig, fired at the privateer, showed that she was broad awake.

Next moment Captain Deadeye hailed. 'Have you mastered the prize crew, Mr Treenail?'

'Aye, aye, sir.'

'Then keep your course, and keep two lights hoisted at your mizzen peak during the night and Blue Peter at the maintopsail yard-arm when the day breaks. I shall haul my wind after the suspicious sail in your wake.'

Another shot, and another, from the brig, the time between each flash and the report increasing with the distance. By this the Lieutenant had descended to the cabin, followed by his people, while the merchant crew once more took the charge of the ship, crowding sail into the body of the fleet.

I followed him close, pistol and cutlass in hand, and I shall never forget the scene that presented itself when I entered. The cabin was that of a vessel of five hundred tons, elegantly fitted up; the panels filled with crimson cloth and edged with gold mouldings, with superb damask hangings before the stern windows and the side berths, and brilliantly lighted up by two large swinging lamps hung from the deck above, which were reflected from, and multiplied in, several plate glass mirrors in the panels. In the recess, which in cold weather had been occupied by the stove, now stood a splendid grand piano, the silk in the open work above the keys corresponding with the crimson cloth of the panels. It was open and a Leghorn bonnet with a green veil, a parasol and two long white gloves, as if recently pulled off, lay on it, with the very mould of the hands in them.

The rudder case was particularly beautiful; it was a richly carved and gilded palm, the stem painted white, and interlaced with golden fretwork, like the lozenges of a pineapple, while the leaves spread up and abroad on the roof.

The table was laid for supper, with cold meat, and wine, and a profusion of silver things, all sparkling brightly; but it was in great disorder, wine spilt, glasses broken, dishes with meat upset and knives, forks, and spoons scattered all about. She was evidently one of those London West Indiamen, on board of which I knew there was much splendour and great comfort.

But, alas! The hand of lawless violence had been there. The Captain lay across the table, with his head hanging over the side of it next to us, and unable to help himself, with his hands tied behind his back, and a gag in his mouth; his face purple from the blood running to his head, and the white of his eyes turned up, while his loud stertorous breathing but too clearly indicated the rupture of a blood vessel on the brain. He was a stout, portly man and, although we released him on the instant, and had him bled, and threw water on his face, and did all we could for him, he never spoke afterwards, and died in half an hour.

Four gentlemanly-looking men were sitting at table, lashed to their chairs, pale and trembling, while six of the most ruffianly-looking scoundrels I ever beheld stood on the opposite side of the table in a row fronting us, with the light from the lamps shining full on them. Three of them were small, but very square mulattoes; one was a South American Indian, with the square, high-boned visage, and long, lank, black glossy hair of his cast. These four had no clothing besides their trousers and stood with their arms folded, in all the calmness of desperate men caught in the very fact of some horrible atrocity, which they knew shut out all hope of mercy. The two others were white Frenchmen, tall, bushy-whiskered, sallow desperadoes, but still, wonderful to relate, with, if I may so speak, the manners of gentlemen. One of them squinted, and had a hare-lip, which gave him a horrible expression. They were dressed in white trousers and shirts with yellow silk sashes round their waists, a sort of blue uniform jackets and blue Gascon caps with peaks, from each of which depended a large bullion tassel, hanging down on one side of their heads.

The whole party had apparently made up their minds that resistance was in vain, for their pistols and cutlasses, some of them bloody, had all been laid on the table, with the butts and handles towards us, contrasting horribly with the glittering equipage of steel, and crystal, and silver things on the snow-white damask table-cloth. They were immediately seized and ironed, to which they submitted in silence. We next released the passengers, and were overpowered with thanks, one dancing, one crying, one laughing and another praying. But, merciful Heaven! What an object met our eyes!

Drawing aside the curtain that concealed a sofa fitted into a recess, there lay, more dead than alive, a tall and most beautiful girl, her head resting on her left arm, her clothes disordered and torn, blood on her bosom and foam on her mouth, with her long dark hair loose and dishevelled and covering the upper part of her deadly pale face, through which her wild sparkling black eyes, protruding from their sockets, glanced and glared with the fire of a maniac's, while her blue lips kept gibbering an incoherent prayer one moment, and the next imploring mercy, as if she had still been in the hands of those who knew not the name. Anon, a low hysterical laugh made our very blood freeze in our bosoms, which soon ended in a long dismal yell, as she rolled off the couch upon the hard deck, and lay in a dead faint.

Alas the day! A maniac she was from that hour. She was the only daughter of the murdered master of the ship, and never awoke, in her unclouded reason, to the fearful consciousness of her own dishonour and her parent's death.

The *Torch* captured the schooner and we left the privateer's men at Barbadoes to meet their reward. Several of the merchant sailors were turned over to the guardship, to prove the facts in the first instance, and to serve his Majesty as pressed men in the second— but scrimp measure of justice to the poor ship's crew.

THE WINDY YULE

I t was in the course of the winter after the decease of Bailie
McLucre that the great loss of lives took place which
everybody agreed was one of the most calamitous things that
had for many a year befallen the town.

Three or four vessels were coming with cargoes of grain from
Ireland; another from the Baltic with Norawa deals; and a third
from Bristol, where she had been on a charter for some Greenock
merchants.

It happened that, for a time, there had been contrary winds,
against which no vessel could enter the port, and the ships,

whereof I have been speaking, were all lying together at anchor in the bay, waiting a change of weather. These five vessels were owned among ourselves, and their crews consisted of fathers and sons belonging to the place, so that, both by reason of interest and affection, a more than ordinary concern was felt for them; for the sea was so rough that no boat could live in it to go near them, and we had our fears that the men on board would be very ill off.

Nothing, however, occurred but this natural anxiety, till the Saturday, which was Yule. In the morning the weather was blasty and sleety, waxing more and more tempestuous till about midday, when the wind checked suddenly round from the nor-east to the sou-west, and blew a gale as if the prince of the powers of the air was doing his utmost to work mischief. The rain blattered, the windows clattered, the shop-shutters flapped, pigs from the lum-heads came rattling down like thunder-claps, and the skies were dismal both with cloud and carry. Yet, for all that, there was in the street a stir and a busy visitation between neighbours, and everyone went to their high windows, to look at the five poor barks that were warstling against the strong arm of the elements of the storm and the ocean.

Still the lift gloomed, and the wind roared, and it was as doleful a sight as ever was seen in any town afflicted with calamity to see the sailors' wives, with their red cloaks about their heads, followed by their hirpling and disconsolate bairns, going one after another to the kirkyard, to look at the vessels where their helpless breadwinners were battling with the tempest. My heart was really sorrowful, and full of sore anxiety to think of what might happen to the town, whereof so many were in peril, and to whom no human magistracy could extend the arm of protection.

Seeing no abatement of the wrath of heaven, that howled and roared around us, I put on my big coat, and taking my staff in my hand, having tied down my hat with a silk handkerchief, towards gloaming I walked likewise to the kirkyard, where I beheld such an assemblage of sorrow, as few men in situation have ever been put to the trial to witness. In the lea of the kirk many hundreds of the town were gathered together; but there was no discourse among them. The major part were sailors' wives and weans, and at every new thud of the blast, a sob rose, and the mothers drew their bairns closer in about them, as if they saw the visible hand of a foe raised to smite them. Apart from the multitude, I observed three or four young lasses standing behind the Whinnyhill families' tomb, and I jaloused that they had joes in the ships, for they often looked to the bay, with long necks and sad faces, from behind the monument.

A widow woman, one old Mary Weery, that was a lameter, and dependent on her son, who was on board the 'Louping Meg' (as the *Lovely Peggy* was nicknamed at the shore), stood by herself, and every now and then wrung her hands, crying, with a woeful voice, 'The Lord giveth and the Lord taketh away, blessed be the name of the Lord.' But it was manifest to all that her faith was fainting within her.

But of all the piteous objects there, on that doleful evening, none troubled my thoughts more than three motherless children that belonged to the mate of one of the vessels in jeopardy. He was an Englishman that had been settled some years in the town, where his family had neither kith nor kin; and his wife having died about a month before, the bairns, of whom the eldest was but nine or so, were friendless enough, though both my gudewife, and other well-disposed ladies, paid them all manner of attention till their father would come home. The three poor little things, knowing that he was in one of the ships, had been often out and anxious, and they were then sitting under the lea of a headstone, near their mother's grave, chittering and creeping closer and closer at every squall. Never was such an orphan-like sight seen.

When it began to be so dark that the vessels could no longer be discerned from the churchyard, many went down to the shore, and I took the three babies home with me, and Mrs Pawkie made tea for them, and they soon began to play with our own younger children, in blithe forgetfulness of the storm; every now and then, however, the eldest of them, when the shutters rattled and the lum-head roared, would pause in his innocent daffing, and cower in towards Mrs Pawkie, as if he was daunted and dismayed by something, he knew not what.

Many a one that night walked the sounding shore in sorrow, and fires were lighted along it to a great extent; but the darkness and the noise of the raging deep, and the howling wind, never intermitted till about midnight, at which time a message was brought to me that it might be needful to send a guard of soldiers to the beach, for that broken masts and tackle had come in, and that surely some of the barks had perished. I lost no time in obeying this suggestion, which was made to me by one of the owners of the 'Louping Meg'; and to show that I sincerely sympathised with all those in affliction, I rose and dressed myself, and went down to the shore, where I directed several old boats to be drawn up by the fires, and blankets to be brought, and cordials prepared, for them that might be spared with life to reach the beach. And I walked the beach with the mourners till the morning.

As the day dawned, the wind began to abate in its violence, and to wear away from the sou-west into the norit; but it was soon discovered that some of the vessels with the corn had perished, for the first thing seen was a long fringe of tangle and grain along the line of the high-water mark, and everyone strained with greedy and grieved eyes, as the daylight brightened, to discover which had suffered.

But I can proceed no further with the dismal recital of that doleful morning. Let it suffice to be known that, through the haze, we at last saw three of the vessels lying on their beam-ends with their masts broken, and the waves riding like the furious horses of destruction over them. What had become of the other two was never known; but it was supposed that they had foundered at their anchors, and that all on board had perished.

The day being now the Sabbath, and the whole town idle,

everybody in a manner was down on the beach, to help and mourn as the bodies, one after another, were cast out of the waves. Alas! Few were the better of my provident preparation, and it was a thing not to be described to see, for more than a mile along the coast, the new-made widows and fatherless bairns mourning and weeping over the corpses of those they loved. Seventeen bodies were, before ten o'clock, carried to the desolated dwellings of their families; and when old Thomas Pull, the betheral, went to ring the bell for public worship, such was the universal sorrow of the town that Nanse Donsie, an idiot natural, ran up the street to stop him, crying, in the voice of a pardonable desperation, 'Wha in sic a time, can praise the Lord?'

THE EDUCATION
OF AN ENGINEER

Anstruther is a place sacred to the muse. She inspired (really to a considerable extent) Tennant's vernacular poem 'Anster Fair', and I have there waited upon her myself with much devotion. This was when I came as a young man to glean engineering experience from the building of a breakwater. What I gleaned, I am sure I do not know; but indeed I had already my own private determination to be an author. I loved the art of words and the appearances of life; and *travellers*, and *headers*, and *rubble*, and *polished ashlar*, and *pierres perdues*, and even the thrilling question of the *string-course*, interested me only (if they interested me at all) as properties for some possible romance or as words to add to my vocabulary. To grow a little catholic is the compensation of years. Youth is one-eyed, and in those days, though I haunted the breakwater by day, and even loved the place for the sake of the sunshine, the thrilling seaside air, the wash of waves on the sea-face, the green glimmer of the divers' helmets far below, and the musical chinking of the masons, my one genuine preoccupation lay elsewhere, and my only industry was in the hours when I was not on duty. I lodged with a certain Bailie Brown, a carpenter by trade, and there, as soon as dinner was despatched, in a chamber scented with dry rose leaves, drew in my chair to the table and proceeded to pour forth literature at such a speed, and with such intimations of early death and immortality, as I now look back upon with wonder.

Only one thing in connection with the harbour tempted me, and that was the diving, an experience I burned to taste of. But this was not to be, at least in Anstruther, and the subject involves a change of scene to the sub-arctic town of Wick.

You can never have dwelt in a country more unsightly than that part of Caithness, the land faintly swelling, faintly falling, not a tree, not a hedge-row, the fields divided by single slate stones set upon their edge, the wind always singing in your ears and (down the long road that led nowhere) thrumming in the telegraph wires. Only as you approached the coast was there anything to stir the heart. The plateau broke down to the North Sea in formidable cliffs, the tall out-stacks rose like pillars ringed about with surf, the coves were over-brimmed with clamorous froth, the sea-birds screamed, the wind sang in the thyme on the cliff's edge. Here and there, small ancient castles toppled on the brim; here and there, it was possible to dip into a dell of shelter, where you might lie and tell yourself you were a little warm, and hear (near at hand) the whin-pods bursting in the afternoon sun, and (farther off) the rumour of the turbulent sea.

As for Wick itself, it is one of the meanest of man's towns and situated certainly on the baldest of God's bays. It lives for herring, and a strange sight it is to see (of an afternoon) the heights of Pulteney blackened by seaward-looking fishers, as when a city crowds to a review or, as when bees have swarmed, the ground is horrible with lumps and clusters. And a strange sight, and a beautiful, to see the fleet put silently out against a rising moon, the sea-line rough as a wood with sails, and ever and again and one after another, a boat flitting by the silver disk.

Into the bay of Wick stretched the dark length of the unfinished breakwater in its cage of open staging, the travellers (like frames of churches) over-plumbing all, and, away at the extreme end, the divers toiling unseen on the foundation. On a platform of loose planks, the assistants turned their air-mills, a stone might be seen swinging between wind and water, underneath the swell ran gaily and, from time to time, a mailed dragon with a window-glass snout came dripping up the ladder. Youth is a blessed season after all; already I did not care two straws for literary glory. Posthumous ambition perhaps requires an atmosphere of roses; the more rugged excitant of Wick east winds had made another boy of me. To go down in the diving-dress, that was my absorbing fancy, and with the countenance of a certain handsome scamp of a diver, Bob Bain by name, I gratified the whim.

It was grey, harsh easterly weather, the swell ran pretty high, and out in the open there were 'skipper's daughters' when I found myself at last on the diver's platform, twenty pounds of lead upon each foot and my whole person swollen with ply and ply of woollen underclothing. One moment, the salt wind was whistling round my night-capped head, the next I was crushed almost double under the weight of the helmet. As that intolerable burden was laid upon me, I could have found it in my heart (only for shame's sake) to cry off from the whole enterprise. But it was too late. The attendants began to turn the hurdy-gurdy, and the air to whistle through the tube. Someone screwed in the barred window of the visor and I was cut off in a moment from my fellow men, standing there in their midst, but quite divorced from intercourse, a creature deaf and dumb, pathetically looking forth upon them from a climate of his own. Except that I could move and feel, I was like a man fallen in a catalepsy. But time was scarce given me to realise my isolation; the weights were hung upon my back and breast, the signal-rope was thrust into my unresisting hand and, setting a twenty pound foot upon the ladder, I began to descend.

Some twenty rounds below the platform, twilight fell. Looking up, I saw a low green heaven mottled with vanishing bells of white, looking around, except for the weedy spokes and shafts of the ladder, nothing but a green gloaming, somewhat opaque but very restful and delicious. Thirty rounds lower, I stepped off on the *pierres perdues* of the foundation, a dumb, helmeted figure took me by the hand, and made a gesture (as I read it) of encouragement and, looking in at the creature's window, I beheld the face of Bain. There we were, hand to hand and (when it pleased us) eye to eye, and either might have burst himself with shouting and not a whisper come to his companion's hearing. Each, in his own little world of air, stood incommunicably separate.

Bob had told me ere this a little tale, a five minutes' drama at the bottom of the sea, which at that moment possibly shot across my mind. He was down with another, settling a stone of the sea-wall. They had it well adjusted, Bob gave the signal, the scissors were slipped, the stone set home, and it was time to turn to something else. But still his companion remained bowed over the block like a mourner on a tomb, or only raised himself to make absurd contortions and mysterious signs unknown to the vocabulary of the diver. There, then, these two stood for a while, like the dead and the living, till there flashed a fortunate thought into Bob's mind, and he stopped, peered through the window of that other world, and beheld the face of its inhabitant wet with tears. The man was in pain! And Bob, glancing downward, saw what was the trouble. The block had been lowered on the foot of that unfortunate–he was caught alive at the bottom of the sea under fifteen tons of rock.

That two men should handle a stone so heavy, even swinging in the scissors, may appear strange to the inexpert. These must bear in mind the great density of the water of the sea, and the surprising results of transplantation to that medium. To understand a little of what these are, and how a man's weight, so far from being an encumbrance, is the very ground of his agility, was the chief lesson of my submarine experience. The knowledge came upon me by degrees. As I began to go forward with the hand of my estranged companion, a world of tumbled stones was visible, pillared with the weedy uprights of the staging, overhead a flat roof of green, a little in front the sea-wall, like an unfinished rampart. And presently in our upward progress, Bob motioned me to leap upon a stone. I looked to see if he were possibly in earnest, and he only signed to me the more imperiously. Now the block stood six feet high. It would have been quite a leap to me unencumbered. With the breast and back weights, and the twenty pounds upon each foot, and the staggering load of the helmet, the thing was out of reason. I laughed aloud in my tomb, and to prove to Bob how far he was astray, I gave a little impulse from my toes. Up I soared like a bird, my companion soaring by my side. As high as to the stone, and then higher, I pursued my impotent and empty flight. Even when the strong arm of Bob had checked my shoulders, my heels continued their ascent, so that I blew out sideways like an autumn leaf and must be hauled in, hand over hand, as sailors haul in the slack of a sail, and propped upon my feet again like an intoxicated sparrow.

Yet a little higher on the foundation, and we began to be affected by the bottom of the swell, running there like a strong breeze of wind. Or so I must suppose. For safe in my cushion of air, I was conscious of no impact, only swayed like a weed, and was now borne helplessly abroad, and now swiftly, and yet with dream-like gentleness, impelled against my guide. So does a child's balloon divagate upon the currents of the air and touch and slide off again from every obstacle. So must have ineffectually swung, so resented their inefficiency, those light crowds that followed the Star of Hades, and uttered exiguous voices in the land beyond Cocytus.

There was something strangely exasperating, as well as strangely wearying, in these uncommanded evolutions. It is bitter to return to infancy, to be supported, and directed, and perpetually set upon your feet, by the hand of someone else. The air besides, as it is supplied to you by the busy millers on the platform, closes the eustachian tubes and keeps the neophyte perpetually swallowing, till his throat is grown so dry that he can swallow no longer. And for all these reasons—although I had a fine, dizzy, muddle-headed joy in my surroundings and longed, and tried, and always failed, to lay hands on the fish that darted here and there about me, swift as humming-birds—yet I fancy I was rather relieved than otherwise when Bain brought me back to the ladder and signed me to mount.

And there was one more experience before me even then. Of a sudden, my ascending head passed into the trough of a swell. Out of the green, I shot at once into a glory of rosy, almost of sanguine light—the multitudinous seas incarnadined, the heaven above a vault of crimson. And then the glory faded into the hard, ugly daylight of a Caithness autumn, with a low sky, a grey sea, and a whistling wind.

Bob Bain had five shillings for his trouble, and I had done what I desired. It was one of the best things I got from my education as an engineer, of which, however, as a way of life, I wish to speak with sympathy. It takes a man into the open air; it keeps him hanging about harbours, which is the richest form of idling; it carries him to wild islands; it gives him a taste of the genial dangers of the sea; it supplies him with dexterities to exercise; it makes demands upon his ingenuity; it will go far to cure him of any taste (if he ever had one) for the miserable life of cities. And when it has done so, it carries him back and shuts him in an office! From the roaring skerry and the wet thwart of the tossing boat, he passes to the stool and desk, and with a memory full of ships, and seas, and perilous headlands, and the shining pharos, he must apply his long-sighted eyes to the pretty niceties of the drawing board, or measure his inaccurate mind with several pages of consecutive figures.

He is a wise youth, to be sure, who can balance one part of genuine life against two parts of drudgery between four walls, and for the sake of the one, manfully accept the other.

R. B. *Cunninghame Graham*

IN A GERMAN TRAMP

The tall, flaxen-haired stewardess Matilda had finished cutting schwartzbrot and had gone to bed. The Danish boarhound slept heavily under the lee of the chicken-coops, the six or seven cats were upon the cabin sofa. With the wind from the south-west, raising a terrific sea and sending showers of spray flying over the tops of the black rocks which fringed the town, the S.S.*Oldenburg* got under way and staggered out into the gut.

The old white city, girt on the seaward side by its breakwater of tall black rocks, the houses dazzlingly white, the crenelated walls, the long stretch of sand, extending to the belt of grey-green scrub and backed in the distance by the sombre forest, lay in the moonlight as distinct and clear as it had been midday. Clearer perhaps, for the sun in a sandy landscape seems to blur the outlines which the moon reveals; so that throughout North Africa night is the time to see a town in all its beauty of effect. The wind lifting the sand, drifted it whistling through the standing rigging of the tramp, coating the scarce-dried paint, and making paint, rigging, and everything on board feel like a piece of shark-skin to the touch.

The vessel groaned and laboured in the surface sea, and on the port quarter rose the rocks of the low island which forms the harbour, leaving an entrance of about half-a-mile between its shores and the rocks which guard the town. West-south-west a little westerly, the wind ever increased; the sea lashed upon the vessel's quarter, and in spite of the dense volumes of black smoke and showers of sparks flying out from the salt-coated smoke-stack, the tramp seemed to stand still. Upon the bridge the skipper screamed hoarsely in Platt-Deutsch down his connection-tube to the chief engineer; men came and went in dirty blue check cotton clothes and wooden shoes; occasionally a perspiring fireman poked his head above the hatch, and looking seaward for a moment, scooped off the sweat from his forefinger, muttered 'Gott freduma,' and went below; even the Arab deck-hands, roused into activity, essayed to set a staysail, and the whole ship, shaken between the storm and the exertions of the crew, trembled and shivered in the yeasty sea.

Nearer the rocks appeared, and the white town grew clearer, more intensely white, the sea frothed round the vessel, and the skipper, advancing to a missionary seated silently gazing across the water with a pallid sea-green face, slapped him upon the back, and with an oath said, 'Mister, will you have one glass of beer?'

The Levite *in partibus*, clad in his black alpaca Norfolk jacket, grey greasy flannel shirt and paper collar, with the whole man surmounted by the inevitable soup-tureen-shaped pith hat, the trade mark of his cofraternity, merely pressed both his hands harder upon his diaphragm and groaned.

'One leetel glass beer, I have it from Olten, fifty dozen of it. Perhaps all to be wasted. Have a glass beer, it will do your shtomag good.'

The persecuted United Presbyterian ambulant broke silence with one of those pious ejaculations which do duty (in the congregations) for an oath, and taking up his parable, fixing the pith tureen upon his head with due precaution, said, 'Captain, ye see I am a total abstainer, joined in the Whifflet, and in addeetion I feel my stomach sort o' discomposed.'

And to him again, good Captain Rindelhaus rejoined, 'Well, Mister Missionary, do you see dat rocks?'

The Reverend Mr McKerrochar, squinting to leeward with an agonising stare, admitted that he did, but qualified by saying, 'there was sic a halgh, he wasna sure that they were rocks at all.'

'Not rocks! Kreuz-Sacrament, dose rocks you see are sharp as razors, and the back-wash off them give you no jance. I dell you, sheep's-head preacher, dat point de way like sign-board and not follow it oop himself, you better take glass beer in time, for if the schip not gather headway in about five minutes you perhaps not get another jance.'

After this dictum, he stood looking into the night, his glass gripped in his left hand, and in his right a half-smoked-out cigar, which he put to his mouth mechanically now and then, but drew no smoke from. The missionary too looked at the rocks with increased interest, and the Arab pilot, staggering up the ladder to the bridge, stolidly pointed to the surf and gave us his opinion that 'he, the captain and the *faqui* would soon be past the help of prayer,' piously adding, 'that it seemed Allah's will, although he thought the Kaffirs, sons of burnt Kaffirs, in the stoke-hole were not firing up.'

With groans and heavings, with long shivers which came over

her as the sea struck her on the beam, the vessel fought for her life, belching great clouds of smoke out into the clear night air. Captain and missionary, pilot and crew, stood gazing at the sea; the captain now and then yelling some unintelligible Platt-Deutsch order down the tube; the missionary fumbling with a bible lettered 'Polyglot', covered in black oil-cloth; the pilot passing his beads between the fingers of his right hand, his eyes apparently not seeing anything; and it seemed as if another twenty minutes must have seen them all upon the rocks.

But Allah perhaps was on the watch; and the wind falling for an instant, or the burnt Kaffirs in the stoke-hole having struck a better vein of coal, the rusty iron sea-coffin slowly gathered headway, staggered as the engines, driven to the highest pressure, seemed to tear out her ribs, and forged ahead. Then, lurching in the sea, the screw occasionally racing with a roar and the black decks dripping and under water, the scuppers being choked with the filth of years, she sidled out to sea, and rose and fell in the long rollers outside the harbour, which came in from the west. Rindelhaus set her on her course, telling the Arab helmsman in the pigeon-English which served them as a means of interchanging their few ideas, to 'keep her head north and by west a little northerly, and let him know when they were abreast of Jibel Hadid,' adding a condemnation of the Arab race in general and the particular sailor, whom he characterised as a 'tamned heaven dog, not worth his kraut.'

The sailor, dressed in loose Arab trousers and a blue jersey, the whole surmounted by a greasy fez, replied, 'Yes, him know Jibel Hadid, Captain, him keep her head north and by west alright,' and probably also consigned the captain and the whole Germanic race to the hottest corner of Jehannum, and so both men were pleased.

The boarhound gambolled on the deck, Matilda peeped up the companion, her dripping wooden shoes looking like waterlogged canoes, and the Scotch missionary began to walk about, holding his monstrous hat on with one hand and hugging his oilskin-covered 'Polyglot' under his left arm. Crossing the skipper in his walk, in a more cheerful humour he ventured to remark, 'Eh! Captain, maybe I could mak' a shape at yon glass of beer the now.' But things had changed, and Rindelhaus looked at him with the usual condescending bearing of the seaman to the mere passenger, and said, 'Nein, you loose your obbordunity for dat glass beer, my friend, and now I have to navigate my ship.'

The *Oldenburg* pursued the devious tenor of her way, touching at ports which all were either open roadsteads or had bars on which the surf boiled with a noise like thunder; receiving cargo in driblets, a sack or two of marjoram, a bale of goatskins or of hides, two or three bags of wool, and sometimes waiting for a day or two unable to communicate until the surf went down. The Captain spent his time in harbour fishing uninterestedly, catching great, bearded, spiky-finned sea monsters which he left to die upon the deck. Not that he was hard-hearted, but merely unimaginative, after the way of those who, loving sport for the pleasure it affords themselves, hotly deny that it is cruel, or that it can occasion inconvenience to any participator in a business which they themselves enjoy. So the poor innocent sea-monsters floundered in slimy agony upon the deck; the boarhound and the cats taking a share in martyring them, tearing and biting at them as they gasped their lives away; condemned to agony for some strange reason, or perhaps because, as every living thing is born to suffer, they were enduring but their fair proportion, as they happened to be fish. Pathetic but unwept the tragedy of all the animals, and we but links in the same chain with them, look at it all as unconcerned as gods. But as the bearded spiky fish gasped on the deck the missionary tried to abridge their agony with a belaying-pin; covering himself with blood and slime, and setting up the back of Captain Rindelhaus, who vowed his deck should not be hammered 'like a skidel alley, all for the sake of half-a-dozen fish, which would be dead in half-an-hour and eaten by the cats.'

The marvels of our commerce, in the shape of Waterbury watches, scissors and looking-glasses, beads, Swiss clocks and musical-boxes, all duly dumped, and the off-scouring of the trade left by the larger ships duly received aboard, the *Oldenburg* stumbled out to sea if the wind was not too strong, and squirmed along the coast. Occasionally upon arrival at a port the sound of psalmody was heard, and a missionary boat put off to pass the time of God with their brother on the ship. Then came the greetings, as the whole party sat on the fiddle-gratings jammed up against the funnel; the latest news from the Cowcaddens and the gossip from along the coast was duly interchanged. Gaunt-featured girls, removed by physical conditions from all temptation, sat and talked with scraggy, freckled, and pith-hatted men. It was all conscience, and relatively tender-hearted, and as the moon lit up the dirty decks, they paraded up and down, happy once more to be secure, even for a brief space, from insult and to feel themselves at home. Dressed in white blouses, innocent of stays, with skirts which no belt known to milliners could ever join to the body or the blouse; with smaller-sized pith hats, sand-shoes and spectacles; their hands in Berlin gloves, and freckles reaching far down upon their necks, they formed a crushing argument in their own persons against polygamy. Still, in the main, all kindly souls, and some with a twinkle in their white-eyelashed, steel-grey eyes, as of a Congregationalist bull-terrier, which showed you that they would gladly suffer martyrdom without due cause, or push themselves into great danger out of sheer ignorance and want of knowledge of mankind. Life's misfits, most of them; their hands early inured to typewriting machines, their souls, as they would say, 'sair hodden doon in prayer'; carefully educated to be ashamed of any scrap of womanhood they might posses. Still they were sympathetic, for sympathy is near akin to tears, and looking at them one divined that they must have shed tears plentifully, enough to wash away any small sins they had committed in their lives.

The men, sunburnt yet sallow, seemed nourished on tinned meats and mineral table-waters; their necks, scraggy and red, protruded from their collars like those of vultures; they carried umbrellas in their hand from early habit of a wet climate, and seemed as if they had been chosen after much cogitation by some unskilled commission, for their unfitness for their task.

They too, dogged and narrow-minded as they were, were yet pathetic, when one thought upon their lives. No hope of converts, or of advancement in the least degree, stuck down on the coast, far off from Dorcas meetings, school-feasts, or anything in which more favoured countries whiles away the Scripture-reader's time; they hammered at their self-appointed business day by day and preached unceasingly, apparently indifferent to anything that passed, so that they got off their due quantity of words a day. In course of time, and after tea and bread-and-butter had been consumed, they got into their boat, struck up the tune of 'Sidna Aissa Hobcum,' and from the taffrail McKerrochar saw them depart, joining in the chorus lustily and waving a dirty handkerchief until they faded out of sight.

Mr McKerrochar, one of those Scottish professional religionists whom early training or their own 'damnable iteration' has convinced of all the doctrine that they preach, formed a last relic of a disappearing type. The antiquated out-and-out doctrine of Hell-fire and Paradise, the jealous Scottish God, and the Mosaic Dispensation which he accepted whole, tinged slightly with the current theology of Airdrie or Coatbridge, made him a formidable adversary of the trembling infidel in religious strife. In person he was tall and loosely built, his trousers bagging at the knees as if a horse's hock had been inside the cloth. Wrong-headed as befits his calling, he yet saw clearly enough in business matters, and might have marked a flock of heathen sheep had he applied his business aptitude to his religious work, or on the other hand he might have made a fortune had he chanced to be a rogue. He led a joyless, stirring life, striving towards ideals which have made the world a quagmire; yet worked towards them with that simple faith which makes a man ten thousand times more dangerous, in his muddle-headed course. Abstractions which he called duty, morality and self-sacrifice, ruled all his life; forcing him ever onward to occupy himself with things which really he had no concern with; and making him neglect himself and the more human qualities of courtesy and love.

And so he stood, waving his pocket-handkerchief long after the strains of 'Sidna Aissa Hobcum' had melted into the night air; his arms still waving as the sails of windmills move round once or twice, but haltingly, after the wind has dropped. Perhaps that class of man seldom or never chews the cud either of sweet or bitter recollection; and if, as in McKerrochar's case, he is deprived of whisky in which to drown his cares, the last impression gone, his mind hammers away, like the keys of a loose typewriter under a weary operator's hands, half aimlessly, till circumstances place new copy under its roller, and it starts off again to work.

He might have gone on waving right through the dog-watch had not the captain with a rough ejaculation stopped his arm. 'Himmel, what for a semaphore, Herr Missionary, is dat; and you gry too, when you look at dat going-away boat...Well, have a glass of beer. I tell you it is not good to look at boats and gry for noddings, for men that have an ugly yellow beard like yours and mine.'

'I wasna greetin', Captain,' said the missionary, furtively wiping his face. 'It was just ane o' thae clinkers, I think they ca' the things, has got intae my eye.'

'Glinkers, mein friend, do not get into people's eyes when der ship is anchored,' Rindelhaus replied. 'Still I know as you feel, but not for missionary boats. You not know Oldenburg, eh? Pretta place, not far from Bremerhaven. Oldenburg is one of the prettaest places in the world. I live there. Hour and half by drain, oot from de port. I just can see the vessels' masts and the funnel smoke as they pass oop and down the stream. I think I should not care too much to live where man can see no ships. Yes, yes. Ah, here come Matilda mit de beer. Mein herz, you put him down here on dis bale of marjoram, and you goes off to bed. I speak here mit de Herr Missionary, who gry for noddings when he look at missionary boat go off into de night.'

'Ah, Oldenburg, ja, yes, I live there. Meine wife she live there, and meine littel Gretchen, she about den or twelve, I don't remember which. Prosit! Herr Missionary, you have no wife, no little Gretchen, eh? So, so, dat is perhaps better for a missionary.'

The two sat looking at nothing, thinking in the painful ruminant way of semi-educated men, the captain's burly North-German figure stretched on a cane deck-chair. About a captain's age he was, that is, his beard had just begun to grizzle, and his nose was growing red, the bunions on his feet knotted his boots into protuberances, after the style of those who pass their lives about a deck. In height above six feet, broad-shouldered and red-faced, his voice of the kind with which a huntsman rates a dog, his clothes bought at a Bremerhaven slop-shop, his boots apparently made by a portmanteau-maker, and in his pocket was a huge silver keyless watch which he said was 'a 'gronometer', and keep de Bremen time.' Instant in prayer and cursing; pious yet blasphemous; kindly but brutal in a Teutonic way; he kicked his crew about as they had all been dogs and yet looked after the tall stewardess Matilda as she had been his child, guarding her virtue from the assaults of passengers, and though alone with her in the small compass of a ship, respecting it himself.

After an interval he broke into his subject, just as a phonograph takes up its interrupted tale, as if against its will.

'So ja, yes, Oldenburg, pretta place. I not see it often though. In all eight years I never stay more to my house than from de morning Saturday to Monday noon, and dat after a four month's trip. Meine wife, she is getting little sdout, and not mind much, for she is immer washing; washing de linen, de house, de steps. She wash de whole ship oop only I never let her come to sea. The Gretchen she immer say, 'Father, why you not stop to home?' You got no littel Gretchen, eh? Well, perhaps better so. Last Christmas I was at Oldenburg. Christmas Eve I buy one tree, and then I remember I have to go to sea next morning about eleven o'clock. So I say noddings all day, and about four o'clock the agent come and tell me that the company not wish me leave Oldenburg upon de Christmas Day. Then I was so much glad I think I wait to eat meine Christmas dinner with meine wife, and talk with Gretchen in the evening while I smoke my pipe. The stove was burning and the table stand ready mit sausage and mit bread and cheese, beer of course, and lax, dat lax they bring from Norway, and I think I have good time. Then I think on de company, what they say if I take favour from them and not go out to sea; they throw it in my teeth for ever, and tell me 'Rindelhaus, you remember we was so good to you upon that Christmas Day.' I tell the agent thank you, but say I go to sea. Meine wife she gry and I say noddings, noddings to Gretchen, and sit down to take my tea. Morning, I tell my little girl, then she gry bitterly and say, 'What for you go to sea?' I kiss meine wife and walk down to the quay; it just begin to snow; I curse the schelm sailors, de pilot come aboard and we begin to warp into the stream. Just then I hear a running on the quay, just like as a Friesland pony come clattering on the stones. I look up and see Gretchen mit her little wooden shoes. She run down to the ship, and say, 'Why you go to sea, father, upon Christmas?' and I not able to say noddings, but just to wave my hand. We warp out into the stream, and she stand grying till she faded out of sight. Sometimes I feel a liddel sorry about dat Christmas Day. But have another glass beer, Herr Missionary, it always do me good.'

Wiping the froth from his moustache with his rough hand he went below, leaving the missionary alone upon the deck.

The night descended, and the ship shrouded in mist grew ghostly and unnatural, whilst great drops of moisture hung on the backstays and the shrouds.

The Arab crew lay sleeping, huddled round the windlass,

looking mere masses of white dirty rags; the seaman keeping the anchor watch looked like a giant, and from the shore occasionally the voices of the guards at the town prison came through the mist, making the boarhound turn in his sleep and growl. The missionary paced to and fro a little, settling a woollen comforter about his neck.

Then, going to the rail, he looked into the night where the boat rearing off his brethren had disappeared; his soul perhaps wandering towards some Limbo as he gazed, and his elastic-sided boots fast glued to the dirty decks by the dried-up blood of the discarded fish.

A LOST MAN

It was a dirty evening, coming on to dusk, and the *Vital Spark* went walloping drunkenly down Loch Fyne with a cargo of oak bark, badly trimmed. She staggered to every shock of the sea; the waves came combing over her quarter, and Dougie the mate began to wish they had never sailed that day from Kilcatrine. They had struggled round the point of Pennymore, the prospect looking every moment blacker, and he turned a dozen projects over in his mind for inducing Para Handy to anchor somewhere till the morning. At last he remembered Para's partiality for anything in the way of long-shore gaiety, and the lights of the village of Furnace gave him an idea.

'Ach! Man, Peter,' said he, 'did we no' go away and forget this wass the night of the baal at Furnace? What do you say to going in and joining the spree?'

'You're feared, Dougie,' said the Captain; 'you're scared to daith for your life, in case you'll have to die and leave your money. You're thinkin' you'll be drooned, and that's the way you want to put her into Furnace. Man! But you're tumid, tumid! Chust look at me - no' the least put aboot. That's because I'm a Macfarlane, and a Macfarlane never was bate yet, never in this world! I'm no' goin' to stop the night for any baal - we must be in the Clyde on Friday; besides, we havna the clothes wi' us for a baal. Forbye, who'll buy the tickets? Eh? Tell me that! Who'll buy the tickets?'

'Ach! You don't need tickets for a Furnace baal,' said Dougie, flicking the spray from his ear, and looking longingly at the village they were nearing. 'You don't need tickets for a Furnace baal as long as you ken the man at the door and taalk the Gaelic at him. And your clothes'll do fine if you oil your boots and put on a kind of a collar. What's the hurray for the Clyde? It'll no' run dry. In weather like this, too! It's chust a temptin' of Providence. I had a dream yonder last night that wasna canny. Chust a temptin' of Providence.'

'I wudna say but that it is,' agreed the Captain weakly, putting the vessel a little to starboard; 'it's many a day since I was at a spree in Furnace. Are you sure the baal's the night?'

'Of course I am,' said Dougie emphatically; 'it only started yesterday.'

'Weel, if you're that keen on't, we'll maybe be chust as weel to put her in till the mornin',' said Para Handy, steering hard for Furnace Bay; and in a little he knocked down to the engines with the usual, 'Stop her, Macphail, when you're ready.'

All the crew of the *Vital Spark* went to the ball, but they did not dance much, though it was the boast of Para Handy that he was a 'fine strong dancer.' The last to come on to the vessel in the morning when the ball stopped, because the paraffin-oil was done, was the Captain, walking on his heels, with his pea-jacket tightly buttoned on his chest, and his round, go-ashore pot hat, as he used to say himself, 'on three hairs.' It was a sign that he felt intensely satisfied with everything.

'I'm feeling chust sublime,' he said to Dougie, smacking his lips and thumping himself on the chest as he took his place at the wheel, and the *Vital Spark* resumed her voyage down the loch. 'I am chust like the eagle that knew the youth in the Scruptures. It's a fine, fine thing a spree, though I was not in the trum for dancing. I met sixteen cousins yonder, and them all in the committee. They were the proud men last night to be having a captain for a cousin, and them only quarry-men. It's the education, Dougie; education gives you the nerve, and if you have the nerve you can go round the world.'

'You werena very far roond the world, whatever o't,' unkindly interjected the engineer, who stuck his head up at that moment.

The Captain made a push at him angrily with his foot. 'Go down, Macphail,' he said, 'and do not be making a display of your ignorance on this ship. Stop you till I get you at Bowling! Not round the world! Man, I wass twice at Ullapool, and took the *Fital Spark* to Ireland wance, without a light on her. There is not a port I am not acquent with from the Tail of the Bank to Cairndow, where they keep the two New Years. And Campbelltown, ay, or Barra, or Tobermory. I'm telling you when I am in them places it's Captain Peter Macfarlane iss the mich-respected man. If you were a rale enchineer and not chust a fireman, I would be asking you to my ludgings to let you see the things I brought from my voyages.'

The engineer drew in his head and resumed the perusal of a penny novelette.

'He thinks I'm frightened for him,' said the Captain, winking darkly to his mate. 'It iss because I am too cuvil to him. If he angers me, I'll show him. It is chust spoiling the boat having a man like that in charge of her enchines, and her such a fine smert boat, with me, and a man like me, in command of her.'

'And there's mysel', too, the mate,' said Dougie; I'm no' bad mysel'.'

Below Minard rocks the weather grew worse again; the same old seas smashed over the *Vital Spark*. 'She's pitchin aboot chust like a washin'-boyne,' said Dougie apprehensively. 'That's the worst of them oak-bark cargoes.'

'Like a washin'-boyne!' cried Para Handy indignantly;' she's chust doing sublime. I was in boats in my time where you would need to be baling the watter out of your top-boots every here and there. The smertest boat in the tred; stop you till I have a pound of my own, and I will paint her till you'll take her for a yat if it wasna for the lum. You and your washin'-boyne! A washin'-boyne wudna do you any herm, my laad, and that's telling you.'

They were passing Loch Gair; the steamer *Cygnet* overtook and passed them as if they had been standing, somebody shouting to them from her deck.

Para Handy refrained from looking. It had always annoyed him to be passed this way by other craft; and in summer time, when the turbine *King Edward* or the *Lord of the Isles* went past him like a streak of lightening, he always retired below to hide his feelings. He did not look at the *Cygnet*.

'Ay, ay,' he said to Dougie, 'if I was telling Mr MacBrayne the umpudence of them fellows, he would put a stop to it in a meenute, but I will not lose them their chobs, poor sowls! Maybe they have wives and families. That'll be Chonny MacTavish takin' his fun of me; you would think he wass a wean. Chust like them brats of boys that come to the riverside when we'll be going up the Clyde at Yoker and cry, '*Columbia*, ahoy!' at us - the duvvle's own!'

As the *Cygnet* disappeared in the distance, with a figure waving at her stern, a huge sea struck the *Vital Spark* and swept her from stem to stern, almost washing the mate, who was hanging on to a stay, overboard.

'Tar! Tar!' cried the Captain. 'Go and get a ha'ad o' that bucket or it'll be over the side.'

There was no response. The Tar was not visible, and a wild look of dread took possession of Para Handy.

'Let us pause and consider,' said he to himself. 'Was the Tar on board when we left Furnace?'

They searched the vessel high and low for the missing member of the crew, who was sometimes given to fall asleep in the fo'c'sle at the time he was most needed. But there was no sign of him. 'I ken fine he wass on board when we started,' said the Captain, distracted, 'for I heard him sputtin'. Look again, Dougie, like a good laad.'

Dougie looked again, for he, too was sure The Tar had returned from the ball with them. 'I saw him with my own eyes,' he said, 'two of him, the same as if he wass a twins; but that iss the curse of drink in a place like Furnace.' But the search was in vain, even though the engineer said he had seen The Tar an hour ago.

'Weel, there's a good man gone!' said Para Handy. 'Och! Poor Tar! It was yon last smasher of a sea. He's over the side. Poor laad! Poor laad! Cot bless me, dying without a word of Gaelic in his mooth! It's a chudgement on us for the way we were carryin' on, chust a judgement; not another drop of drink will I drink, except maybe beer. Or at New Year time. I'm blaming you, Dougie, for making us stop at Furnace for a baal I wudna give a snuff for. You are chust a disgrace to the vessel with your smokin' and your drinkin' and your ignorance. It iss time you were livin' a better life for the sake of your wife and femily. If it wass not for you makin' me go into Furnace last night, The Tar would be to the fore yet, and I would not need to be sending a telegram to his folk from Ardrishaig. If I wass not steering the boat, I would break my he'rt greetin' for the poor laad that never did anybody any herm. Get oot the flag from below my bunk, give it a syne in the pail, and put it at half-mast and we'll go into Ardrishaig and send a telegram–it'll be a sixpence. It'll be a telegram with a sore he'rt, I'll assure you. I do not know what I will say in it, Dougie. It will not do to break it too much to them. Maybe we will send them two telegrams—that'll be a shilling. We'll say in the first wan 'your son, Colin, left the boat today,' and in the next wan we will say, 'he iss not coming back, he is drooned.' Och! Och! Poor Tar, amn't I sorry for him? I was chust going to put up his wages a shillin' on Setturday.'

The *Vital Spark* went in close to Ardrishaig pier just as the *Cygnet* was leaving after taking in a cargo of herring-boxes. Para Handy and Dougie went ashore in the punt, the Captain with his hands washed and his watch-chain on as a tribute of respect for the deceased. Before they could send off the telegram it was necessary that they should brace themselves for the melancholy occasion.

'No drinking. Chust wan gless of beer,' said Para Handy, and they entered a discreet contiguous public-house for this purpose.

The Tar himself was standing at the counter having a refreshment, with one eye wrapped up in a handkerchief.

'Dalmighty!' cried the Captain, staggered at the sight, and turning pale. 'What are you doing here with your eye in a sling?'

'What's your business?' retorted The Tar coolly. 'I'm no' in your employ anyway.'

'What way that?' asked Para Handy sharply.

'Did you no' give me this black eye and the sack last night at the baal, and tell me I wass never to set foot on the *Vital Spark* again? It was gey mean o' you to go away withoot lettin' me get my dunnage oot, and that's the way I came here with the *Cygnet* to meet you. Did you no' hear me roarin' on you when we passed?'

'Weel done! Weel done!' said Para Handy soothingly, with a wink at his mate. 'But ach! I wass only in fun Colin; it was a jeenk; it was chust a baur aalthegither. Come away back to the boat like a smert laad. I have a shilling here I wass going to spend anyway. Colin, what'll you take? We thought you were over the side and drooned, and you are here, quite dry as usual.'

David W. Bone

THE BLUE PETER

Ding...dong...ding...dong.

The university bells toll out in strength of tone that tells of south-west winds and misty weather. On the street below my window familiar city noises, unheeded by day, strike tellingly on the ear—hoof-strokes and rattle of wheels, tramp of feet on the stone flags, a snatch of song from a late reveller, then silence, broken in a little by the deep mournful note of a steamer's siren, wind-borne through the Kelvin Valley, or the shrilling of an engine whistle that marks a driver impatient at the junction points.

Sleepless, I think of my coming voyage, of the long months, years perhaps, that will come and go ere next I lie awake hearkening to the night voices of my native city. My days of holiday–an all too brief spell of comfort and shore living–are over; another peal or more of the familiar bells and my emissary of the fates–a Gorbals cabman, belike–will be at the door, ready to set me rattling over the granite setts on the direct road that leads by Bath Street, Finnieston, and Cape Horn–to San Francisco. A long voyage and a hard. And where next? No-one seems to know! Anywhere wind blows and square-sail can carry a freight. At the office on Saturday, the shipping clerk turned his palms out at my questioning.

'Home again, perhaps. The colonies! Up the Sound or across to Japan,' he said, looking in his *Murray's Diary* and then at the clock, to see if there was time for him to nip home for his clubs and catch the 1.15 for Kilmacolm

Nearly seventeen months of my apprenticeship remain to be served. Seventeen months of a hard sea life, between the masts of a starvation Scotch barque, in the roughest of seafaring, on the long voyage, the stormy track leading westward round the Horn.

It will be February or March when we get down there. Not the worst months, thank Heaven! But bad enough at the best. And we'll be badly off this voyage, for the owners have taken two able seamen off our complement. 'Hard times!' they will be saying. Aye! Hard times–for us, who will now have to share two men's weight in working our heavily sparred barque.

Two new apprentices have joined. Poor little devils! They don't know what it is. It seemed all very fine to that wee chap from Inveraray who came with his father to see the ship before he joined. How the eyes of him glinted as he looked about, proud of his brass-bound clothes and badge cap. And the mate, all smiles, showing them over the ship and telling the old Hielan' clergyman what a fine vessel she was, and what an interest he took in boys, and what fine times they had on board ship, and all that! Ah yes–

fine times! It's as well the old chap doesn't know what he is sending his son to! How can he? We know–but we don't tell. Pride! Rotten pride! We come home from our first voyage sick of it all....Would give it up but for pride....Afraid to be called 'stuck sailors'....of the sneers of our old schoolmates....So we come home in a great show of bravery and swagger about in our brass-bound uniform and lie finely about the fine times we had....out there!....And then nothing will do but Jimmy next door must be off to the sea too–to come back and play the same game on young Alick! That's the way of it!

Then when the mate and them came to the half-deck, it was, 'Oh yes, Sir! This is the boys' quarters, Well! Not always like that, Sir–when we get away to sea, you know, and get things ship-shape. Oh, well no! There's not much room aboard ship, you see. This is one of our boys–Mister Jones.' (Jones, looking like a miller's man– he had been stowing ship's biscuits in the tanks–grinned foolishly at the mate's introduction.) 'Mister!' 'We're very busy just now, getting ready for sea. Everything's in a mess, as you see, Sir. Only joined myself last week. But, oh yes! It will be all right when we get to sea–when we get things shipshape and settled down, Sir!'

Oh yes! Everything will be all right then, eh? Especially when we get off the Horn, and the dingy half-deck will be awash most of the time with icy water. The owners would do nothing to it this trip, in spite of our complaints. They sent a young man down from the office last week who poked at the covering boards with his umbrella and wanted to know what we were growling at. Wish we had him out there–off Diego Ramirez. Give him something to growl about with the ship working, and green seas on deck, and the water lashing about the floor of the house, washing out the lower bunks, bed and clothing that we had fondly hoped would keep us moderately dry in the next bitter night watch. And when (as we try with trembling, benumbed fingers to buckle on the sodden clothes) the ill-hinged door swings to, and a rush of water and a blast of icy wind chills us to the marrow, it needs but a hoarse, raucous shout from without to crown the summit of misery. 'Out there, the watch! Turn out!' in a tone that admits of no protest. 'Turn out, damn ye, an' stand by t' wear ship.'

(A blast of wind and rain rattles on my window-pane. *Ugh!* I turn the more cosily amid my blankets).

Oh yes! He would have something to growl at, that young man who asked if the 'Skipp-ah' was aboard, and said he 'was deshed if he could see what we had to complain of.'

He would learn, painfully, that a ship, snugly moored in the south-east corner of the Queen's Dock (stern-on to a telephone call-box), and the same craft, labouring in the teeth of a Cape Horn gale, present some points of difference; that it is a far cry from 58° South to the Clyde Repair Works, and that the business of shipping is not entirely a matter of ledgers.

Oh well! Just have to stick it, though. After all, it won't always be hard times. Think of the long, sunny days drowsing along down the 'Trades', of the fine times out these in 'Frisco, of the joys of strenuous action greater than the shipping clerk will ever know, even if he should manage to hole out in three. Seventeen months! It will soon pass, and I'll be a free man when I get back to Glasgow again. Seventeen months, and then–then–

Ding...dong...Ding...dong...Ding...dong...

Quarter to! With a sigh for the comfort of a life ashore, I rise and dress. Through the window I see the Square, shrouded in mist, the nearer leafless shrubs swaying in the chill wind, pavement glistening in the flickering light of the street lamps. A dismal morning to be setting off to the sea! Portent of head winds and foul weather that we may meet in Channel before the last of Glasgow's grime and smoke-wrack is blown from the rigging.

A stir in the next room marks another rising. Kindly old '*Ding...dong*' has called a favourite brother from his rest to give me convoy to the harbour. Ready for the road, he comes to my room. Sleepy-eyed, yawning.

'Four o'clock! *Ugh!* Who ever heard of a man going to sea at four in the morning! Ought to be a bright summer's day, and the sun shining and flags flying and...' A choked laugh. 'Glad I'm not a sailorman to be going out on a morning like this! Sure you've remembered everything? Your cab should be here now. Just gone four. Heard the bells as I was dressing.'

Rattle of wheels on the granite setts—sharp metallic ring of shod heels—a moment of looking for a number—a ring of the doorbell.

'Perty that's tae gang doon tae th' Queen's Dock wi' luggage....A' richt, Mister! Ah can cairry them ma'sel....Aye! Weel! Noo that ye menshun it, Sur...oan a mornin' like this....Ma respeks, gents!'

There are no good-byes. The last has been said the night before. There could be no enthusiasm at four on a raw November's morning; it is best that I slip out quietly and take my seat, with a last look at the quiet street, the darkened windows, the quiet, familiar belfry of St Jude's.

'A' richt, Sur. G'up, mere! Haud up, mere, ye...!'

At a corner of the Square the night policeman, yawning whole-heartedly, peers into the cab to see who goes. There is nothing to investigate; the sea-chest, sailor-bag and bedding, piled awkwardly on the 'dickey', tell all he wants to know.

'A sailor for aff!'

Jingling his keys, he thinks maybe of the many braw lads from Lochinver who go the same hard road.

Down the deserted, wind-swept streets we drive steadily on, till house lights glinting behind the blinds and hurrying figures of a night-shift show that we are near the river and the docks. A turn along the waterside, the dim outlines of the ships and tracery of mast and spar looming large and fantastic in the darkness, and the driver, questioning, brings up at a dim-lit shed, bare of goods and cargo—the berth of a full-laden outward-bounder.

My barque—the *Florence*, of Glasgow—lies in a corner of the dock, ready for sea. Tugs are churning the muddy water alongside, getting into position to drag her away from the quay wall; the lurid side-light gleams on a small knot of well-wishers gathered at the forward gangway exchanging parting words with the local seamen of our crew. I have cut my time but short. 'Come on there, you!' is my greeting from the harassed chief mate. 'Are you turned a ------ passenger, with your gloves and your overcoat? You should have been here an hour ago! Get a move on ye now, and bear a hand with these warps....Gad! A drunken crew an' skulkin' 'prentices, an' the Old Man growlin' like a bear with a sore ------.'

Grumbling loudly, he goes forward, leaving me the minute for 'good-bye,' the late 'remembers,' the last long hand grip.

Into the half-deck, to change hurriedly into working clothes. Time enough to note the guttering lamp, evil smell, the dismal aspect of my home afloat–then, on deck again, to haul, viciously despondent, at the cast-off mooring ropes.

Forward, the crew–drunk to a man–are giving the chief mate trouble, and it is only when the gangway is hauled ashore that anything can be done. The cook, lying as he fell over his sailor bag, sings *t'wis yer vice, ma gen-tul Merry!* in as many keys as there are points in the compass, drunkenly indifferent to the farewells of a sad-faced woman, standing on the quayside with a baby in her arms. Riot and disorder is the way of things; the mates, out of temper with the muddlers at the ropes, are swearing, pushing, coaxing–to some attempt at getting the ship unmoored. Double work for the sober ones, and for thanks–a muttered curse. Small wonder that men go drunk to the sea; the wonder is that any go sober!

At starting there is a delay. Some of the men have slipped ashore for a last pull at a neighbourly 'half-mutchkin,' and at muster four are missing. For a time we hold on at single moorings, the stern tug blowing a 'hurry-up' blast on her siren, the captain and a river pilot stamping on the poop, angrily impatient. One rejoins, drunken and defiant, but of the others there is no sign. We can wait no longer.

'Let go, aft!' shouts the captain. 'Let go, an' haul in. Damn them for worthless sodjers, anyway! Mister'—to a waiting Board of Trade official—'send them t'Greenock, if ye can run them in. If not, telephone down that we're three ABs short....Lie up t'th'nor'ard, stern tug, there. Hard a-port, Mister? All right! Let go all, for'ard!' ... We swing into the dock passage, from whence the figures of our friends on the misty quayside are faintly visible. The little crown raises a weakly cheer, and one bold spirit (with his guid-brither's 'hauf-pey note' in his pocket) shouts a bar or two of 'Wull ye no' come back again!' A few muttered farewells. And the shore folk hurry down between the wagons to exchange a last parting word at the Kelvinhaugh.

'...*Dong....ding....DONG....DONG....*'

Set to a fanfare of steam whistles, Old Brazen Tongue of Gilmorehill tolls us benison as we steer between the pierheads. Six sonorous strokes, loud above the shrilling of workshop signals and the nearer merry jangle of the engine-house chimes.

Workmen, hurrying to their jobs, curse us for robbing them of a 'quarter,' the swing-bridge being open to let us through.

'Come oan! Hurry up wi' that auld jeely-dish an' sees a chance tae wur wark,' they shout in a chorus of just irritation.

A facetious member of our crew shouts, 'Wot-oh, old stiy-at-'omes. Cahmin' aat t' get wandered?'

And a dockman answers 'Hello, Jake. Man, th'sailormen maun a' be deid when th'mate gied you a sicht! Jist you wait tae he catches ye fanklin' th'crojeck sheets!'

We swing slowly between the pierheads, and the workmen, humoured by the dockman's jest, give us a hoarse cheer as they scurry across the still-moving bridge.

In time-honoured fashion our Cockney humourist calls for, 'Three cheers f'r ol' Pier'ead, boys' and such of the 'boys' as are able chant a feeble echo to his shout.

The tugs straighten us up in the river, and we breast the flood cautiously, for the mist has not yet cleared and the coasting skippers are taking risks to get to their berths before the stevedores have picked their men. In the shipyards workmen are beginning their day's toil, the lowe of their flares lights up the gaunt structure of ships to be. Sharp at the last wailing note of the whistle, the din of strenuous work begins, and we are fittingly drummed down the reaches to a merry tune of clanging hammers–the shipyard chorus 'Let Glasgow Flourish!'

Dawn finds us off Bowling, and as the fog clears, gives us misty views of the Kilpatrick Hills. Ahead, Dumbarton Rock looms up, gaunt and misty, sentinel o'er the lesser heights. South, the Renfrew shore stretches broadly out under the brightening sky–the wooded Elderslie slopes and distant hills and, nearer, the shoal ground behind the lang Dyke, where screaming gulls circle and wheel. The setting out is none so ill now, with God's good daylight broad over all, and the flags flying–the 'Blue Peter' fluttering its message at the fore.

On the poop, the captain (the 'Old Man,' be he twenty-one or fifty) paces to and fro–a short sailor walk, with a pause now and then to mark the steering or pass a word with the river pilot. Of medium height, though broad to the point of ungainliness, Old Jock Leish (in his ill-fitting broadcloth shore-clothes) might have passed for a prosperous farmer, but it needed only a glance at the keen grey eyes peering from beneath bushy eyebrows, the determined set of a square lower jaw, to note a man of action, accustomed to command. A quick, alert turn of the head, the lift of shoulders as he walked, arms swinging in a seaman-like balance, and the trick of pausing at a windward turn to glance at the weather sky, marked the sailing shipmaster–the man to whom thought and action must be as one.

Pausing at the binnacle to note the direction of the wind, he gives an exclamation of disgust.

'A dead muzzler, Pilot. No sign o' a slant in the trend o' th' upper clouds. Sou'west, outside, I'm afraid....Mebbe it's just as weel; we'll have t' bring up at the Tail o' th' Bank anyway, for these three hands, damn them....An' th' rest are useless....Drunk t' a man, th' mate says. God! They'd better sober up soon, or we'll have to try 'Yankee music' t' get things shipshape!'

The pilot laughed. 'I thought the 'Yankee music' touch was done with at sea now,' he said. Merchant Shippin' Act, and that sort of thing, Captain?'

'Goad, no! It's no' by wi' yet, an' never will be as long as work has to be done at sea. I never was much taken with it mysel but, damn it, ye've got to sail the ship, and ye can't do it without hands. Oh, a little of it at the setting off does no harm. They forget about it before long. But at the end of a voyage, when ye're getting near port, it's not very wise. No, not very wise. An' besides, you don't need it!'

The pilot grins again, thinking maybe of his own experiences, before he swallowed part of the anchor, and Old Jock returns to his walk.

Overhead the masts and spars are black with the grime of a 'voyage' in Glasgow Harbour and 'Irish pennants' fluttering wildly on spar and rigging tell of the scamped work of those whose names are not on our 'Articles'. Sternly superintended (now that the mate has given up all hope of getting work out of the men), we elder boys are held aloft, reeving running gear through the leads in the maintop. On the deck below the new apprentices gaze in open-mouthed admiration at our deeds. They wonder why the mate should think such clever fellows laggard, why he should curse us for clumsy sodgers, as a long length of rope goes (wrongly led) through the top. In a few months more they themselves will be criticising the 'hoodlums', and discussing the wisdom of the Old Man in standing so far to the south'ard.

Fog comes on us dense at Port Glasgow and incoming steamers, looming large on the narrowed horizon, steer sharply to the south to give us water. Enveloped in the driving wraiths we hear the deep notes of moving vessels, the clatter of bells on ships at anchor, and farther down, loud over all, the siren of the Cloch, bellowing a warning of thick weather beyond the Point. Sheering cautiously out of the fairway, we come to anchor at the Tail of the Bank to wait for our 'pier-head jumps.'

At four in the afternoon, a launch comes off with our recruits and our whipper-in explains his apparent delay. 'Hilt nor hair o' the men that left ye hae I seen. I thocht I'd fin' them at Dirty Dick's when the pubs opened...but no, no sign, an' a wheen tailor buddies wha cashed their advance notes huntin' high an' low! I seen yin o' them ower by Mclean Street wi' a nicht polis wi'm t' see he didna get a heid pit on'm - *sss!* A pant! So I cam' doon here, an' I hiv been lookin' for sailormen sin' ten o'clock. Man, they'll no' gang in thae wind-jammers, wi' sae mony new steamers speirin' hauns, an' new boats giein' twa ten fur th' run tae London....Thir's th' only yins I can get, an' ye wadna get them, but that twa's feart o' the polis an' Jorgensen wants t'see th' month's advance o' th' lang yin!'

The captain eyes the men and demands of one, 'Been to sea before?'

'Nach robh mhi? Twa years I wass a 'bow rope' in the *I-o-na*, an' I wass a wheelhouse in the Allan Line.'

A glance at his discharges confirms his claim, slight as it is, to seamanship, and Duncan McInnes, of Sleat in Skye, after being cautioned as to his obligations, signs his name and goes forward.

Patrick Laughlin has considerable difficulty in explaining his absence from the sea for two years, but the captain, after listening to a long, rambling statement....'i' th' yairds...riggin' planks fur the rivitter boys....Guid-brither a gaffer in Hamilton's at the Poort ... shoart time'... gives a quick glance at the alleged seaman's cropped head and winks solemnly at the Shipping-master, who is signing the men on. Hands being so scarce, however, Patrick is allowed to touch the pen.

One glance at the third suffices. Blue eyes and light, colourless hair, high cheekbones and lithe limbs, mark the Scandinavian. Strong, wiry fingers and an indescribable something proclaim the sailor, and though Von Schmit can hardly say 'yes' in English, he looks the most likely man of the three.

The Shipping-master, having concluded his business, steps aboard his launch, leaving us with a full crew, to wait the weather clearing and the fair wind that would lift us down Channel.

Daybreak next morning shows promise of better weather, and a light SSE wind with a comparatively clear sky decides the Old Man to take the North Channel for it. As soon as there is light enough to mark their colours, a string of flags brings off our tug-boat from Princes pier, and we start to heave up the anchor. A stout coloured man sets up a 'chantey' in a very creditable baritone and the crew, sobered now by the snell morning, give sheet to the chorus.

> *Blow, boy-s, blow, - for Califor-ny, oh!*
> *For there's lots of gold, so I've been told,*
> *On the banks - of the Sa-cramen-to!*

The towing hawser is passed aboard, and the tug takes the weight off the cable. The nigger having reeled off all he knows of 'Californy,' a Dutchman sings lustily of 'Sally Brown.' Soon the mate reports, 'Anchor's short, Sir,' and gets the order to weigh. A few more powerful heaves with the seaman-like poise between each—*'Spent my mo-ney on Sa-lley Brown!'*—and the shout comes, 'Anchor's a-weigh!'

Down comes the Blue Peter from the fore, whipping at shroud and backstay in quick descent—our barque rides ground-free, the voyage begun!

The light is broad over all now, and the Highland hills loom dark and misty to the nor'ard. With a catch at the heart, we pass the well-known places, slowly making way, as if the flood-tide were striving still to hold us in our native waters. A Customs boat hails, and asks of us, 'Whither bound?'

'Frisco away!' we shout, and they wave us a brief God-speed. Rounding the Cloch, we meet the coasting steamers scurrying up the Firth.

'Ow'd ye like t' be a stiy-at-'ome, splashin' abaht in ten fathoms, like them blokes, eh?' The Cockney asks me, with a deep-water man's contempt in his tone.

How indeed? Yearning eyes follow their glistening stern-wash as they speed past, hot-foot for the river berths.

The tide has made now. A short period of slack water, and the ebb bears us seawards, past the Cowal shore, glinting in the wintry sunlight, the blue smoke in Dunoon valley curling upward to Kilbride Hill, past Skelmorlie Buoy (tolling a doleful benediction), past Rothesay Bay, with the misty Kyles beyond. The Garroch Head, with a cluster of Clyde Trust Hoppers, glides abaft the beam, and the blue Cock o' Arran shows up across the opening water. All is haste and bustle. Aloft, spider-like figures against the tracery of the rigging, cast down sheets and clew lines in the one place where they must go. Shouts and hails. 'Fore cross-trees, there! Royal buntline inside th' crin'line, *in*-side, damn ye!'

'Aye, aye! Stan' fr' under!'

...*rrup!* A coil of rope hurtling from a height comes rattling down to the rail, to be secured to its own particular belaying-pin. Out of a seeming chaos comes order. Every rope has its name and its purpose, and though we have 'sodgers' among us, before Arran is astern we are ready to take to the wind. Off Pladda we set staysails and steer to the westward, and, when the wind allows, hoist topsails and crowd the canvas on her. The short November day has run its course when we cast off the tow rope.

As we pass the standing tug, all her hands are hauling the hawser aboard. Soon she comes tearing in our wake to take our last letter ashore and to receive the captain's 'blessing.' A heaving-line is thrown aboard, and into a small oilskin bag are put our hastily written messages and the captain's material 'blessing.' Shades of Romance! Our last link with civilisation severed by a bottle of Hennessy's Three Star!

The tugmen (after satisfying themselves as to the contents of the bag) give us a cheer and a few parting 'skreichs' on their siren and, turning quickly, make off to a Norwegian barque, lying-to, off Ailsa Craig.

All hands, under the mates, are hard driven, sweating on sheet and halyard to make the most of the light breeze. At the wheel I have little to do; she is steering easily, asking no more than a spoke or two when the Atlantic swell, running under, lifts her to the wind. Ahead of us a few trawlers are standing out to the Skerryvore Banks. Broad to the North, the rugged, mist-capped Mull of Cantyre looms up across the heaving water. The breeze is steady, but the barometer tells of wind or mist ere morning.

Darkness falls, and coast lights show up in all airts. Forward, all hands are putting a last drag on the topsail halyards, and the voice of the nigger tells of the fortunes of—'*Renzo, boys, Renzo!*'

THE OUTGOING
OF THE TIDE

From the unpublished Remains of the Reverend John Dennistoun,
sometime minister of the Gospel in the parish of Caulds,
and author of *Satan's Artifices Against the Elect*.

Men come from distant parts to admire the tides of Solloway, which race in at flood and retreat at ebb with a greater speed than a horse can follow. But nowhere are there queerer waters than in our own parish of Caulds at the place called the Sker Bay, where between two horns of land a shallow estuary receives the stream of the Sker. I never daunder by its shores, and see the waters hurrying like messengers from the great deep, without the solemn thoughts and a memory of Scripture words on the terror of the sea. The vast Atlantic may be terrible in its wrath, but with us it is no clean open rage, but the deceit of the creature, the unholy ways of quicksands when the waters are gone, and their stealthy return like a thief in the night-watches.

But in the times of which I write there were more awful fears than any from the violence of nature. It was the day of my ministry in Caulds, for then I was a bit callant in short clothes in my native parish of Lesmahagow; but the worthy Doctor Chrystal, who had charge of spiritual things, has told me often of the power of Satan and his emissaries in that lonely place. It was the day of warlocks and apparitions, now happily driven out by the zeal of the General Assembly. Witches pursued their wanchancy calling, bairns were spirited away, young lassies selled their souls to the evil one, and the Accuser of the Brethren in the shape of a black tyke was seen about cottage doors in the gloaming. Many and earnest were the prayers of good Doctor Chrystal, but the evil thing, in spite of his wrestling, grew and flourished in his midst. The parish stank of idolatry, abominable rites were practised in secret, and in all the bounds there was no-one had a more evil name for this black traffic than one Alison Sempill, who bode at the Skerburnfoot.

The cottage stood nigh the burn in a little garden with lilyoaks and grosart-bushes lining the pathway. The Sker ran by in a linn among hollins, and the noise of its waters was ever about the place. The highroad on the other side was frequented by few, for a nearer-hand way to the west had been made through the Lowe Moss. Sometimes a herd from the hills would pass by with sheep, sometimes a tinkler or a wandering merchant, and once in a long while the laird of Heriotside on his grey horse riding to Gledsmuir. And they who passed would see Alison hirpling in her garden, speaking to herself like the illwife she was, or sitting on a cutty-stool by the doorside with her eyes on other than mortal sights. Where she came from no man could tell. There were some said she was no woman, but a ghost haunting some mortal tenement. Others would threep she was gentrice, come of a persecuting family in the west, that had been ruined in the Revolution wars. She never seemed to want for siller; the house was a bright as a new preen, the yaird better delved than the manse garden; and there was routh of fowls and doos about the small steading, forby a wheen sheep and milk-kye in the fields. No man ever saw Alison at any market in the countryside, and yet the Skerburnfoot was plenished yearly in all proper order. One man only worked on the place, a doited lad who had long been a charge to the parish, and who had not the sense to fear danger or the wit to understand it. Upon all others the sight of Allison, were it but for a moment, cast a cold grue, not to be remembered without terror.

It seems she was not ordinarily ill-faured, as men use the word. She was maybe sixty years in age, small and trig, with her grey hair folded neatly under her mutch. But the sight of her eyes was not a thing to forget. John Dodds said they were the een of a deer with the devil ahint them, and indeed they would so appal an onlooker that a sudden unreasoning terror came into his heart, while his feet would impel him to flight. Once John, being overtaken in drink on the roadside by the cottage, and dreaming that he was burning in hell, woke and saw the old wife hobbling towards him. Thereupon he fled soberly to the hills, and from that day became a quiet-living, humble-minded Christian.

She moved about the country like a wraith, gathering herbs in dark loanings, lingering in kirkyards, and casting a blight on innocent bairns. Once Robert Smillie found her in a ruinous kirk on the Lang Muir where of old the idolatrous rites of Rome were practised. It was a hot day, and in the quiet place the flies buzzed in crowds, and he noted that she sat clothed in them as in a garment, yet suffering no discomfort. Then he, having mind of Beelzebub, the god of flies, fled without a halt homewards; but, falling in the Coo's Loan, broke two ribs and a collar-bone, the whilk misfortune was much blessed to his soul. And there were darker tales in the countryside, of weans stolen, of lassies misguided, of innocent beasts cruelly tortured, and in one and all there came in the name of the wife of the Skerburnfoot.

It was noted by them that kenned best that her cantrips were at their worst when the tides in the Sker Bay ebbed between the hours of twelve and one. At this season of the night the tides of mortality run lowest, and when the outgoing of those unco waters fell in with the setting of the current of life, then indeed was the hour for unholy revels. While honest men slept in their beds, the auld rudas carlines took their pleasure. That there is a delight in sin no man denies, but to most it is but a broken glint in the pauses of their conscience. But what must be the hellish joy of those lost beings who have forsworn God and trysted with the Prince of Darkness, it is not for a Christian to say. Certain it is that it must be great, though their master waits at the end of the road to claim the wizened things they call their souls. Serious men, notably Gidden Scott in the Back of the Hill and Simon Wauch in the shieling of Chasehope, have seen Alison wandering on the wet sands, dancing to no earthly music, while the heavens, they said, were full of lights and sounds which betokened the presence of the prince of the powers of the air. It was a season of heart-searching for God's saints in Caulds, and the dispensation was blessed to not a few.

It will seem strange that in all this time the presbytery was idle, and no effort was made to rid the place of so fell an influence. But there was a reason, and the reason, as in most like cases, was a lassie. Forby Alison there lived at the Skerburnfoot a young maid, Ailie Sempill, who by all accounts was as good and bonnie as the other was evil. She passed for a daughter of Alison's, whether born in wedlock or not I cannot tell; but there were some said she was no kin to the auld witch-wife, but some bairn spirited away from honest parents. She was young and blithe, with a face like an April morning and a voice in her that put the laverocks to shame. When she sang in the kirk, folk have told me that they had a foretaste of the music of the New Jerusalem, and when she came by in the village of Caulds old men stottered to their doors to look at her. Moreover, from her earliest days the bairn had some glimmerings of grace. Though no minister would visit the Skerburnfoot, or if he went, departed quicker than he came, the girl Ailie attended regular at the catechizing at the Mains of Sker. It may be that Alison thought she would be a better offering for the devil if she were given the chance of forswearing God, or it may be that she was so occupied in her own dark business that she had no care of the bairn. Meanwhile the lass grew up in the nurture and admonition of the Lord. I have heard Doctor Chrystal say that he never had a communicant more full of the things of the Spirit. From the day when she first declared her wish to come forward to the hour when she broke bread at the table, she walked like one in a dream. The lads of the parish might cast admiring eyes on her bright cheeks and yellow hair as she sat in her white gown in the kirk, but well they knew she was not for them. To be the bride of Christ was the thought that filled her heart; and when at the fencing of the tables Doctor Chrystal preached from Matthew nine and fifteen, 'Can the children of the bride-chamber mourn, as long as the bridegroom is with them?' it was remarked by sundry that Ailie's face was liker the countenance of an angel than of a mortal lass.

It is with the day of her first communion that this narrative of mine begins. As she walked home after the morning table she communed in secret and her heart sang within her. She had mind of God's mercies in the past, how He had kept her feet from the snares of evildoers which had been spread around her youth. She had been told unholy charms like the seven south streams and the nine rowan berries, and it was noted when she went first to the catechizing that she prayed 'Our Father which wert in heaven,' the prayer which the illwife Alison had taught her, meaning by it Lucifer who had been in heaven and had been cast out therefrom. But when she came to years of discretion she had freely chosen the better part, and evil had ever been repelled from her soul like

Gled water from the stones of Gled brig. Now she was in a rapture of holy content.

The drucken bell - for the ungodly fashion lingered in Caulds— was ringing in her ears as she left the village, but to her it was but a kirk-bell and a goodly sound. As she went through the woods where the primroses and whitethorn were blossoming, the place seemed as the land of Elam, wherein there were twelve bells and three-score and ten palm trees. And then, as it might be, another thought came into her head, for it is ordained that frail mortality cannot continue long in holy joy. In the kirk she had been only the bride of Christ; but as she came through the wood, with the birds lilting and the winds of the world blowing, she had mind of another lover. For this lass, though so cold to men, had not escaped the common fate. It seemed that the young Heriotside, riding by one day, stopped to speir something or other, and got a glisk of Ailie's face, which caught his fancy.

He passed the road again many times, and then he would meet her in the gloaming or of a morning in the field as she went to fetch the kye. 'Blue are the hills that are far away' is an owercome in the countryside, and while at first on his side it may have been but a young man's fancy, to her he was like the god Apollo descending from the skies. He was good to look on, brawly dressed, and with a tongue in his head that would have willed the bird from the tree. Moreover, he was of gentle kin, and she was a poor lass biding in a cot-house with an ill-reputed mother. It seems that in time the young man, who had begun the affair with no good intentions, fell honestly in love, while she went singing about the doors as innocent as a bairn, thinking of him when her thoughts were not on higher things. So it came about that long ere Ailie reached home it was on young Heriotside that her mind dwelt, and it was the love of him that made her eyes glow and her cheeks redden.

Now it chanced that at that very hour her master had been with Alison, and the pair of them were preparing a deadly pit. Let no man say that the devil is not a cruel tyrant. He may give his folk some scrapings of unhallowed pleasure; but he will exact tithes, yea of anise and cummin, in return, and there is aye the reckoning to pay at the hinder end. It seems that now he was driving Alison hard. She had been remiss of late, fewer souls sent to hell, less zeal in quenching the Spirit, and above all the crowning offence that her bairn had communicated in Christ's kirk. She had waited overlong, and now it was like that Ailie would escape her toils. I have no skill of fancy to tell of that dark collogue, but the upshot was that Alison swore by her lost soul and the pride of sin to bring the lass into thrall to her master. The fiend had bare departed when Ailie came over the threshold to find the auld carline glunching by the fire.

It was plain that she was in the worst of tempers. She flyted on the lass till the poor thing's cheek paled.

'There you gang,' she cried, 'troking wi' thae wearifu' Pharisees o' Caulds, whae daurna darken your mither's door. A bonnie dutiful child, quotha! Wumman, hae ye nae pride? No even the mense o' a tinkler lass?'

And then she changed her voice, and would be as soft as honey. 'My puir wee wee Ailie! Was I thrawn till ye? Never mind, my bonnie. You and me are a' that's left, and we mauna be ill to ither.'

And then the two of them had their dinner, and all the while the auld wife was crooning over the lass. 'We maun 'gree weel,' she says, 'for we're like to be our lee-lane for the rest o' our days. They tell me Heriotside is seeking Joan o' the Croft, and they're sune to be cried in Gledsmuir kirk.'

It was the first the lass had heard of it, and you may fancy she was struck dumb. And so with one thing and another the auld witch raised the fiends of jealousy in that innocent heart. She would cry out that Heriotside was an ill-doing wastrel, and had no business to come and flatter honest lasses. And then she would speak of his gentle birth and his leddy mother, and say it was indeed presumption to hope that so great a gentleman could mean all that he said. Before long Ailie was silent and white, while her mother rimed on about men and their ways. And then she could thole it no longer, but must go out and walk by the burn to cool her hot brow and calm her thoughts, while the witch indoors laughed to herself at her devices.

For days Ailie had an absent eye and a sad face, and so it fell out that in all that time young Heriotside, who had scarce missed a day, was laid up with a broken arm and never came near her. So in a week's time she was beginning to hearken to her mother when she spoke of incantations and charms for restoring love. She kenned it was sin; but though not seven days syne she had sat at the Lord's table, so strong is love in a young heart that she was on the very brink of it. But the grace of God was stronger than her weak will. She would have none of her mother's runes and philters, though her soul cried out for them. Always when she was most disposed to listen some merciful power stayed her consent. Alison grew thrawner as the hours passed. She kenned of Heriotside's broken arm, and she feared that any day he might recover and put her stratagems to shame. And then it seems that she collogued with her master and heard word of a subtler device. For it was approaching that uncanny time of the year, the festival of Beltane, when the auld pagans were wont to sacrifice to their god Baal. In this season warlocks and carlines have a special dispensation to do evil, and Alison waited on its coming with graceless joy.

As it happened, the tides in the Sker Bay ebbed at this time between the hours of twelve and one and, as I have said, this was the hour above all others when the powers of darkness were most potent. Would the lass but consent to go abroad in the unhallowed place at this awful season and hour of the night, she was as firmly handfasted to the devil as if she had signed a bond with her own blood. For then, it seemed, the forces of good fled far away, the world for one hour was given over to its ancient prince, and the man or woman who willingly sought the spot was his bond-servant for ever. There are deadly sins from which God's people may recover. A man may even communicate unworthily, and yet, so be it he sin not against the Holy Ghost, he may find forgiveness. But it seems that for this Beltane sin there would be no pardon, and I can testify from my own knowledge that they who once committed it became lost souls from that day. James Deuchar, once a promising professor, fell thus out of sinful bravery and died blaspheming; and of Kate Mallison, who went the same road, no man can tell. Here, indeed, was the witch-wife's chance, and she was the more keen, for her master had warned her that this was her last. Either Ailie's soul would be his, or her auld wrinkled body and black heart would be flung from this pleasant world to their apportioned place.

Some days later it happened that young Heriotside was stepping home over the Lang Muir about ten at night—it being his first jaunt from home since his arm had mended. He had been to the supper of the Forest Club at the Cross Keys in Gledsmuir, a clanjamfry of wild young blades who passed the wine and played at cartes once a fortnight. It seems he had drunk well, so that the world ran round about and he was in the best of tempers. The moon came down and bowed to him, and he took his hat off to it. For every step he travelled miles, so that in a little he was beyond Scotland altogether and pacing the Arabian desert. He thought he was the Pope of Rome, so he held out his foot to be kissed, and rolled twenty yards to the bottom of a small brae. Syne he was the King of France, and fought hard with a whin-bush till he had banged it to pieces. After that nothing would content him but he must be a bogle, for he found his head dunting on the stars and his legs were knocking the hills together. He thought of the mischief he was doing to the auld earth, and sat down and cried at his wickedness. Then he went on, and maybe the steep road to the Moss Rig helped him, for he began to get soberer and ken his whereabouts.

On a sudden he was aware of a man linking along at his side.

He cried, 'A fine night,' and the man replied.

Syne, being merry from his cups, he tried to slap him on the back. The next he kenned he was rolling on the grass, for his hand had gone clean through the body and found nothing but air. His head was so thick with wine that he found nothing droll in this.

'Faith, friend,' he says, 'that was a nasty fall for a fellow that has supped weel. Where might your road be gaun to?'

'To the World's End,' said the man, 'but I stop at the Skerburnfoot.'

'Bide the night at Heriotside,' says he. 'It's a thought out of your way, but it's a comfortable bit.'

'There's mair comfort at the Skerburnfoot,' said the dark man.

Now the mention of the Skerburnfoot brought back to him only the thought of Ailie and not of the witch-wife, her mother. So he jaloused no ill, for at the best he was slow in the uptake.

The two of them went on together for a while, Heriotside's fool head filled with the thought of the lass. Then the dark man broke the silence.

'Ye're thinkin' o' the maid Ailie Sempill,' says he.

'How ken ye that?' asked Heriotside.

'It is my business to read the herts o' men,' said the other.

'And who may ye be?' said Heriotside, growing eerie.

'Just an auld packman,' said he—'nae name ye wad ken, but kin to mony gentle houses.'

'And what about Ailie, you that ken sae muckle?' asked the young man.

'Naething,' was the answer—naething that concerns you, for ye'll never get the lass.'

'By God, and I will!' says Heriotside, for he was a profane swearer.

'That's the wrong name to seek her in, anyway,' said the man.

At this the young laird struck a great blow at him with his stick, but found nothing to resist him but the hill-wind.

When they had gone on a bit the dark man spoke again. 'The lassie is thirled to holy things,' says he. 'She has nae care for flesh and blood, only for devout contemplation.'

'She loves me,' says Heriotside.

'Not you,' says the other, 'but a shadow in your stead.'

At this the young man's heart began to tremble, for it seemed that there was truth in what his companion said, and he was ower drunk to think gravely.

'I kenna whatna man ye are,' he says, 'but ye have the skill of lassies' hearts. Tell me truly, is there no way to win her to common love?'

'One way there is,' said the man, 'and for our friendship's sake I will tell it you. If ye can ever tryst wi' her on Beltane's Eve on the Sker sands, at the green link o' the burn where the sands begin, on the ebb o' the tide when the midnight is by but afore cock-crow, she'll be yours, body and soul, for this world and for ever.'

And then it appeared to the young man that he was walking by his lone up the grass walk of Heriotside with the house close by him. He thought no more of the stranger he had met, but the words stuck in his heart.

It seems that about this very time Alison was telling the same tale to poor Ailie. She cast up to her every idle gossip she could think of.

'It's Joan o' the Croft', was aye her owercome, and she would threep that they were to be cried in the kirk on the first Sabbath of June. And then she would rime on about the black cruelty of it, and cry down curses on the lover, so that her daughter's heart grew cold with fear. It is terrible to think of the power of the world even in a redeemed soul. Here was a maid who had drunk of the well of grace and tasted God's mercies, and yet there were moments when she was ready to renounce her hope. At those awful seasons God seemed far off and the world very nigh, and to sell her soul for love looked a fair bargain. At other times she would resist the very devil and comfort herself with prayer; but aye when she spoke there was the sore heart, and when she went to sleep there were the weary eyes. There was no comfort in the goodliness of spring or the bright sunshine weather, and she who had been wont to go about the doors lightfoot and blithe was now as dowie as a widow woman.

And then one afternoon in the hinder end of April came young Heriotside riding to the Skerburnfoot. His arm was healed, he had got him a fine new suit of green, and his horse was a mettle beast that well set off his figure. Ailie was standing by the doorstep as he came down the road, and her heart stood still with joy. But a second thought gave her anguish. This man, so gallant and braw, would never be for her; doubtless the fine suit and the capering horse were for Joan of the Croft's pleasure. And he in turn, when he remarked her wan cheek and dowie eyes, had mind of what the dark man said on the muir, and saw in her a maid sworn to no mortal love. Yet the passion for her had grown fiercer than ever, and he swore to himself that he would win her back from her phantasies. She, one may believe, was ready enough to listen. As she walked with him by the Sker water his words were like music to her ears, and Alison within-doors laughed to herself and saw her devices prosper.

He spoke to her of love and his own heart, and the girl hearkened gladly. Syne he rebuked her coldness and cast scorn upon her piety, and so far was she beguiled that she had no answer. Then from one thing and another he spoke of some true token of their love. He said he was jealous, and craved something to ease his care.

'It's but a small thing I ask,' says he; 'but it will make me a happy man, and nothing ever shall come atween us. Tryst wi' me for Beltane's Eve on the Sker sands, at the green link o' the burn where the snads begin, on the ebb o' the tide when midnight is by but afore the cock-crow. 'For,' said he, 'that was our forebears' tryst for true lovers, and wherefore no' for you and me?'

The lassie had grace given her to refuse, but with a woeful heart, and Heriotside rode off in black discontent, leaving poor Ailie to sigh her lone. He came back the next day and the next, but aye he got the same answer. A season of great doubt fell upon her soul. She had no clearness in her hope, nor any sense of God's promises. The Scriptures were an idle tale to her, prayer brought her no refreshment, and she was convicted in her conscience of the unpardonable sin. Had she been less full of pride she would have taken her troubles to good Doctor Chrystal and got comfort; but her grief made her silent and timorous, and she found no help anywhere. Her mother was ever at her side, seeking with coaxings and evil advice to drive her to the irrevocable step. And all the while there was her love for the man riving in her bosom and giving her no ease by night or day. She believed she had driven him away and repented her denial. Only her pride held her back from going to Heriotside and seeking him herself. She watched the road hourly for a sight of his face, and when the darkness came she would sit in a corner brooding over her sorrows.

At last he came, speiring the old question. He sought the same tryst, but now he had a further tale. It seemed he was eager to get her away from the Skerburnside and auld Alison. His aunt, the Lady Balcrynie, would receive her gladly at his request till the day of their marriage. Let her but tryst with him at the hour and the place he named, and he would carry her straight to Balcrynie, where she would be safe and happy. He named that hour, he said, to escape men's observation for the sake of her own good name. He named that place, for it was near her dwelling, and on the road between Balcrynie and Heriotside, which fords the Sker Burn. The temptation was more than mortal heart could resist. She gave him the promise he sought, stifling the voice of conscience; and as she clung to his neck it seemed to her that her heaven was a poor thing compared with a man's love.

Three days remained till Beltane's Eve, and throughout the time it was noted that Heriotside behaved like one possessed. It may be that his conscience pricked him, or that he had a glimpse of his sin and its coming punishment. Certain it is that, if he had been daft before, he now ran wild in his pranks, and an evil report of him was in every mouth. He drank deep at the Cross Keys, and fought two battles with young lads that angered him. One he let off with a touch on the shoulder, the other goes lame to this day from a wound he got in the groin. There was a word of the procurator-fiscal taking note of his doings, and troth, if they had continued long he must have fled the country. For a wager he rode his horse down the Dow Craig, wherefore the name of the place is the Horseman's Craig to this day. He laid a hundred guineas with the laird of Slipperfield that he would drive four horses through the Slipperfield loch, and in the prank he had his bit chariot dung to pieces and a good mare killed. And all men observed that his eyes were wild, his face grey and thin, and that his hand would twitch as he held the glass, like one with the palsy.

The Eve of Beltane was lown and hot in the low country, with fire hanging in the clouds and thunder grumbling about the heavens. It seems that up in the hills it had been an awesome deluge of rain, but on the coast it was still hot and lowering. It is a long road from Heriotside to the Skerburnfoot. First you go down the Heriot Water, and syne over the Lang Muir to the edge of Mucklewham. When you pass the steadings of Mirehope and Cockmalane you turn to the right and ford the Mire Burn. That brings you on to the turnpike road, which you will ride till it bends inland, while you keep on straight over the Whinny Knowes to the Sker Bay. There, if you are in luck, you will find the tide out and the place fordable dryshod for a man on a horse. But if the tide runs, you will do well to sit down on the sands and content yourself till it turn, or it will be the solans and scarts of the Solloway that will be seeing the next of you.

On this Beltane's Eve the young man, after supping with some wild young blades, bade his horse be saddled about ten o'clock. The company were eager to ken his errand, but he waved them back. 'Bide here,' he says, 'and birl the wine till I return. This is a ploy of my own on which no man follows me.'

And there was that in his face as he spoke which chilled the wildest, and left them well content to keep to the good claret and the soft seat and let the daft laird go his own ways.

Well and on, he rode down the bridlepath in the wood, along the top of the Heriot glen, and as he rode he was aware of a great noise beneath him. It was not the wind, for there was none, and it was not the sound of thunder, and aye as he speired at himself what it was it grew louder till he came to a break in the trees. And then he saw the cause, for Heriot was coming down in a furious flood, sixty yards wide, tearing the roots of the aiks, and flinging red waves against the dry-stone dykes. It was a sight and sound to solemnise a man's mind, deep calling unto deep, the great waters of the hills running to meet the great waters of the sea. But Heriotside recked nothing of it, for his heart had but one thought and the eye of his fancy one figure. Never had he been so filled with love of the lass, and yet it was not happiness but a deadly secret fear.

As he came to the Lang Muir it was geyan dark, though there was a moon somewhere behind the clouds. It was little he could see of the road, and ere long he had tried many mosspools and sloughs, as his braw coat bare witness. Aye in front of him was the great hill of Mucklewham, where the road turned down by the Mire. The noise of the Heriot had not long fallen behind him ere another began, the same eerie sound of burns crying to ither in the darkness. It seemed that the whole earth was overrun with water. Every little runnel in the bog was astir, and yet the land around him was as dry as flax, and no drop of rain had fallen. As he rode on the din grew louder, and as he came over the top of Mirehope he kenned by the mighty rushing noise that something uncommon was happening with the Mire Burn. The light from the Mirehope shieling twinkled on his left, and had the man not been dozened with his fancies he might have observed that the steading was deserted and men were crying below in the fields. But he rode on, thinking of but one thing, till he came to the cot-house of

Cockmalane, which is nigh the fords of the Mire.

John Dodds, the herd who bode in the place, was standing at the door, and he looked to see who was on the road so late.

'Stop;' says he, 'stop, Laird Heriotside. I kenna what your errand is, but it is to no holy purpose that ye're out on Beltane Eve. D'ye no hear the warning o' the waters?'

And then in the still night came the sound of Mire like the clash of armies.

'I must win over the ford,' says the Laird quietly, thinking of another thing.

'Ford!' cried John in scorn. 'There'll be nae ford for you the nicht unless it be the ford o' the River Jordan. The burns are up, and bigger than man ever saw. It'll be a Beltane's Eve that a' folk will remember. They tell me that Gled valley is like a loch, and that there's an awesome folk drooned in the hill. Gin ye were ower the Mire, what about crossin' the Caulds and the Sker?' says he, for he jaloused he was going to Gledsmuir.

And then it seemed that that word brought the laird to his sense. He looked the airt the rain was coming from, and he saw it was the airt the Sker flowed. In a second, he has told me, the works of the devil were revealed to him. He saw himself a tool in Satan's hands, he saw his tryst a device for the destruction of the body, as it was assuredly meant for the destruction of the soul, and there came on his mind the picture of an innocent lass borne down by the waters with no place for repentance. His heart grew cold in his breast. He had but one thought, a sinful and reckless one–to get to her side, that the two might go together to their account. He heard the roar of the Mire as in a dream, and when John Dodds laid hands on his bridle he felled him to the earth. And the next seen of it was the laird riding the floods like a man possessed.

The horse was a grey stallion he aye rode, the very beast he had ridden for many a wager with the wild lads of the Cross Keys. No man but himself durst back it, and it had lamed many a hostler lad and broke two necks in its day. But it seemed it had the mettle for any flood, and took the Mire with little spurring. The herds on the hillside looked to see man and steed swept into eternity; but though the red waves were breaking about his shoulders and he was swept far down, he ay held on for the shore. The next thing the watchers saw was the laird struggling up the far bank, and casting his coat from him, so that he rode in his sark. And then he set off like wildfire across the muir towards the turnpike road. Two men saw him on the road and have recorded their experience. One was a gangrel, by name McNab, who was travelling from Gledsmuir to Allerkirk with a heavy pack on his back and a bowed head. He heard a sound like the wind afore him, and, looking up, saw coming down the road a grey horse stretched out to a wild gallop and a man on its back with a face like a soul in torment. He kenned not whether it was devil or mortal, but flung himself on the roadside, and lay like a corp for an hour or more till the rain aroused him. The other was Sim Dolittle, the fish-hawker from Allerfoot, jogging home in his fish-cart from Gledsmuir fair. He had drunk more than was fit for him, and was singing some light song, when he saw approaching, as he said, the pale horse mentioned in the Revelations, with Death seated as the rider. Thoughts of his sins came on him like a thunderclap, fear loosened his knees, he leaped from the cart to the road, and from the road to the back of a dyke. Thence he flew to the hills, and was found the next morning far up among the Mire Crags, while his horse and cart were gotten on the Aller sands, the horse lamed and the cart without the wheels.

At the tollhouse the road turns inland to Gledsmuir, and he who goes to Sker Bay must leave it and cross the wild land called the Whinny Knowes, a place rough with bracken and foxes' holes and old stone cairns. The tollman, John Gilzean, was opening his window to get a breath of air in the lown night when he heard and saw the approaching horse. He kenned the beast for Heriotside's and, being a friend of the laird's, he ran down in all haste to open the yett, wondering to himself about the laird's errand on this night. A voice came down the road to him bidding him hurry; but John's old fingers were slow with the keys, and so it happened that the horse had to stop and John had time to look up at the gash and woeful face.

'Where away the nicht sae late, laird? says John.

'I go to save a soul from hell,' was the answer.

And then it seems that through the open door there came the chapping of a clock.

'Whatna hour is that?' asks Heriotside.

'Midnicht,' says John, trembling, for he did not like the look of things.

There was no answer but a groan, and horse and man went racing down the dark hollows of the Whinny Knowes.

How he escaped a broken neck in that dreadful place no human being will ever tell. The sweat, he has told me, stood in cold drops upon his forehead; he scarcely was aware of the saddle in which he sat; and his eyes were stelled in his head, so that he saw nothing but the sky ayont him. The night was growing colder, and there was a small sharp wind stirring from the east. But, hot or cold, it was all one to him, who was already as cold as death. He heard not the sound of the sea nor the peesweeps startled by his horse, for the sound that ran in his ears was the roaring Sker Water and a girl's cry. The thought kept goading him, and he spurred the grey till the creature was madder than himself. It leaped the hole which they call the Devil's Mull as I would step over a thistle, and the next he kenned he was on the edge of the Sker Bay.

It lay before him white and ghastly, with mist blowing in wafts across it and a slow swaying of the tides. It was the better part of a mile wide, but save for some fathoms in the middle where the Sker current ran, it was no deeper even at flood than a horse's fetlocks. It looks eerie at bright midday when the sun is shining and whaups are crying among the seaweeds; but think what it was on that awesome night with the powers of darkness brooding over it like a cloud. The rider's heart quailed for a moment in natural fear. He stepped his beast a few feet in, still staring afore him like a daft man. And then something in the sound or the feel of the waters made him look down, and he perceived that the ebb had begun and the tide was flowing out to sea.

He kenned that all was lost, and the knowledge drove him to stark despair. His sins came in his face like birds of night, and his heart shrank like a pea. He knew himself for a lost soul, and all that he loved in the world was out in the tides. There, at any rate, he could go too, and give back that gift of life he had so blackly misused. He cried small and soft like a bairn, and drove the grey out into the waters. And aye as he spurred it the foam should have been flying as high as his head; but in that uncanny hour there was no foam, only the waves running sleek like oil. It was not long ere he had come to the Sker channel, where the red moss-waters were roaring to the sea, an ill place to ford in midsummer heat, and certain death, as folks reputed it, in the smallest spate. The grey was swimming, but it seemed the Lord had other purposes for him than death, for neither man nor horse could drown. He tried to leave the saddle, but he could not; he flung the bridle from him, but the grey held on, as if some strong hand were guiding. He cried out upon the devil to help his own, he renounced his Maker and his God; but whatever his punishment, he was not to be drowned. And then he was silent, for something was coming down the tide.

It came down as quiet as a sleeping bairn, straight for him as he sat with his horse breasting the waters, and as it came the moon crept out of a cloud and he saw a glint of yellow hair. And then his madness died away and he was himself again, a weary and stricken man. He hung down over the tides and caught the body in his arms and then let the grey make for the shallows. He cared no more for the devil and all his myrmidons, for he kenned brawly he was damned. It seemed to him that his soul had gone from him and he was as toom as a hazel-shell. His breath rattled in his throat, the tears were dried up in his head, his body had lost its strength, and yet he clung to the drowned maid as to a hope of salvation. And then he noted something at which he marvelled dumbly. Her hair was drookit back from her clay-cold brow, her eyes were saut, but in her face there was the peace of a child. It seemed even that her lips were smiling. Here, certes, was no lost soul, but one who had gone joyfully to meet her Lord. It may be that in that dark hour at the burn-foot, before the spate caught her, she had been given grace to resist her adversary and flung herself upon God's mercy.

And it would seem that it had been granted, for when he came to the Skerburnfoot there in the corner sat the weird-wife Alison, dead as a stone and shrivelled like a heather-birn.

For days Heriotside wandered the country or sat in his own house with vacant eye and trembling hands. Conviction of sin held him like a vice; he saw the lassie's death laid at his door, her face haunted him by day and night, and the word of the Lord dirled in his ears telling of wrath and punishment. The greatness of his anguish wore him to a shadow, and at last he was stretched on his bed and like to perish. In his extremity worthy Doctor Chrystal went to him unasked and strove to comfort him. Long, long the good man wrestled, but it seemed as if his ministrations were to be to no avail. The fever left his body, and he rose to stotter about the doors; but he was still in his torments, and the mercy-seat was far from him. At last, in the back-end of the year, came Mungo Muirhead to Caulds to the autumn communion, and nothing would serve him but he must try his hand at this storm-tossed soul. He spoke with power and unction, and a blessing came with his words, the black cloud lifted and showed a glimpse of grace, and in a little the man had some assurance of salvation. He became a pillar of Christ's Kirk, prompt to check abominations, notably the sin of witchcraft, foremost in good works; but with it all a humble man, who walked contritely till his death. When I came first to Caulds I sought to prevail upon him to accept the eldership, but he aye put me by, and when I heard his tale I saw that he had done wisely. I mind him well as he sat in his chair or daundered through Caulds, a kind word for everyone and sage counsel in time of distress, but withal a severe man to himself and a crucifier of the body. It seems that this severity weakened his frame, for three years syne come Martinmass he was taken ill with a fever, and after a week's sickness he went to his account, where I trust he is accepted.

John MacDougall Hay

GILLESPIE'S COUP

In foul weather Gillespie walked the wharves and quays, and nosing about among the herring-boxes and fish-guts, would ask the fishermen and smacksmen news of the fishing. This was accounted to him for sociability. He entered into the interests of their trade and knew the baffling tides of their fortune, and picked up information, carelessly noting everything of importance that fell.

Especially he watched the methods of the herring buyers. These were two. Either out on the loch in smacks which, when a full cargo was taken aboard, set sail for Glasgow. If there was no prospect of wind they offered a low price for the herring because of the risk of transport. On Saturday mornings the smacksmen refused to buy at all. Other buyers waited on the quay to which those fishermen came who found no market among the smacks. On the days of a 'big fishing' the fishermen had sometimes to throw whole skiffs-loads into the harbour for want of a market. The quay buyers were meagre men. They rarely risked more than twenty boxes, which they sent to Glasgow by luggage steamer; other trifling boxes they bought on commission for merchants in Rothesay, Dunoon and Helensburgh. Gillespie was soon master of their methods. He noticed they were a fraternity. If one of them happened to be a little earlier on the quay than the others he bought up the fish, to share them later on with the slug-a-beds. Gillespie pointed out to the fishermen this heinous lack of competition.

He studied the flow and ebb of the Glasgow Fish Market, and keenly watched the Baltic ports as a haven for salt herring. He discovered that Manchester and Liverpool would take unlimited supplies of fresh herring packed on ice. And he waited patiently. No one knew that he had leased from the laird the long row of stores and curing-sheds stretching along the shore road from the quay. On a June morning of perfect calm, when ducks were swimming about in the harbour, a skiff was seen coming in at the Perch, deep to the gunwhales. The men on the beams were sitting on herring as they rowed. She was followed by a second, a third, a fourth, and a fifth, under clouds of gulls. The smacksmen had refused to buy. The half-dozen buyers on the quay were in a flutter, running about like hens, sharing their empty stock. They bought some seventy boxes between them. There yet remained four and a half boats of herring. The fishermen were now offering these at any price, instead of being offered; at five shillings a box, four shillings, three, two, one. Standing on the quay and looking down upon these fishermen in their loaded boats, one caught a look of pathos upon their rugged faces, tawny with sweat threshed out of them in a fifteen-mile pull in the teeth of the tide. Their tired eyes were grey like the sea, their blue shirts with short oilskin sleeves were laced with herring scales; herring scales smeared the big fishing boots which come up over the knee; their hands were slippery with herring spawn; even their beards and pipes were whitened. Everywhere a flood of light poured down. It stiffened and blackened the blood of the bruised fish, and the heat brought up that tang of fish and that savour of brine which have almost an edge of pain, so sharp, haunting and fascinating are they in the nostrils of men who have been bred as fishers and have lived upon the salt water. The spectacle was compelling in its beauty, in its suggestion of prodigal seas and of the tireless industry and cunning craft of man; and at the same time sad with the irony of circumstance–niggard dealers haggling, shuffling, sniffing in the background. The dotard buyers shook their heads, though their mouths watered. They could not cope with one hundreth part of the fish. It was too early in the season for curing. Besides, they had no empty stock. One of them, in slippers, with a narrow face and rheumy eyes, gave a doleful shake of his head.

'No use, boys. It's the big market for them.' The 'big market' was the sea.

What a heartbreaking task was there; to basket all these fish into the sea. These fishermen had laboured all the night and toiled home through the long, blazing morning. The fish were worth ten shillings a box in Glasgow. To basket herring up on the quay and into the boxes, the music of chinking gold was in it; but into the harbour–how green and still it was–that was hell.

A deep silence fell down the length of the quay. One by one the fishermen, with dumb faces, sat down on the gunwhales, the oars, or the beams, eyeing the load of fish. An old man seated on the stern of the second boat lifted a massive head slowly and took off his round bonnet. He seemed to be invoking Heaven. As they had come homewards in the break of day to the sweep of the oars, he was given the tiller, being too old for that long pull. As he leaned upon the tiller he had dreamed in the somnolent morning of the spending of money. The sun glanced and shone on his round, bald head. The streaks of grey hair were smeared with herring scales. He opened his mouth as if to speak, then closed it hopelessly in acquiesence of Fate. The frustrate words were more eloquent of despair than any rhetoric. Someone forward said 'Ay! ay!' and sighed deeply. The old man bent and lifted a herring. He held it a moment aloft in the glittering sunlight; then he tossed it into the sea. It fell with a plout which seemed to crash in through the tremendous silence. Every eye followed it, wriggling down to the bottom. The old man nodded to the crews.

'Gull's meat, boys! Gull's meat,' and he collapsed in the stern beam, huddled up, a piteous, forlorn wisp, stupidly nursing the old rusty round bonnet in his hands.

An air of profound sorrow hung over the boat. She seemed chained in white, gleaming manacles. It was not precious food that was aboard any longer, but ballast.

The uneasy shuffling of men's feet on the causewayed quay, all the idlers in the town had assembled, was now the only sound which broke the silence. In the clean face of bountiful heaven it was an indecency, a crime, to cast that bulk of food back to the sea, which lay with the patience and the sombre expectation of the grave on its sparkling face.

'Sanny, my man, hold up your pow.' The words were spoken in a quiet and penetrating voice. As if he were a child on a bench at school, the old man lifted his bowed head and looked into a red, jolly face. Every eye was turned with Sandy's upon Gillespie, who stood alone, leaning against the head pile of the quay, with his baffling whimsical gaze steady on the old man's face.

'Ye've had a touch, Sanny.' We call a real big haul 'a touch.'

'Ay! Gillespa', a bonny touch, tae feed the gulls.'

Gillespie was broadly laughing without making any audible sound.

'That's no' work for a man that has been fifty years at the fishin', Sanny.'

Everyone present had pricked ears. A subtle change had come into the atmosphere. It was indescribably charged with hope. The old man lifted up his bonnet and put it on his head. It was an act partly of reverence, partly signalising that a crisis had been past.

'Boys.' Gillespie's quick gaze swept round the boats and his voice rang out cheerily. 'I'll buy the five boats at a shilling a box.'

An uneasy silence fell down the quay. Men glanced at one another, and then stole an amazed look at Gillespie. A voice, like the crack of a whip on the still air, rang out from one of the boats.

'By Goad, but you're a man.'

Andrew Rodgers padded softly in his slippers up to Gillespie, his slit eyes blinking as if he had arisen from sleep. He came of a race of fish-men. His father had cadged herring through Bute, buying them in a little lugger. He was tacitly recognised as chief of the coterie of buyers, all of whom deferred to him. He lived in a house overlooking the quay, and was accustomed to have the fishermen wait on him. They awakened him in the early morning by throwing mud and chuckies on his window-pane. He knew that Gillsepie had 'a big thing' in the stuff, but where was his empty stock? Besides, it was impossible to get the fish to Glasgow that day. The luggage steamer was gone. The next day at evening was the soonest the fish could reach the city. The market would then be closed. The stuff would have to lie on the Broomielaw till the following day. Three whole days in this heat. The bellies would be out of the fish. He smiled up in Gillespie's face sardonically.

'Fine, man, fine; is it manure ye're buyin'?'

As he looked down on the shimmering bulk of fish his face was contorted with a spasm of hatred. He, the best buyer on the quay, not so much as asked a by your leave. The other buyers, the idlers, and fishermen looked on at the duel. Gillespie from his broad jovial height purred down on the acidulous little man.

'Hoots! Andy, I've gien ower the fermin'; I'm goin' to try my hand at the buyin'.'

'Ye'd better go to the school first an' learn a wee.'

'I've bocht at a shullin'. Can you buy them chaper?'

A roar of laughter went up from the quay. Gillespie, still smiling, said, 'I'll stan' doon an' gie ye a chance yet, Andy.'

'I winna tek' the damn lot at fivepence.'

'No, man.'

The withering words stung

'You should learn to buy fish afore ye leave the back o' the coonter. Ye'll come doon heavily on this,' snapped Andy.

The other buyers felt this was a just warning. The man was a fool to take all that perishable stuff on his hands.

'Andy, my man.' Gillespie spoke as if chiding a fractious child. 'They're gran' herrin', are they no? Worth half-a-soavrin' the box.'

Andy's inane laugh cackled loudly over the quay.

'Half-a-soavrin'!' The idea spurted out ribald laughter. He shuffled about in his slippers. 'Up wi' your herrin', boys, Gillespie's going to fill them in sweetie boxes.'

All the buyers wheezed with foolish mirth; but old Sandy stood up in the stern with flashing eyes and whipped the carved tiller from the rudder head.

'If I was as near ye, Andy, as I'm far from ye, I'd mek' ye feel the wecht o' this.' He swung the tiller about his head. 'Gillespa's bocht the fish. That's more than ye could do, ye louse. Ye hevna the hert o' a pooked dooker.'

In the midst of the laughter Andy roared, 'Away up to the shop in the Square, Sandy, an' cairry doon the sweetie boxes.'

Gillespie laid a hand on his shoulder. 'Come wi' me, Andy, an' I'll show ye my sweetie boxes.' He turned to the boats. 'You, Ned, an' you, Polly, an' you, an' you,' he pointed with his forefinger to the young men of the crews, 'come an' cairry doon the sweetie boxes.'

All the quay and half the crews, babbling, followed Gillespie. He turned to the left, passed along the dike of the Square, above the quay, stopped at the first of the doors in the long line of sheds and stores belonging to the laird, and took a key out of his pocket.

'Are they your stores?' snapped Andy.

Gillespie nodded.

'Well, I'm damned, boys; an' never a word aboot it.'

This key's a wee roosty,' answered Gillespie, and turning it gratingly pushed open with knee and hand the big red door. From ceiling to floor the store was packed with splinter-new herring barrels and boxes, tier upon tier. Quietly, unassumingly, Gillespie had had a score or so of these boxes and barrels brought down to him from Glasgow in every gabbart and puffer which had borne coal for his ree. The surprise of the rented stores was nothing to this.

'Goad, boys,' someone in the background shouted, 'Gillespa' hes a forest o' barrels.'

The crowd surged forward, peering at the miracle. Gillespie had forgotten Andy. That cheap sort of triumph had no appeal for him.

'Now, boys! Now, boys!' he cried briskly, rubbing his hands; 'doon wi' the boxes to the quay. I'm in a hurry.'

Andy was athirst. 'Where in the name o' Goad did ye steal the barrels?'

Gillespie shouldered past him. 'Dae ye no' see I'm thrang, man?' His tone was faintly irascible. 'The bit sweetie boxes cam' frae the shop.' And with a jerk of his hand he brought the first tier of barrels to the floor.

'Hurray now, boys; I must catch the market.' He kicked a barrel to the door. There was an air of capacity and mastery about the man.

'He'll likely hae a steamer in the other store.' Andy's very eyes rolled with irony.

'When the herrin's filled I'll show ye the steamer. An' noo, Andy, ye'll hae to stan' aside. Ye're wastin' time.' Gently but firmly he shoved the waspish man from the doorway. Old Sandy suddenly stepped forward and and took Andy's place. The shadow of the boxes darkened his wizened countenance. He held up his hand. 'Wan meenut, boys.' Gillespie straightened his back.

'Are you goin' in for buyin', Gillespa'?'

Gillespie nodded impatiently.

'Boys! I've been a fisherman a' my days, an' no for fifty strucken years hae I seen what I saw the day. Thae men,' his condemning eyes swept over the buyers, 'wad hae left us on oor backside. Never a tail that I fish will I sell to ony man noo but Gillespa' Strang as long's God leaves braith in my body.' He smacked his palm with his clenched fist.

'Hear! Hear! Hurrah! Hurrah!'

From that moment Gillespie was the man of the fleet. The deep throated hurrahing was the knell of the buyers. Someone in the crowd began to boo.

'Way there, boys!' Gillespie appeared shouldering one of his brand-new boxes, followed by one of the crew with one box on his shoulder and trailing another by its bicket.

The idle buyers lined the 'Shipping Box' at the quay, watching dourly as box after box was filled from the teeming cran baskets. The quay rang under the iron-heeled sea-boots, stamping under the weight of the baskets. Gillespie, Sandy the Fox, and Jeck the Traiveller stood by the boxes. At midday three of the boats were discharged and had gone to anchor. Gillespie held a brief consultation with the fishermen, who ceased filling the boxes.

'By Goad!' whispered Andy, 'he's fed up.'

'I'm no sae sure o' that,' said Queebec, a fiery-faced buyer, and discerner of men, who in his youth had made a voyage to Quebec. He was discovering in himself a certain respect for Gillespie.

They left the 'Shipping Box' and joined the circle about Gillespie, who nodded cheerily to them. 'Hot work this, boys,' and went on speaking to the fishermen. 'Ye understan' I'll send ye doon a gallon o' beer an' biscuits an' cheese.'

'Did ye hear thon?' Andy whispered behind his hand, 'beer an' cheese.' The thing was unheard of.

'Right O!' cried young Polly, 'we're your men every day.'

Above the quay and adjacent to the stores was a large oblong Square, surrounded on three sides by a four-foot dike. The fourth side was partly built in with the dike, but a space was left to approach it from the quay by a flight of three broad steps. Sandy the Fox, who had been hastily summoned from Gillespie's coalree, entered the store, along with three fishermen. They reappeared each at the corner of a huge tarpaulin, which they dragged into and spread out in the Square.

'He's rented the Square as weel frae the laird,' said Tamar Lusk, an active, bent, bow-legged man, who combined the buying of a meagre box of herring with the selling of ice-cream, vegetables and newspapers. 'There's nothin' ye can teach Gillespie.' He meant to sting Andy, whom he hated with years of herring-buying hatred, because Andy cheated him like a fox. Andy, however, was too petrified to feel the jibe, and Tamar lunged again.

'Gillespie's the boy; he'll sweep us a' off the quay in wan whup.'

'The waff o' a newspaper'll sweep you aff, ye bloomin' Eyetalian. What's the salt for, Ned?' He wheeled on a fisherman who was rolling a heavy, grinding barrel, its new wood tarnished with mud. The fisherman straightened his back, took out his clay from the top waistcoat pocket, and borrowed a match from Andy. He was a tall man, slow of speech, with a grave eye.

'Gillespie's goin' tae show you boys how to work wi' herrin'.' There was an accent of pity in his voice. 'He's for roilin' them in salt.'

'In salt! Where did he get the salt?'

The grey eye smiled. 'In the sweetie boxes behind the coonter,' and was on his way again behind a puff of smoke.

Cran basket after cran basket was carried up the stone steps and poured on the tarpaulin. Gillespie and Sandy the Fox stood, each at one end of the growing pile, with a shallow tin plate, in his left hand, with which he scooped up salt from a barrel, drew his right hand across the salt, and hailed it down on the fresh fish, as a sower sows seed. The Square was full of the tinkling sound of the falling salt. Jeck the Traiveller sat on an upturned herring box, and as every cran was emptied on the pile, the fisherman shouted 'Tally!'

'Tally oh!' answered Jeck, and dropped a herring into a small basket. In this way the count of the crans was kept.

Another of the boats was discharged. The fishermen, wet with sweat, drank their beer and ate their biscuits and cheese. They had never been fed before in discharging fish, and the last bolt in the door of their hearts was drawn. Andy had been whispering, 'No wonder he was keen on your stuff at a shillin' a box wi' a' that stock. Catch him biddin' when they were at five shillin's.'

For all that the fishermen esteemed Gillespie as a man of bowels, who had plucked their fish from the 'big market.' And where was his own market? And now beer and cheese. He was their comrade, the fisherman's friend.

'I hope to Goad,' cried old Sandy, as he drew the back of his hand across his mouth, 'he'll get a pound a box. He's the best man in Brieston that Goad ever put braith intae.'

Work was begun again and the second boat discharged. The salted fish gleamed high in the Square. Barrels were rolled from the store, and filled with shovels from the pile. Andy, putting on a supercilious face, went up the stairs leisurely, meaning to pick a sure bone at his ease. 'Hey, Gillespa'! I thought ye were in a hurry?'

'A mile a minute's the speed,' came back the genial answer.

'Weel, I never saw herrin' roiled that wy before.'

'No?'

'The wy it used tae be done was to fill the barrels, an' salt the herrin' as they were goin' frae the can basket tae the barrel. Ye've been gien' yersel' double labour.'

'Ye micht he told me earlier,' said Gillespie unabashed.

'Oh! Ye think ye ken everything; I just let ye hev' your own wy.'

'Weel! Weel! A' that, Andy. I'll tell you something my faither's faither learned doon by the Heads o' Ayr. Aye roil them first ootside the barrels.'

'Ay,' came the sarcastic rejoinder.

'Ye see, Andy, when ye roil them in the barrels they sink terrible wi' the shakin' on the steamers an' the trains, an' when they reach the mercat it's no a fu' barrel ye're offerin'. The fish-merchants lik' a fu' barrel. An' the herrin' keep their bellies better this wy; but you'll ken best, Andy.'

He was not only buying herring, he was teaching them something new about their business.

'Ye'll hae tae get up early in the morn wi' tackets in your boots afore ye get to windward o' Gillespie,' wheezed the asthmatic Queebec.

'Ay! He's no' a scone o' yesterday's bakin',' Tamar Lusk gloated.

As each barrel was filled Gillespie covered it with a top of canvas cloth, nailing the cloth round with tacks.

'He can cooper as weel. I'll never leave the ice-cream shop again.' But Andy cursed Tamar for a fool.

The whitened tarpaulin lay empty in the sun; and then the men, finishing their beer and cheese, eyed the three-hundred-odd barrels of fish, proud of their labour, and discussed the new order. On everyone's tongue was a word of commendation or friendship for Gillespie. His action was heroic. He had stood gallantly in the breach of the sea.

'Does the damn fool think roiled herrin'll keep in this weather?' Andy had again found a platform in Gillespie's inability to dispose of the fish. 'An' what o' the fresh herrin' in the boxes?' he asked. 'Manure! Fair manure! They'll be stinkin' afore they get to the mercat.'

'It's you has the black hert, Andy,' roared old Sandy. 'It's time your day was done on the quay. Goad be thankit, there's wan man that can buy fish, mercat or no mercat.'

Precisely at that moment that one man was handling two telegrams across the counter at the Post Office, one to a Manchester firm, which ran: 'Sending 330 barrels large herring in salt.' The other was to a merchant in the Glasgow Fish Market. 'Sending 645 boxes large herrings by special steamer; arrive night.' The Glasgow Fish Market would be closed before the hour of arrival, but early the following morning, Gillespie knew, a long line of lorries would be on the Broomielaw; the lumpers would be waiting. Gillespie's herring would be the first in the market next day; at nine o'clock sharp the auctioneer would have them under his hammer, while the herring smacks would only be trailing round the Garroch Head, six hours from market. Gillespie would have the market to himself.

'Manure! Fair manure. He'll be fined for bringing refuse into Glesca,' sniped Andy.

'Weel, Andy, I was never so puzzled since the day I saw white porpoises off Newfoundland.' Queebec scratched his pow solemnly. At the old quay, used for discharging coal, some four hundred yards further in the harbour, lay a puffer, which had brought a cargo from Ardrossan for Gillespie's ree.

'Are ye dischairged?' Gillespie asked a black-bearded man who was drying his hairy arms in a rough towel.

'Naethin' left but fleas,' was the succinct answer.

Gillespie lightly swung himself aboard forward. 'Where are ye for?'

'The Port.'

'Goin' back light?'

The bearded man freed his face from the towel.

'As licht,' he answered, 'as a pauper's belly.'

'I'll gie ye some ballast as far's the Broomielaw.'

The bearded man's eyes twinkled. 'Deid cats?' he inquired.

'Deid herrin'. Will ye mek a run for me to Glesca?'

'Lik' hey-my-nanny,' said the master mariner, becoming alert.

'Ye'd be burnin' your coal onywy.' Gillespie was meditative. 'You'll be gled o' the price o' the coal.'

'I winna objec'.'

'Twenty pound for the run.'

The bearded man pulled a solemn face, though secretly he was glad of the found money.

'Ye were goin' back licht,' and Gillespie added significantly, 'I'll soon be wantin' another cargo o' coal if this fishin' continues.'

'Streitch it to twenty-five.'

Gillespie made a rapid calculation. For the number of boxes and barrels twenty-five pounds worked at sixpence a package. The freight by luggage steamer was three shillings. He laid his hand on the jocose mariner's arm, and sucked in his breath.

'You an' me'll no' quarrel ower a five-poun' note. I'll mak it twenty-five pounds if ye drive her an' get up the night.'

'I'll can do't in seeven 'oors, nate; the sewin' machine's in good order.' He jerked his thumb towards the engines.

'Get her doon to the quay then; I'll get the fishermen to gie ye a hand with the stuff.'

'Hae ye many?'

'Oh! A pickle, a pickle,' cried Gillespie as he mounted the breast wall. He appeared in the Square with a large pile of labels, a box of tacks and a hammer, and briskly instructed the fishermen to roll the barrels on to the quay.

'Rowl them ower the quay heid,' shouted Andy, derisively, 'it'll save them frae the dung-heap in Glesca.'

Gillespie, who was standing beside the first barrel, imperturbably beckoned Andy with the hammer.

'Step ower, Andy, an' ye'll see their destination.'

Gillespie tacked a large red label on the side of the barrel. The name and address of a fish salesman in Manchester was printed on the card in large, black type. He handed a label to Andy.

'It's a wee further than Glesca, Andy.'

Andy flung the label in the mud, spat, and stamped on it.

'Dinna be sae wastefu' o' guid gear, Andy,' said Gillespie, his mouth full of tacks. 'I had to pay postage on thae labels a' the wy frae Manchester.' Nimbly he went from barrel to barrel tacking on the labels. In the midst of this work a puffer came steaming down the harbour. An ordinary sight, scarcely noticed. Suddenly a stentorian voice rang out across the water. 'The quay ahoy! Catch this line.'

It was a common thing for such craft to put in at the quay for oil or stores. No one surmised, and the puffer was warped up. Gillespie appeared with a bundle of slings from the store of the luggage steamer, which lay behind the 'Shipping Box'. The coal bucket of the puffer was unhooked from the end of the chain and steam turned on the winch.

'Goad! But he's chartered the puffer.' Queebec danced in excitement from one leg to the other. 'He's fair bate us. I kent he'd something up his sleeve; he was that quate an' smilin'.'

The thing was so astonishing, so tremendous, to these men who never bought more than twenty or thirty boxes at a time, that they could only stare in silence. To have a store crammed with stock; to have unlimited barrels of salt and have rented the Square—all that was nothing; but to have chartered a steamer! A dim conception of the bigness of this man and of his audacity began to impregnate their minds. He seemed no more than a boy, with his jovial red face and lithe swinging walk; yet he caused their trafficking in fish to appear to them a piece of shy, dawdling inefficiency. This man in one morning suddenly became gigantic, and these sparrows of Dothan saw that their day of hopping on the quay was done. There was nothing to do but to retire from the shadow of an eagle.

'He'll hae the first o' the market the morn,' wheezed Queebec, who in a dull way felt angry with Andy.

'Boys-a-boys, but he'll hev' the haul.' The ice-cream vendor's mouth fairly watered.

'Every barrel'll be a pound in Manchester,' cried Queebec.

The stem of Andy's pipe snapped between his teeth. He spat out the fragment and walking across the quay accosted the black-bearded mariner.

'Where are ye goin'?' he asked bluntly.

'Yattin'.'

The witticism stung Andy.

'Ye damn big fool; ye'll no' get the price o' paint for your rotten funnel oot o' Gillespa'.'

The black-bearded man, who had a wad of notes in his hand, the freight on the coal and the herring just paid by Gillespie, estimated Andy. A guffaw over at the 'Shipping Box' caused a surge of dark-red blood to swamp his face; his bull-dog neck began to swell; his dark eyes to blaze beneath their bushy eyebrows.

'Ca' me a damn fool, div ye? Me, Jock Borlan' o' Govan. I'll salt your whisker for ye an' tek it to Glesca in a barrel for pickle pork, ye swine. See that,' he held up the wad of notes, ' a bit praisint frae Gillespie Strang to my wife, by Jing!' Backhanded he swung the wad hard across Andy's cheek.

'That's Jock Borlan's wy, by Jing!'

Andy danced in front of him, screaming with rage.

'Get oot o' my way,' the mariner threatened Andy with the wad. 'Wur ye ever at the thaieter? Whaur are ye for, div ye say? I'm for the Langlands Road tae tak my wife to the thaieter the nicht.' He walked ponderously down upon Andy, stamping at the slippered toes.

Andy leapt back, rubbing his cheek and screaming, 'I'll pey ye, ye big Glesca keelie. I'll pey ye for this.'

'Ye'll never pey like Gillespie Strang,' cried the bearded man, jocose again. 'Gillespie Strang's pey,' he tapped the wad with a thick forefinger. 'My wife an' me's gaun to the thaieter the nicht by Jing!'

The eager song of the winch clanked over the quay as tier after tier of the boxes was slung aboard. At the same time the barrels were being rolled in on two planks. In an hour and a half the puffer cleared, the black-bearded sailorman roaring an invitaion to Andy, 'Ir ye comin' to the thaieter the nicht?'

Punctually to the minute at noon on Saturday Gillespie paid the fishermen in his shop.

'That's better than the big market, Sanny.'

'Ay! You bate, Gillespa'; a full hairbour wad be a toom stomach for some o' us.'

'Weel boys,' he said briskly, rubbing his hands, 'I hope I'll pay ye ten times as much next Setterday.'

In this way Gillespie announced that buying would be a permanent part of his business. He retired to his back-shop and, seated at an aged black mahogany desk full of pigeon holes, made up his 'returns':

	£	s.	d.
1020 boxes............................	51	0	0
Freight Glasgow................	25	0	0
ditto Liverpool..............	39	0	0
Salt......................................	5	0	0
	120	16	3

His eyes had a profound look of regret. The Manchester herring had been a test and a risk, but fortunately the weather had been foul on the English coast. He had had a telegram from Manchester—twenty two shillings a barrel. Yes! His eyes had a profound look of regret. He ought to have sent all the stuff to the English market—only it was a risk. He made his entry carefully:

	£	s.	d.
333 barrels at 22s.............	363	0	0
645 boxes at 12 6d.........	403	2	6
Balance	645	6	3

He chewed the end of the pen.

'Nane sae ill for a green hand.' He nodded, wiped the pen, put it behind his ear, carefully put the ledger away, and passed into the front shop, whistling softly between his teeth. He put a sweet in his mouth, passed to the door, and stood regarding the herring

133

fleet, supine in the calm over their anchors. He had prestige. He had bowels of sympathy. He was the man of the town.

Neil M. Gunn

TO THE FLANNANS

W e had been arranging for my friend's annual trip to the Flannan Isles, those lonely green-clad rocks we had tried to pick up on the horizon of the Atlantic. Each summer season he takes out a boatload of over thirty sheep about a year old and carries back a load of sheep he left there twelve months before. Two trips are necessary to evacuate all the sheep, for on the rich grazing of the Flannans they grow wonderfully, and incidentally, produce a mutton that cannot be equalled for flavour. It seemed an arduous method of sheep-farming, conducted on so small a scale, but just how arduous and adventurous I had no idea until the trip was over.

Everything, I was told, depends on the weather, and the start may have to be postponed from day to day, even week to week, for this can be one of the most dangerous seas in the world. But omens were good, and we parted for the night after the fiery cross had been sent round the crew. The start was to be at six in the morning, and I need not stir until I got a shout. I was awake at six, and lay hearkening for a sound, until I remembered that folk on this decent island kept the Creator's time. But when by half-past seven there was still no human movement, I decided that the trip was off. Half an hour later a cup of tea was brought to me. Yes, they were going, said the lady of the gentle smile, but there was no special hurry.

Ah well, it's the West! I decided, hurrying all the same, because I did not want to keep anyone back. On the way to the boat, I met the old man and asked, 'Were you waiting for me?'

'No,' he answered pleasantly. 'We are just waiting for Alastair's cow to calf.'

Now, the previous day, from early morning until late at night, Alastair and I had become friends in the way that it takes a recalcitrant Kelvin engine to make men friends. Hour after hour we had worked at it, analysed each piece of machinery, and said all that could be said—and often a little more. For Alastair was first engineer and I was signing on as his next in command. I flattered myself, after my experience with my own boat's engine, that there was nothing about a Kelvin I didn't know inside out. But I was wrong. There was a piece of mechanism called an 'impulse starter' which I had never met. About nine o'clock at night we decided that a certain two springs were weak, and I got into a telephone box to ring up a man in Stornoway who had those springs. I first made contact in Carloway, and after that a voice answered me from here and there over the island, from any place but Stornoway. Supposing someone was ill, I asked, how could contact be made with a doctor, how could arrangements be made for getting an urgent hospital case to Stornoway? Just couldn't be

done! Was the answer. It seemed a bit madder than usual, even for
the West. Bernera alone carries a population of some five or six
hundred. But there it was. We had already asked an engineer in
Stornoway to stand by for a call about nine o'clock. We had made
arrangements for any necessary piece of mechanism to be brought
over in a private car. And here we were, unable to get in touch!
We went back to the engine and fixed her up sufficiently well to
do the passage—with any luck.

During these arduous proceedings I had not heard about the
cow, but it now seemed she was a fortnight overdue, and as there
had been trouble at the last birth—well, she was a good cow and
we all appreciated Alastair's feelings. Two new members of the
crew were on the scene, young limber fellows, and the third—to
make six of us in all—was due to be picked up *en route*. Everything
was got shipshape. Then we all went and had a solemn look at the
cow. Alastair thought she might calf in an hour. We hung about
for over an hour, then decided to go home. It was a good sea day.
It looked as if we could not now get to the Flannans before dark,
and I wanted photographs of certain rock-faces. But clearly the
chances were we would not now go this day. Perhaps tomorrow...

It was a pity, but no one was upset. In ships' charter-parties
there is always allowance made for what is called an Act of God.
As for the ordinary mortal who could not have foreseen its
application to the behaviour of a cow, he is always learning. The
skipper and I presently parted, with the suggestion on his side that
I should complete my sleep. About eleven o'clock I was brought a
bowl of thick cream and a saucer of raw oatmeal and, as I supped,
remembered my distant childhood, for not since then had I last
seen this rich concoction. I decided to go outside and have a last
look towards the sea. A figure coming, saw me, paused, and began
to semaphore.

That wise brute of a cow had at last given birth to a calf as black
as herself and bigger than any brand new calf I had ever seen.
Alastair was smiling and gave the starting-handle of the old engine

so firm a swing that it hit back at him, knocking his wrist useless for the time being and turning his colour grey. He had, besides, been up all night with the cow. One of the young men got on to the handle, and after half an hour we had the engine warm enough to keep going. Once hot, we knew she would be all right. Soon the anchor was up and we were heading out of the inlet, barely six hours late. I looked at Alastair, saw he was grey still, and remembered the bottle of medicine I had brought for just such an emergency as this.

Folk may talk as they like about our Caledonian spirit, and there is, no doubt, a time for all things. Scientifically, however, one is compelled to recognise the evidence of the senses, and if what happened to Alastair in a few moments was not the result of my medicine, then it was pure miracle.

We had a long, long wait for a man at a pier over in Lewis; but the third Kenneth did not keep us waiting and leapt nimbly from his native rock. Our crew was now complete and we set off for an island where grazed the young sheep that were to be taken to the Flannans. I began wondering how, without any dogs, they would gather the sheep and get them on board. My wonder increased when the boat slowed up opposite a spit of rock, for there was obviously no pier, no suggestion even of a primitive jetty. The four members of the crew leaped ashore, leaving the old man (our Skipper) and myself to make fast the boat by the rock. I watched them disappear over the low crest of the island. There was silence for a long time, then a distant shouting, then sheep coming round above the west shore—followed by the four men spread out, waving their arms, and whooping. I could not help laughing. It was like the boyhood game of Red Indians. When the sheep saw us and the boat, they stopped. This was the first difficult moment. The whooping increased. The sheep came on a little; then stopped again. One sheep turned its head away, seeking escape. Before the thought had got right into that solitary head, however, one of the lads had torn a soft turf from the ground and let fly. There was a burst of moss on the forehead and - the sheep came on. Came on and paused again. Swung to this side, to that. But came on; inexorably driven by the flailing arms and jumping feet of the nimble shepherds. Surely they would never come on to the rock, to the bare rock? They were now against it, crowding together. While we on board kept quiet and motionless, the whooping behind closed its ranks, cunning in sheep knowledge, grew ever more urgent, compulsive, until something must break. One sheep came on to the rock; two, three...Over the rock towards the boat, crowding, pushing, until the weight behind made one sheep jump on deck; two, three...The Skipper caught the first one and dropped it down into the hold, then the second, the third...In a few minutes we were pushing off from the rock, two of us with our heads hanging down into the hold and agreeing that the full load consisted of either thirty or thirty-one.

It had been an exhilarating bit of work, attended by luck, too, for if the sheep had at any moment broken back through the cordon, it would have been much more difficult to drive them a second time. Keep them on the run; don't let them think; and, above all, don't let them know they can break through.

It was now after two o'clock, and though I did not feel hungry—for a bowl of thick cream mixed with raw oatmeal is hardly an evanescent delicacy—I accepted a lump of new white bread, a solid hunk of cheese, and a dish of undeniable tea. For it was farewell to Bernera at last, and now for the Flannan Isles.

Seasickness is a sort of curse. For those who are liable to it, the sea is a place of dread, if not of horror. There are people who maintain that you expect to get seasick, therefore you will. I am quite sure this is mostly wrong. Yet the mind must have a considerable amount to do with it. Two years before, when my wife and I started off alone in our small cruiser, both of us expected to be sick. But we did not worry about it, because, even seasick, one can manage a reasonably sized boat. We were at sea for over two months and during that time slept ashore only three nights. We experienced some very bad weather, and not least when swinging and tossing at anchor in some windy bay. Yet during all that time neither of us had a suggestion of seasickness. The theory we came to was that responsibility for keeping the boat afloat did not give us time to be seasick! The stormiest sea we found exciting and, at moments, exhilarating.

The many miles of ocean between Bernera and the Flannans are not often calm, and as we stood out, close by Gallan Head, we could see it was not exactly smooth today. The heavy cross-swell was boiling on the skerries, smashing against the rock walls, and spouting upward from blue, through living green, to purest white. How wildly Gallan Head boils its cauldron! One of the crew, a young man who has sailed to South America, said this was a more dangerous piece of sea than is likely to be met in most places. Apparently the tide runs for twelve hours in each direction, so that a counter-wind has time to pile up the waters in an exceptional manner. For the rest, there was nothing between us and America, barring St Kilda.

The *Rhoda* is thirty-five feet long and, with her stern cut away in Zulu fashion, is a splendid sea-boat. She rose and slid down and rolled with that complicated living action which, if one had to move at all, made one move warily. I anchored myself in a corner on deck, and lying back, admired the rock walls of that wild western coast. To the south, Scarpa Island could be discerned, a great haunt of sea-birds. The sun pierced the heavy cloud here and there with fiery beams of light.

'We'll have a good passage,' said the Skipper quietly.

After an hour or two I began to feel the chill of the sea, and getting up was, in a moment and to my complete surprise, properly sick. I wonder if it will ever be possible for a man to surmount the feeling of humiliation, touched with anger, at being seasick? I doubt it. But when Kenneth heard of the cream and the raw meal and the cheese, he nodded sympathetically.

'Do you know,' he said, 'that if I take that cream and meal I feel it heavy on me for days. In fact, I would have been sick myself.' Which is, at least, an illustration of the courtesy that can be encountered in these parts!

An hour or so later, I went below, where the fire was warm and an oily smell of cooking fish arose with the steam from the open pot.

This triangle in the bow of the boat, with its bunks on either side, is what east-coast fishermen call 'the den.' Its atmosphere is necessarily somewhat tangible at the best of times. When things have to be battened down, it can be very rich. It was nice and thick now, and when the Skipper lit up his pipe with its load of black twist, I tried a cigarette myself. I was still not feeling on top of the weather, and it was decided that perhaps a little of the medicine that had succeeded so well with Alastair might do no harm. So we toasted each other in friendly tones. I was reclining on a bare wooden seat, but did not feel it hard, and the hand at the wheel was sympathetic enough to the seas to keep me from being violently thrown off. What an art the business of steering is! Any member of the crew in his bunk (as one of them remarked later) could tell at once when the Skipper himself took the wheel, for he alone knew all the movements of the sea and met them with the smooth certainty of the master. In real danger, they would not let him leave the wheel.

As we chatted away in the yellow light of the oil lamp, I asked him if he had ever encountered really dirty weather on this trip. He smiled. Many a time that! And the worst was not so many years ago. On that occasion, a storm beat up while they were in the shelter of the Flannan rocks, and they lay there for days. Solid walls of sea came in through the narrow canyon between the two islands. 'The boat all over was a lather of foam bubbles.' Then the wind began to shift, and their position became extremely perilous. In fact, the only thing for it was to take to sea and risk it. And this they did. A steam drifter, caught in that storm, could not believe her eyes when she came on them making for land, and with the gallantry of the sea, of which ordinarily we hear so little, stood by them hour after hour. 'It was a stormy passage. At home they thought we were lost, for they had no word of us all those days. But she's a good boat.'

Later, one of the crew told me the real story. The Skipper, of course, was permanently fixed at the wheel, with their lives in his steering hand, looking ahead and looking behind. From behind every now and then came a vast sea. You saw it coming far off like a mountain, and if you could, you got out of its way by steering to either hand. Every sea had to be watched and dealt with, hour after hour, while the spindrift blew from the raging crests, and water, little by little, was shipped.

'I never thought we'd live through it. I was in the hold, swinging sometimes from the coamings as if I was hanging to a trapeze! We must keep her light at all costs. We had killed a lot of rock-birds, and, with the water and what not, began throwing them overboard. Then once I looked up to see how the Skipper was doing. There he was, calm as ever. But as I looked I saw him lean over with his left hand—like that—and pull something up out of the sea. Do you know what it was? One of the birds we had thrown over! He leant sideways a second time. Another bird! He did not know we had pitched them out. He thought they had got washed overboard, and he wasn't losing anything while the going was still possible!' You could see the wild scene in the eye of the younger speaker, the scene and that touch of the fantastic, the incredible, that made us both laugh.

A voice came to the hatch and shouted down, 'A French smack!'

The Skipper at once went on deck. I was trying to make up my mind to follow him, when one of the crew descended the short ladder and said we should be there in half an hour. And the French smack?

'She's disappearing round towards the big island. She's poaching lobsters.' He smiled.

There was no sign of the French smack when I got on deck, but here were the Flannan Isles, and I gazed at their great rock faces and green crests with some awe.

Outposts in the Atlantic, they had about them that air of the remote and wild, shut off by incalculable seas, sustaining the shock of thunderous water, pierced by the myriad screaming birds, and haunted by an inhuman loneliness that has to be felt to be dimly understood.

To most people who know of the Flannans there is also added the tragedy of the lighthouse, that unsolved mystery of the sea. It arrests thought now and holds it in an emotion timeless and static as the rocks themselves.

But the moment had come for action, as we nosed into the swinging waters between the cliff walls of the two islands to the south of the big island (Eilean Mór). An anchor went overboard for'ard, and we slid in slowly stern first to the rock on our right. With a foot on the stern-post, and gripping a three-pronged light anchor or grappling-iron with rope attached, one of the lads got ready. On the heave of the waters the boat rose and fell six or eight feet. Some three or four yards off-shore, he threw the grappling-hook on to the rock ledges and pulled, but the hook came away. Not until he had tried many times did one of the prongs catch in a crevice and hold. The stern was brought nearer the rock. Then, about a yard away (for we dared not go nearer), as the stern came up, he leapt–and landed, grabbing and holding on to the rock. The remaining two Kenneths and Alastair followed one after the other, leaping across the narrow aperture of the deep sea that boiled under their feet. They looked up the broken cliff face and began to climb. It was steep enough, but manifestly not impossible for anyone with a sound head. Besides they knew the way, and slipped along sideways under a projecting bluff, and round, and up and on. Presently they entered the region of a very green vegetation, white with what appeared to be blossom, and in a short time after that they had gone out over the top.

'Will they bring the sheep down there?' I asked.

'Oh yes,' said the Skipper. 'This is the easiest place.'

'How many?'

'We put six on to it this time last year, but that's not to say they will be there now.'

'Do they fall over sometimes?'

'Yes. But...I don't know. I wouldn't say that the rock is always to blame.' He smiled in his quiet way. It occurred to me that a fishing vessel after days, or perhaps weeks, at sea might not be altogether averse to some fresh meat.

Our conversation was interrupted by distant shouts, and in a moment we saw the heads of sheep tossed up against the skyline. The beasts came on, and the four men appeared, whooping and flailing their arms in terrifying style. As the slow advance down the rocks proceeded, how I regretted that I could not use my camera, for it was now nine o'clock at night, and the light, under the grey sky, was hopeless for taking photographs.

'There are only four sheep?'

'Yes,' answered the Skipper. 'Only four.' His voice and expression conveyed no slightest annoyance or regret. Two of his sheep had gone, and, apparently, that was that. The true attitude of the man born to the hazard of the sea. One felt that there was no deliberate restraint or repression. The attitude was natural. And, in fact, the loss was never again referred to.

After their year's residence on this island rock, the sheep were not only in splendid condition, with wool of an unbelievable cleanness, but as nimble on their feet as goats. There was more than one exciting moment when a beast all but broke back from the edge through the cordon. Then a man leapt in a way that rivalled the sheep, while one hand grabbed and let fly a sod— flower, root and earth. The aim was always accurate and convinced the sheep without hurting it. We laughed when at one critical moment a squawking puffin was hurled through the air. For all this was taking place directly above us and to the accompaniment of a thousand screaming birds. They squatted on their inaccessible ledges; they darkened the air. Puffins, fulmars, guillemots, razorbills, petrels, gulls, kittiwakes, cormorants, they all nest here.

This was no reconstruction of the past, as one sometimes sees it on a film. The Skipper actually paid a rent for the grazing on these rocks. This was part of his livelihood. Yet, as a 'shot', it certainly impressed me more than anything of the kind I had ever seen in a cinema.

Down the broken rock to the ledges, the overhanging bluffs, directly above the boat, until the sheep had to be persuaded to go the last and only way. And, after a final dangerous break, they went, until they were penned on the last ledge of all. The boat was drawn in until, in that heaving sea, its stern-post was clearing the rocks by the narrowest permissible margin. Then a sheep was caught and, as the boat rose, heaved at the man on the stern-post, who caught it and swung it on board.

When all four sheep were thus loaded, the reverse process started. One by one, six sheep were thrown at the two men on the ledge, who caught them and set them on their way up the rocks. They had, in fact, to climb after them, pushing them on in front, until the green vegetation was reached. Whereupon the lads gave a last shout for luck and turned back. I watched the sheep. Their consternation was obvious. One looked at the green stuff—and tried it vaguely. Before we pushed off from that rock, all six were busily browsing, while they slowly climbed.

'But you can't go up there!' I exclaimed, as the boat slid in stern first to the rock wall of the opposite island.

Yes, they could today, but not always. If the rock was wet, for example, the feet would get no hold. Though, even then, they had seen themselves use a scarf or other garment for treading on. 'It's worse than it looks from the boat,' one of them assured me out of a long experience of the black and often treacherous surface.

The grappling-hook was thrown about a dozen times before at last it got what seemed to me a very precarious grip. The boat was eased in as near as possible, and, as she rose from the plunge, the oldest Kenneth leapt–and landed. I began to feel uncomfortable. The others followed him. The rock above them was a sheer black wall, but a narrow ledge, sloping to the sea, ran to their left and gave on to a miniature funnel. One after another, without any hesitation, they went nimbly along the dangerous ledge and climbed up the funnel–and thus in a few minutes the worst of it was over, though we watched them for a long time hauling themselves up over the broken surfaces above.

'How many have you here?'

'Three,' said the Skipper. 'Though I'm only expecting two, because one of them was ailing.'

'As no poacher would think of tackling that rock, perhaps you'll get all three!' I suggested.

He smiled back. 'Perhaps so,' he said.

Looking at the sheer rock, one could not help reflecting: for three sheep! Even much less than that: one year's growth on three sheep–with the possible loss of a whole sheep! One could hardly help an involuntary, if unspoken, tribute to this Skipper and these men. What grand company they were–willing, good-natured, courteous, and full of pluck!

Here was the other side to that dark picture of the 'dole' and all it was supposed to represent in economic efficiency and lack of initiative. What a sad mess had been made of Highland economics! How tragic the misunderstanding of what was not merely an economic problem but a whole way of living.

I thought of the grumbling of southern farmers, whose dogs moved a thousand sheep from one fenced pasture to another.

In his blood the true Highlander is still a hunter and a seaman. Twenty-four hours on end he will stand incredible discomfort and danger if all his energies are employed, if life gets its thrill from continuous movement with a definite object in view. But he has got to live, and if the result of his labours does not amount to the certainty of 'dole' payments that can be got without such labours, naturally being human, he is inclined to take, like the rest of us, the easiest and safest economic way out.

We heard the shout. They were coming. Far above us we saw— three sheep, one as sturdy and nimble as another.

'They're all there!'

'Ay,' said the Skipper.

A game in persuasion! Each sheep took a hurried yard or two and stood; a yard or two and stood; glancing to right and left; anxious to break back, but terrified of the leaping noisy humans behind. They could still go another yard or two...

'There's one island round the back there—we'll go to it next time—that is very difficult,' said the Skipper. 'Do you see that ledge away up there on the right? Well, it was like that, only worse. A sheep went right on to it and stuck there, and nothing that the boys could do would make it move. It was just big enough to hold the sheep and it was right over the sea.' Seventy feet of a drop, I judged, into a boiling sea (with a possible knock on the bulge of the rock midway). 'Well, at last Alastair climbed down onto the ledge itself and gripped the sheep, and after a little struggle he got it up.'

This story reminded me of my rebellious stomach, and I certainly did not want to be a spectator of any such feat at the moment. Fortunately, nothing untoward happened. Men and sheep came down the funnel together and along the treacherous ledge. Three sheep were heaved out, and persuaded along the ledge, and up the funnel.

'Did you ever have an accident?'

'Never, I am happy to say,' replied the Skipper.

And so we left that dark rock and made for our last landing, the island with the lighthouse, for it was the largest of the Flannan group and would take the remainder of our cargo, over twenty sheep.

We were approaching the east landing, and already on the cement stairs that had been set in the living rock we could see two figures from the Flannan lighthouse. The cliffs on the east side of Eilean Mór attain to a height of some 300 feet. The top is a green tableland sloping to the west, where the height above sea level is but 200 feet. We could see the crane on a hewn platform in the face of the rock far above high-water mark. Its long white arm is used for hoisting merchandise and, occasionally, human beings in slings from the deck of a relief ship. For the greater part of the year there is probably no other way by which a man could get landed on this island. But the swell was not so bad tonight, even if the light was fading, and we stood in stern first in the usual manner.

Our rope was now caught by expert hands. Our leading seaman leapt on to the cement steps, nimbly avoiding the swirls of water, and in a few moments unloading the remainder of the sheep we had brought from Bernera began. One by one they started to mount the steps that slanted up the face of the cliff. Occasionally a beast left the steps and tried to advance upon the precipice itself, but after a yard or two had to admit defeat. It was a laborious business, and I thought we were lucky to get them all landed without mishap. The Skipper suggested I should go up to see the lighthouse, so I waited for the plunging stern to come up, leapt for the concrete step, and slid on its slime a successful yard. The Skipper and Alastair remained behind to look after the boat.

We were all invited to his home by the friendly, quiet-mannered head lighthouse-keeper, but on the way up we wondered whether it would not be wiser first of all to collect our sheep and get them on board. The daylight was going fast, for it must now have been after eleven o'clock, and though it would not get quite dark, still, there were three or four hours ahead when it would certainly be darker. While the hunt started I was invited up to see the lens.

A lighthouse has always had a peculiar attraction for me. In earliest boyhood I could count on a clear night seven flashes

across a wide sea. And now and then, in later years, the image of
the lighthouse has come to mind. As the great prismatic sphere
slowly revolves it throws over the dark waters its beam of light.
Impartially it shines forth, like sun or moon. Indeed, it is when sun
or moon and all the stars are gone in a roaring blackness that it
takes their place and, in its smaller orbit, fulfils their directing
purpose with equal certainty. It is then, as the flashes cross a
skipper's eyes and he counts and times them, that he learns where
he is, and thereupon proceeds with confidence into the
tempestuous night.

On top of the ladder I sat looking at the bright globe that
revolved with slow steadfastness. I looked around me and out
upon a darkening world. Cleanliness, and order, and discipline,
and–light.

I came out of the lighthouse to find men and sheep rushing
through the gloom as in a mimic battle, converging on those
hundreds of cement steps that zigzagged down the cliff. And at
last a sheep broke through! A figure pursued at full tilt, but, as it
turned out, the sheep won. It took a fair time to heave the many
sheep on deck, for the boat was plunging a lot, as if the swell had
increased. Once I thought I saw a sheep in the surf after an
unsuccessful heave (these beasts were much heavier than those we
had brought over), but in the end they were got safely on board;
and this, everything taken into account, in the deep gloom of that
midnight, was a remarkable enough feat.

The crew relaxed, wiping their foreheads, and when the
hospitable head of the lighthouse suggested that a cup of tea or
coffee might be refreshing, we did not disagree, but there and then
turned and began climbing again the multitude of steps–all, that is,
except the Skipper and Alastair, who, well content with the night's
exertions, stuck to the *Rhoda*. As for the single sheep that had won
a temporary respite, it would be duly collected on the next trip.

After being hospitably entertained, we came out again into the
night, all feelings of exertion or strain gone in the mood of ease

and relaxation. The crying of the sea-birds in the cliffs seemed to have increased. I could hear the continuous booming of the sea. Then the whole atmosphere of the place seeped inward in that darkness that was faint with light, and there was born the emotion of an ultimate loneliness, as if one stood on a storm-lashed outpost of the world.

I looked up at the light. Day and night a man was on duty there. Every half-hour the mechanism was wound up that kept the great crystal globe revolving. In calm and tempest, its beam swept over the dark seas. The light that never failed. And then I remembered that once the light had failed.

The Skipper had told me how one night over in Uig, in Lewis, a gamekeeper could not see the light. But, perhaps, the atmosphere was thick outside? For how could the light fail? The following night–there was no light. It was mid-December in the year 1900. The absence of the light was reported, and on the 26th of December the Northern Lighthouse steamer drew in towards the east landing. Once a month, if weather permitted, this steamer visited the lighthouse with whatever gear or provisions were required, and landing one man, took another off, for the men worked on a continuous shift of two months on the island and one off. But now there was no sign of life about the lighthouse, no response to the steamer's signal, and, as a small boat was lowered and got away, there were no figures on the steps.

It was not difficult to imagine the scene, even to experience in some measure, not only the concern and trepidation, but that deeper, eerier emotion of insecurity that invades the mind at such a moment. Up those cement steps, up the narrow double line of rail by which heavy goods are hauled up to the store, up the bare slope in front, up to the lighthouse itself, white and silent.

They reached the lighthouse, but found no-one. The last entry in the log-book was made at 9a.m. on the 15th of December. The morning's work had been completed. The lamps were trimmed and charged. The lenses had been polished. All was shipshape and in order. They searched the outhouses, searched every corner of the island, but no trace of them has ever been found. Why and how they disappeared must now for ever remain one of the mysteries of the sea.

There are one or two theories. In the living-room there was evidence of a hastily interrupted breakfast. One chair had been knocked back. Apparently something had called the men's attention urgently. On the three nights preceding the 15th, the log-book shows that a tremendous gale had been blowing from the west. It has been suggested that the mind of one of the men gave way under the strain, that he got up precipitately and made for the cliff, that the two others followed him, and, in the final struggle, all three went over.

But this is very unlikely, because lighthouse-keeping implies a certain temperament to begin with, and, anyway, by the morning of the 15th the gale had blown itself out. There would still, of course, be terrific seas running; but the wearing roar of the wind, and, indeed, the danger of being swept over the cliffs by the sheer force of that wind, had gone.

The evidence in which our Skipper believes—and no man living knows these seas as he does—was collected round the west landing. At the east landing there was no trace of any violence from the storm. But at the west landing, against which the storm had smashed, there had been a remarkable happening. Some 112 feet above sea-level, a wooden box firmly fixed in a cranny of the rocks, and holding ropes, crane handles, and other gear, had been smashed open and its contents scattered far and wide.

Even in calm weather, this western coast knows these tremendous swells. The Skipper had lost his previous boat by just such a swell invading his normally secure anchorage at the inner end of a Bernera inlet. Many yards above high-water mark the brimming water rose, converting for the moment a land knoll into an island, setting up in the process a whirling motion. In the course of the night this miniature maelstrom had, by spinning the vessel round, fouled the two anchor chains and thrown her upon the rocks where she was broken up.

And what was a sheltered narrow Bernera inlet compared with these rocks in this open sea? And that, after a three-day gale of terrific intensity! The lighthouse had only been established a year. The men would not know all the ways and currents of the ocean against the rock formations. In fact, subsequent observations proved that in calm weather the sea can pile itself up in a sudden and treacherous manner against the west landing.

The crane was some forty feet below the box and seventy feet above the sea. After the reverberating impact from a vast wave, the men may have hurried to the landing and, descending the steps, tried to collect their gear. A new wave comes sweeping towards them, to be thrown by the formation of the rocks into a climbing, upreaching mountain of green water. We know that one such wave reached over 112 feet. And we know that nothing living could at a lower level hang on when its immense weight and mass broke upon the cliff.

As I walked down the slope with the head keeper at the darkest hour of the night (it was now one o'clock in the morning), we came on the narrow-gauge rail that disappeared towards the west landing. It was hardly the time and the place to introduce the subject of the mystery of the Flannans.

'Do you use the west landing much?' I asked casually.

'Not much,' he answered. 'There are nasty swells there.'

We made no other allusion to it. But one thing he did say, which I shall remember. I can hardly think that I would make the banal remark that it was lonely here or ask him if he felt lonely. Perhaps it was out of some momentary community of mood that he said, 'No, I cannot say that I ever feel lonely. I like it.' And I felt, rightly or wrongly, that I understood him.

Above the crying of the sea-birds and the booming of the waves, there was a feeling of the loneliness that has peace at its heart. For perhaps loneliness can be a terrifying thing, in itself, only to him who fears his own company. But to him who has no such fear, loneliness may bring peace and, on occasion, a quiet exaltation. It may have been some such conception of loneliness and peace that drew the old Celtic missionaries of the early church to exactly such outposts as Eilean Mór. Indeed, the Flannan group is named after St Flannan, an Irish saint of the seventh century, who is believed by tradition to have lived for years on Eilean Mór. The ruins of his simple oratory can be seen behind the lighthouse.

An arm was ready to catch us as we leapt from the slippery step to the stern-post, after having bade the men of the lighthouse goodbye. Out into the open sea and the plunge and roll of the heavy cross-swell. How steadfast looked the lighthouse on its black wall of rock, how serene its beam! For many a mile it would accompany us through the night.

'You'll be more comfortable below,' said the Skipper. 'It's getting very cold.'

So we went down, and the Skipper lowered a berth that had been hanging against the boat's side. The simple mattress, being rarely used these days, added a faint odour of mildew to the atmosphere, but its dampness bred a gradual warmth and comfort. I took off my oilskins and lay on my back. The Skipper, on the other side, did not lower his bunk, but merely stretched himself on the hard board of the seat. For a long time we smoked and talked. Once or twice one of us went up on deck to see how the lads were getting on. They were crowded behind a wind-shelter, with the compass before them. None of them appeared to have thought of turning in, though there were four good bunks in the den.

'It's cosy here,' I said.

Yes, many a night he had spent in this small space; and many a night in the dens of fishing boats on many seas. It was fine to listen to him talking in his quiet pleasant voice. But the picture that sticks most vividly in my mind concerns these same Flannan rocks, when Alastair and himself used to go lobster-fishing there on the *Rhoda* in the depth of winter. Sometimes it would be icy cold, and the sea, as one could imagine, would hardly be very smooth. Hauling and cleaning and baiting the lobster-pots was a bitterly cold job. In truth, often it would freeze you to the marrow. But when the work was over, *then* to come down into the den here, with its warm fire, and settle in for the night, while the boat herself rode the elements. Ah, it was homely and fine!

One could feel the warmth of it, the companionship of men in hard and dangerous toil. Long thoughts about it drifted through my mind. The inshore fishing, surely the most natural way of fishing, had to a large degree been ruined by economic causes beyond the power of these fishermen to control. Economic causes? Let us have moments of human companionship when even to discuss profit-hunting and greed may be forgotten. Let us listen to one another's voices in the den of a small boat on a stormy sea. There is a chance then that human values may be seen in reasonable perspective; there is a certainty that the mystery of human life, and the companionship and goodness that so miraculously come out of it, will at least be perceived. The rotten bait slips back into the sea.

We dozed, and spoke, and sometimes one of the crew came down to get a warming. The sky was black and it was keeping very dark, but soon they should be picking up the land.

We picked up the land, and presently were in the tumult round Gallan Head. After the pranks that had been played by my internal economy, there had supervened a certain bodiless feeling that was by no means unpleasant. The clock had made a double round since we had gazed expectantly at Alastair's cow, but it seemed a longer stretch of time than that.

Two or three miles more, and we ran into the shelter of the island of Pabaidh Mhór, into a calm sea with white sands on the Lewis shore. The morning was now advanced, but no smoke came from the croft cottages, and the land lay still and strangely fresh under the grey sky. Often summer mornings in this western world have to a marked degree this curiously arrested air of enchantment. After long physical toil or endurance, the mind, too, at such moments is conscious of release from the body and all its desires, all its urgent moods. The voice goes quiet, and the spirit floats in an air of friendliness and fellowship. Strife seems an odd phenomenon, a madness of the uncleansed flesh, and the thought of it, in the abstract, is something to smile at.

from **SHIPS AND SHIPMEN**

The Brassbounder's new ship lay at Yorkhill, and I was bidden to come down and inspect her glories. The day, it chanced, was fine; even had there been no new vessel to see, the prospect of looking up and down the lighted river at the coloured funnels was irresistible.

I was only one of the crowd. It seemed that thousands were there to gape at the panelling of the saloons and think how jolly it would be to sleep in one of those trim white cots. A formal affair of the kind is always painfully artificial. You feel so crude and curious and conventional against the inherent romance of a ship.

A picture hat doesn't go with a gyroscopic compass, somehow, and it is awful to have to say 'How interesting!' when the mechanism of bulkhead doors is explained. A ship deserves better of human curiosity.

These great liners, of course, are marvels of sophistication in their way. Etchings in the alleyways, and pink shades over the lamps, and all that. But such things are irrelevant to the main interest. It's the proud, strong, beautiful efficiency of a ship that counts; the weep of the long decks and the marvellous co-ordination of her controls. The rubberneck misses these things in a foolish enthusiasm for pretty interiors.

So I broke away from the procession. An electrician was at work on the bridge, producing reassuring noises from bells and poignant little red lights on complicated switchboards. To him I was indebted for some dramatic facts about the bulkheads. Seven minutes it takes after the crash. The crash, you observe. No room for grand pianos alongside that idea.

Then they were filling the holds with sacks, that came swinging up from the quay on the prehensile jibs of noiseless cranes. The holds are very deep, pits that seem to be bottomless. Hundreds of sacks swung up and then down into the depths, under the tacit control of a stevedore who communicated his wishes with an eloquent right hand. Tons and tons of stuff: it was good to watch the process till you began to apprehend the significance of a voyage across the Atlantic. Here was wealth and responsibility. Then the aggrieved voice of a labourer on the quay, shouting:

'Are ye no' full yet?'

He pronounced 'full' to rhyme with 'dull'. But the stevedore motioned with his hand to the mechanician in the glass cabin of the crane, and the work went on—while the procession of people in their best bibs and tuckers looked at the music-room carpets and said: 'How perfectly lovely!'

I dodged below to explore the bowels of the ship for myself. It was a tactic badly planned. The procession sucked me in to share its exploration of the kitchens. More sophistication here. The place was like a laboratory. You couldn't envisage any son of a sea-cook in this gleaming repository of copper boilers and electric ovens and silver grills. Only scientists, fastidious technicians dare toy with these shining levers and read the thermometers. No salt junk was ever to come out of here, no steaming cups of coffee for men who shivered on icicled spars.

But the procession delighted in it. 'How awfully interesting!' we said, and tested the temperature of the cauldrons with gloved hands. And this was the first-class dining-room! How convenient! And how handsome! Those individual tables are so awfully jolly!

They did not even look down into the white cavern of the engine-room; but I hung back there, waiting—for something that I could not define to myself. It came at last. Out of the depths there rose a voice that spoke in the unadulterated accent of Greenock.

'For crivven's sake, Alec,' it said passionately, 'keep yer flakin' eye on thae gauges!'

A window was opened. Here was reassurance. At last, I was getting near the soul of the ship.

Greenock in the engine-room, of course. I could see them down there, between watches, in a stuffy mess-room, recalling hectic days in the Rue-End. The tradition was not broken by the upholsterers. It would be all right when the procession cleared out, and the bells clanged, and the throbbing propellers pushed her out to curtsey to the rushing seas. The procession was merely an incident in the life of the ship.

While it gurgled and cooed its appreciation of the gymnasium, I climbed to the boat-deck and encountered there a small man with a drooping moustache and bandy legs. He was dashing about, a coil of wire in one hand, followed by a lanky halflin with sandy hair.

'Here, Pe'er,' he cried to his satellite. 'There's anither wee joab up here. C'mon and we'll get on to it.'

All the men who mattered were busy. It was not the sight-seeing that counted; the great thing was to get the ship ready for sea. To this task hundreds of silent artisans were addressing themselves– the stevedore at No.2 hold, Greenock in the engine-room, Pe'er on the boat-deck. Strength, skill and energy were coming to life under the hands of those unpolished but energetic accoucheurs. Mother Clyde and her acolytes had a reputation to sustain.

That was the splendid feature of the spectacle. The mills of efficiency were grinding slowly but small, and the procession was only in the way. Get her ready, ready for sea–make her fit and eager for the first bout with the Atlantic. The panelling did not matter; only the ship with the long, strong, stately hull.

Dodging the procession again, I blundered in among a gang that was engaged in washing down the decks under the stern eye of the first officer. It was the first throb of the clockwork discipline of a ship at sea. Nobody in this gang was going to take the slightest heed of a lady visitor's suede shoes. Then, as I left the ship, steam was hissing eagerly from behind the funnel. Grouped on the quay, and dwarfed by the sheer sides of her, the procession had relinquished its temporary hold on the vessel. Now she was divorced from landlubberly influences. She had passed, for ever, into the keeping of the seamen.

When I looked back from the head of the dock, even the artisans were knocking off. Only, up on the dizzy plateau of the boat-deck, there trotted Pe'er and his mate, still feverishly engaged in getting on to the wee joab.

* * * * *

The East Wind cracked his vicious whip along the length of Princes Pier and drove the crowd, in huddled groups, to seek shelter in the echoing passage-ways and staircases of the red station buildings. For some unknown, wildly-surmised reason the tender delayed its appearance at the quay. Out at the anchorage the black liner lay ready, wisps of steam fretting round the funnels, the Blue Peter pointing towards the West at the cold command of the wind; but the crowd of emigrants, trebled in bulk by related women, children, and dogs, had to prolong the dreary farce of making a cheery business of parting.

The little group nearest me was doing its level best. It consisted of Jamie, a shipyard worker plainly; Jamie's mother, a weary-faced little woman, looking out through brown, apprehensive eyes from between the tight-drawn folds of a snuff-coloured shawl; Jamie's sister, a big lass in a cheap blanket coat with a baby asleep on her breast; and Jamie's intended, a pale, pretty thing, whose nervousness expressed itself mainly in guffaws of incredibly loud and vulgar laughter. That was how they did their best—by laughing; at anything. Quick, excessively hearty bursts, followed by strained silences, during which the beady eyes of Jamie's mother and the pale eyes of Jamie's intended devoured his strong, confident, careless face.

It was no place for women. Jamie's sister, content with her baby, was placid enough, but these others should have stayed at home and got over it in privacy. But they were too hungry for sensation and love. Mother and intended were competitors to the death for the affection of Jamie. They would see him away together, keeping each other well in sight.

Jamie's mother, being a mother, was solicitous in a practical way. Her questions shot out to him sharply.

'Ye've got the spare socks handy, Jamie?'

'Ugh, ay!' said Jamie, gloomily, resenting the feminine fuss. Then, relenting, to cheer her up: 'I'll no' wear oot ma socks that quick—I'll be seeck for the next week.'

Loud laughter from Jamie's intended—a high, shrill burts of it. Jamie's sister cut in on the tail of the laugh.

'Ye shouldna' ha' took yon haddie fur yer breakfast.'

A master-stroke of wit. Jamie's intended had to be shaken back into sobriety. It was all so funny. Then the laughter died. That cold fatal thought crept into the minds of them all once again. Silence.

The eyes of Jamie's mother gloated on his, which were averted as if he wished to photograph the grouping of the hills above Helensburgh and carry away a last, loved picture of old Scotland. His intended peeled the paper from a caramel. His sister tenderly wiped the mouth of her baby with the fringe of the shawl. Then Jamie's intended made another heroic effort.

'Nane o' yer jinin' the Mormons!' and cackled with laughter. 'I'm no' wantin' to be second fiddle to a big Yankee wumman.'

Loud laughter. Jamie turned from the hills with an admiring smile for his intended.

'Don't you fear, Sarah,' he declared stoutly. 'I'll keep ye the place at the tap o' the table.'

Another burst of hilarity. It stopped as quickly as it began. Then Jamie's mother, swinging the door-key in her thin hand, spoke gravely.

'They're an awfu' dangerous lot, the Mormons,' she said, apprehending all the temptations that might be put before her boy.

It was plain why Jamie was going away. A glance up the river-front let me see the empty berths, where a hundred sterns of ships a-building were wont to hang above the tide. Thinly, on the east wind, came the rattle of a single pneumatic riveting machine—and we used to hear them thundering in chorus. Bad times. To emigrate was all a decent, active lad could do. And here was Jamie, off to Philadelphia in the morning.

The river and the country round about were not at their best. No overburdening sense of their beauty and the dearness of their associations could hurt the emmigrant on this sad day of March. The haze from the east had taken the colour out of the sea and the hills and blurred the outlines of distant things. Yet—and yet Home was recognisable. That wooded point of Rosneath and the bluff peninsula of Ardmore; the swell of Ben Buidhe's three tops and the more jagged peaks of Argyll behind; the stern rise of the Rock above Dumbarton and the sweep of the old grey town round the flank of the Renfrewshire uplands—surely Jamie could not ignore them. And his womenfolk here–his mother, old and done, you know; and his sister, another man's now and careless; and his intended–it might be a long time...

'Cheer up Jamie,' said his sister, suddenly, 'ye're no' deid yet.'

'No' me!' cried Jamie, reissuing from his dreams. Then, at a loss, 'It's awful cold.'

'Mind you whit I tell't ye aboot thae thick semmits,' said his mother anxiously.

So it went on. The humorous resources of the party gave out. The bursts of laughter were few and far apart, and when they did occur, they were too loud to be honest, too curt and hard to relieve the tension. The thin fingers of Jamie's mother tightened round the key, Jamie's intended jigged uneasily to her humming of a tawdry tune and chewed caramels. Only his sister, nourishing her young, was far from the strained tragedy of the moment. Then Jamie shedded pretence and spoke fretfully.

'That boat–waitin' here a' day–daith o' cold.'

He frowned and moved out of shelter to scan the Firth. He turned back at once and picked up his bundle.

'She's comin',' he said curtly.

Without another word, he stooped and kissed the pale cheek of his mother. Not a word, no demonstration but that momentary gesture.

One lost grip of the situation. The surge forward of the crowd and its noises broke up the perspective. Jamie disappeared into the mob, his sister and his intended on either side. The girl was sobbing bitterly, and he had his arm around her. One could see that he was pouring comfort in her ear. Then confusion: shouts of admonition from the officials, of false hilarity from the crowd. A whistle blew. The old song rose against the wind, mournfully,

> Will ye no' come back again?
> Will ye no' come back again?
> Better lo'ed ye canna be–
> Will ye no' come back again?

A toneless voice, speaking at my elbow, brought me back to immediate things.

'That's oor Jamie gone,' said Jamie's mother quietly.

It was not a cry of sentiment, or self-pity, or grief. It was a statement of fact by one who had yet to realise its import, who made it just in order that she might understand. Jamie was gone. He had stooped and kissed her lightly and gone, keeping his comfort and his affection for that chit who chewed caramels and laughed. But—gone! After all these years of care and anxiety; away like that, with the ghost of a kiss and never a word to her. Off to Philadelphia in the morning! And it was finished....Jamie's mother did not quite understand.

She stood looking at me, a sort of baffled confusion in her eyes. She was trying very hard to appreciate the price she was being called upon to pay for being the mother of a man.

'Oor Jamie's gone,' she said again—almost raptly, you would have thought. But still it was beyond her. Perhaps the emptiness of the house would help her to understand.

The sob of the parting-song came down the wind; and it was a song of passionate despair, with not a glimmer of hope in it.

Cherry Drummond

BOMBS AT SEA

Victoria Drummond was the first woman to become Chief Engineer on a British
merchant ship

O
n our last Sunday in England, I went ashore early,
crossed the harbour and climbed the steep road, little
more than a lane beaten deep into the soil by centuries of
traffic and the feet of generations of Cornishmen. Turning into a
meadow near the crest of the hill I found a shady bank and settled
down for a completely lazy and happy afternoon. The whole air
was heavy with the scent of wild flowers and new mown hay.
Beneath me the inlet stretched dark between green meadows and
yellow cornfields, and the harbour mouth shimmered in the bright
light. Beyond, a white fringe of breakers marked the Channel, deep
blue and stretching into limitless haze.

Here in that place of peace, on that perfect day, the War became remote and unthinkable. Yet beyond the haze-dimmed horizon, the forces were already in motion for a grim struggle on which the fate of my country would depend, the Battle of the Atlantic.

On 23rd August I telephoned Mummy and Frances and told them we were off. Crossing the Atlantic in a convoy seemed somehow more of an adventure than threading one's way across the Channel in a minefield or cruising up the Med with the British Expeditionary Force. It was going into Tom Tiddler's ground with a vengeance, submarines and planes would both be on the lookout for us.

After I got back to the *Bonita* I was busy getting everything ready for sailing, running the fridge for the sea storage and so on. As dusk settled over the town and harbour, tugs forward and aft manoeuvred the deeply-loaded *Bonita* round the bends in the canal and we headed seawards on the first stage of our journey.

Hundreds of people turned out and waved to us. It was a long and laborious business in the engine room and entailed innumerable movements of engines. 'Full Ahead' to 'Full Astern' alternatively for several hours. I envied the officers on the bridge or on deck who could see and exchange greetings and farewells with their friends on the jetties as we drifted slowly past the town. It was dark when we cleared the entrance and the pilot left taking our last letters for home. The telegraph rang 'Full Ahead', then 'Full Away' and the ship swung slowly to her course, lifting gently like some great animal waking from sleep as she felt the deep ground-swell of the Atlantic. The night was dark and the land soon faded into the blackness as we steered well south to avoid the danger of mines in the shallower waters. Shortly before midnight flares were dropped, presumably from enemy planes, but well astern of us and we did not come within their fatal radius. Through the night we drove the engines at their maximum, working full speed in the hope of clearing the danger area during the hours of darkness.

We were a Panamanian ship with a Hungarian captain, in effect an alien, so we were not thought to need the protection of a convoy.

Next day we saw a dozen St Malo fishing boats with sails strung out in a long line. I thought they looked so pretty, but the mate, Mr Warner, muttered darkly that they came from St Malo, which was in enemy hands. All was smooth and calm and I thought nothing more of it. We had taken up sea watches and I was on the normal second's watch of 4-8.

On the morning of Sunday 25th August I came up on deck after my watch and was talking to Mr Warner when we saw more of the St Malo fishing boats. The second mate was also with us.

'I don't like those fishing boats we passed this morning,' the mate said, 'and last night too. They are spying on us. What are they doing fishing here? The water is too deep and we are 300 miles out from the nearest land.'

He had hardly said this when there was a burst of firing from a plane that had just appeared overhead. It was 8.55 a.m. Within two minutes I was in the engine room, standing by the main engines. I gave her all the speed I could, for I knew that our only hope of survival was to dodge the bombs. Herbert the fireman was in the stokehold where he stood no chance at all if the ship were hit, and indeed there was little chance of survival even in the engine room. I called Herbert up and Tommy, the greaser, to stand on the main platform by me. Hardly had I done this than vibrations began shaking the ship. Never had I known anything like it. The bombing at Portland had been bad, but this was ten thousand times worse.

We got it, all right, and I thought we must be hit as the vibration was so terrific. I counted eight separate bursts of firing from the guns. All the lagging came off the pipes and fell like snow. The feeling was as if the ship were lifted up and dropped each time. With the bombs, the machine-gun fire and the engines of the plane, the noise was terrific and magnified even more in the enclosed space of the engine room. In fact, with all the noise going on, the ship's engines seemed almost silent.

Flying debris hit the main water service pipe to the main engine and scalding water began to gush out; the end of the speaking tube to the bridge broke off too. I had stuffed my ears with cotton waste to deaden the noise but pulled it out to hear the captain's orders. None came through. We were on our own. I got the engineers to open out the fuel injectors and the main steam throttle, and then I pointed to the door.

'Get out,' I shouted.

By this time oil from somewhere was running down my face and I could only see out of one eye. The engine was a hissing, bubbling inferno and everything that could shake or bang rattled like marbles in a drum. The ship must be doomed, I knew that now. My duty was to keep the engines going as long as they would turn. For the rest of the crew their chance of safety lay in being outside and getting to the boats. Tommy hesitated, then he too went, and I was alone.

Was this the end, I wondered, banged and buffeted in this inferno of noise and steam? It didn't seem a good way to go.

How many times had the plane bombed the ship? Was it three, was it four? Each time we were miraculously unharmed. I began, against all reason, to hope.

Suddenly the noise of the bombs and firing stopped. I heard a slight noise behind me and saw that Tommy and Herbert were back. I scrawled a chit to tell the chief that the engine room water service pipe and the end of the voice tube to the bridge were damaged and I wished to repair them. It was 9.25 a.m. and it was all over.

The plane had exhausted her bombs, finished her bullets and gone. Not a single bomb had hit us. It was a miracle, due in part to the brilliant seamanship of Captain Herz, who had held the ship steady on course and then, as the bomber was ready to unload, had jinked the bow away in time to avoid the bombs, putting her hard to port or hard to starboard so that they were always just behind. I thought perhaps it was also due to the fact that the engines were kept going so he could avoid the bombs.

When it was all over the chief came down and took charge of the engine room. The donkeyman came down with a bullet in his hand which he had picked up off the deck. After I had examined the boiler and engine room for damage and seen to the pipe and tube, I went up on deck and we all looked for bullets and bits of bomb. The plane had been a large four-engined bomber, they thought a converted airliner, so she could not turn easily and had to go about five miles, take a huge circle, and come back.

Even though she came over four times, flying just over the mast, not one of the twenty-five bombs she dropped hit us, though they fell within ten or fifteen feet of the ship. The water was all black, like ink, where some had fallen. These were thought to have been mustard gas. The explosive bombs detonated at a greater depth, getting under the hull to blow the ship sky high! It was a marvellous escape.

I went round with the captain and Mr Warner to see the damage. One bullet had gone right through the deck sheet of the poop and hit the deck in the crew's quarters. One had gone through the deck above our bathroom and made a long dent. Another had gone through the deck above the second mate's room, through the ceiling of his cabin, through his bunk, through his chest of drawers and made holes in lots of his clothes. We found the bullet in the bottom drawer, resting among his silk pyjamas. There were two kinds of bullets; one large and copper-covered, one small and steel.

The port lifeboat was holed and the bullets cut grooves in the iron decks and through the hatch covers. If we had had a gun, I think we could have knocked spots off her. The mate said, 'If we had taken to the boats we would have had 300 miles to go, which at a rate of about four miles an hour, would have taken seventy-seven hours.' We had lovely new ship's biscuits in the boats, and I tried a bit of one, but thought little of it.

After it was all over the ship's cat and kitten came out and sat on the hatch, not minding a bit. The cat cleaned her whiskers and the kitten played with little bits of string. We all felt a bit like the cat and the kitten, I think, with the relief of it.

THE SAILING SHIP

M rs Regan yelled at her son.
  'Get up, ye lazy pig! Rise up an' look for work an' don't
shame me before the neebors!'

  She stopped sweeping the floor and approached the set-
in bed, brandishing the brush over him with insane gestures. The
veins bulged in her scrawny neck, her eyes were crazy, she was red
from her brow to the top of her breast, like a person in the throes
of suffocation.

  'Get up, d'ye hear? Get out o' this house an' never come back,
ye lazy coward! Ye'll no' be lyin' there day-in day-out an' neebors

whisperin'.' She came closer, sneering. 'D'ye ken whit they call ye? Johnny Regan, the dirty conshie, the wee gentleman that's too good for work!'

He stared in silent misery at the wall, holding in his rage, conquering the inherited violence in his blood. How he hated her! He would always hate her. Always! When she was long dead and gone, her memory would be nauseous! His hands gripped the undersheet in the vehemence of restraint. She screamed down at him.

'A conshense objaictor! My, ye're a rare son! A conshense objaictor an' socialist! Ma braw Terence is lyin' deid in France, while you're lyin' here safe an' weel!'

Why must she taunt him so horribly, making his itch to inflict the brutality he had witnessed so often since childhood? He had gone to prison, driven by wild idealism, believing his action would end life like this!

He turned on his pillow and said quietly, 'Ach, shut up, will you? Don't make yourself uglier than you are!'

He could have plucked out his tongue. He had not meant to say that. But her nagging would enrage a saint! She became speechless and struck him with the broom handle, hard, vicious blows. Any reference to her disfigurement always infuriated her.

One of her aimless blows hit his elbow and he felt sick with sudden pain. He must stop this! He leapt from bed, as he was, in pants and semmit, and seized the broom handle.

'Stop it now, Mother! Stop it, for God's sake! D'ye hear me!' He shouted, pleading at her crazed face. 'Have you gone mad? You'll hurt yourself!'

But he could not wrest the brush from her, and he regarded, with horrified interest, her thin, red arms, amazed at her strength. Then rage gusted through him like a blast furnace. One good blow would settle her! He trembled, blinded by emotion, and let go his hold. She began receding from him as though from a ghost, walking slowly backwards, holding the broom straight in front of her, terrified by the burning fixity of his gaze. He followed, slowly, ominously, with clenched fists. As she got round the lop-sided table, she darted from the room, slamming the door after her.

For several minutes he stood trembling and staring as if she was still there; then, aware that his bare feet were wet with the sodden tea-leaves she always threw down to lay the summer dust, he exclaimed, 'Ach, hell!' and stepped uncomfortably to the shallow window-bay, where his socks and trousers lay heaped on a chair. He pulled them and his boots on and sat regarding the street. Inflamed by a base desire to rush into the kitchen after her, he clapped his hands to his eyes. 'No! For Christ's sake! Not that!' His own mother! He ought to pity her and all warped people. A sense of the waste of life deeply affected him. One set of people embarrassed or bored by possessing much more than they needed, while others were continually distressed by the lack of common human needs. Five years after the appalling waste of beautiful human energy and lives in war, he saw it still around him in slums, unemployment, preventable disease and ignorance.

Waste!

No one could call him a coward. He would have shouldered a rifle in a revolution. Let them whisper 'Coward' behind his back; none of them had the courage to step up and say. But returned soldiers had said: 'Ah wish Ah'd had the pluck tae be a conshie, like you, Johnny. It was four years of hell.' And those same men were unemployed, their lives as aimless and empty as his own. How gladly he would man any gun used to batter these tenements to the ground!

Why did he linger on here anyway? Some queer loyalty was keeping him, some faint hope of a return of the humble prosperity and friendliness and cheer that once had brightened this sad house. If only that recurring sickness did not afflict him. He would have adventured from here long ago. That two years' imprisonment, with underfeeding on bad food, had left him with some mysterious weakness. For days it disabled him; and these nights, crushed with three others in the bed, it was impossible to sleep for the heat and the bugs.

He stood up vigorously and hustled into his waistcoat and jacket, trying, by activity, to divert his thoughts from their dark channel. What was the matter with him? He was only twenty-six and Life, fascinating, beautiful, waited for him to turn his youth to account.

He thought of going into the kitchen for a wash, but he knew that she would set her tongue on him, and once more his feelings darkened. He looked at his collar and tie on the back of the chair. Why worry? Why bother putting them on? Why worry about anything? He strode into the lobby and met her waiting there, sullenly contrite.

'D'ye want ony breakfast, son?' she asked.

He opened the door and passed out.

'I'm not hungry!' he cast back at her.

Ay, sure she would give him breakfast, he reflected as he turned out of the dark close into the main road. With his father and two brothers out of work like himself, bread and margarine and stewed tea was all the poor soul had to offer him this morning. And she would have nagged him like one of the Furies while he ate it. His heart turned back to her; he should never forget that she wasn't responsible for those mad fits; her nerves were fretted raw by worry and care; he believed she loved him, but he was aware that affection is a delicate thing, driven deep into people and lost behind the tough exterior they develop to face a sordid life.

Ach, if only he had a Woodbine! He raked his pockets for a stub. Across the street he saw a man stoop and pick a fag-end from the gutter, wipe it on his sleeve and stuff it into his clay pipe. His ache for a smoke tempted him to do the same, but with no food in him the idea made him squeamish. Never mind! He might get a few hours' casual work. Then his pockets would jingle!

The sky was sprinkled with gay clouds that sailed and shone as if there were no unemployment and slums in the world. At least he

could smile at the sky! Perhaps the sea was like that today,
limitless, deep azure, with ships roving about it like those clouds.
He saw a cloud shaped like a swimming man, with arms and legs
stretched in the breast-stroke. It sailed to a good wind, and he
watched it awhile, wondering how long it would keep its form, till
the wind tore it and bundled it into another shape. He laughed,
and his heart stood up in him cheerful and fearless, his shoulders
squared and he walked with manlier step.

From every by-street, the sounds of the hordes of tenement
children, on holiday these times, came to him; laughing and
calling, each day they marvellously discovered happiness, like
some lovely jewel, in the gutters and back courts of the big city.
His soul joined with them as they sported and ran, and he was
lightened with belief that war and poverty would sometime vanish
away like an evil dream and that wakened Man would stand
amazed at his blundering and turn to find happiness as simply and
innocently as those ragged children were finding it now.

So exalted, he realised he had walked, without tiring, the four
miles from his home to the docks. He entered the wide gates and
strolled through the crowds of idle dockers, vigorously discussing
football, religion or politics in the assertive Scottish manner. Small
chance of his getting work here! And even if he did, he would
have to quit if the union delegate demanded to see his
membership badge and card. But he was not saddened. The
dazzled waters of the harbour immediately foiled his
disappointment, and he inhaled the breath of travel and the smell
of merchandise from the abounding light and heat. Flashing
pinions curved in the blaze; he sensed them like a wreath around
his head and smiled at the pigeons crooning their passion and
quarrelling on the warehouse roofs, or seeking spilled grain and
Indian corn among the very feet of the men.

He watched a big tramp steamer manoeuvring into the first great
basin. It was the only vessel there, and he recalled the prosperous
days of the port, when every basin was so crowded with masts and

funnels that it was hardly possible to row a dinghy between the herded ships. He sauntered around and, lifting his head to watch a wheeling gull, saw the towering masts and cross-trees of a sailing ship peering over the stern of a steamship. It was ten years since he had beheld a sailing ship and one of such a size as the height of those masts hinted she must be, and he almost ran towards her in delighted excitement.

He stood close and contemplated her with amazement as though she was a phantom which had sailed out of the past of buccaneers and pirates and which might at any moment fade from sight. She was a long, slim three-master, newly painted a pale blue, with the name *France* glittering in solid brass letters on her prow that pointed proudly at the bluff stern of the steamship like an upheld spear. She looked all too slender for her great calling; her spars were crowded white with resting gulls, still as sculpted birds, and as Regan gazed past them at the sky he was taken by desire to get a job on her.

He walked smartly up the gangway. There was apparently no one aboard, and he was elated by his solitary experience as he looked along the clean, bare decks where every hatch was battened down and everything stowed away. If only he might get work on her! That would be a manly break with the mean life of the tenements. Once he had faced the seas with her, he could never return to that life again. There was hardly a part of the ship he could have named, but he placed his hand fondly on her hot rail as though he had sailed with her for many years and knew her intimately. He leant over the side and saw hundreds of monkey-nuts floating, bright in the narrow space between the quay and the ship. He had not noticed them when he hurried forward, with all his eyes for her, but now he saw them plentifully scattered about the dock and on the travelling crane, under which they shone like nuggets of gold on the coal-dust lying where a vessel had been coaled.

Monkey-nuts! They must have fallen from the hoisted sacks;

they must have been her cargo; she had come from the tropics! His fancy wandered into passionate depths of tropical forests, he heard the chattering scream of monkeys, saw small bodies swing and little eyes flash in the green gloom; and he felt convinced that the tropic heat, soaked deep in her planks, was mounting from her decks through the soles of his feet into his body.

He turned to see an amazingly tall, broad man in sea-going uniform stepping up from a cabin away forrard. His heart bounded. Here was his chance! He walked towards him, summoning all his spirit to ask for a job, without the vaguest idea what to say, regretting his ignorance and inexperience of sea-life. The sailor, tanned and handsome, with blond hair gleaming under his officer's cap, stopped and looked dumbly at Regan, who felt most painfully at that moment the complete absence of breakfast in his belly.

Trembling, he removed his cap and said shakily, 'Good morning, Sir! Do you need any sailors?' while he felt his blood scald his cheeks and seemed to himself the utterest fool alive.

The officer stared a moment, then took a long, twisted black cheroot from his mouth and waved it vaguely about, as if taking in the whole harbour.

'All my grew iss 'ere!' he said. It was a Scandinavian voice. 'I haf no yobs! You haf been a sailor? Ya? No?' He replaced his cigar and stared stonily, then removed it and burst out with an uproarious laugh, pointing it at the dizzy masts. 'You could yoomp up there, ya? No, I sink you are yoost too schmall!'

Regan wanted to run off the ship. What a bloody fool he was! Fancy the likes of him expecting to get a berth, with hundreds of seasoned men unemployed! He felt mortified by the officer's scorn of his physique. He was the last and slightest of eight strong brothers, but he had never been regarded as a weakling.

'Hi!' The officer was calling him back, and hope flared up in him again. As he approached, the officer took a cheroot from his outside breast pocket and offered it silently, with a vast grin on his face. Regan accepted it and descended to the dock where he stuffed his pockets with monkey-nuts and sat on the big iron wheel of the crane eating them and flicking the shells over the quayside. He shrugged his shoulders. Ach, well! At least he could admire the beauty of the ship if he couldn't sail with her!

He loved the way her slim bows curved, like the flanks of a fawn. *France*, that was a light little name that suited her beautiful poise. He had heard it said that the Clyde would never see a windjammer again; that they had all been requisitioned, dismasted and turned into steamships for war service. And here was a lovely one whose decks he had walked!

When he was sick of monkey-nuts, he begged for a match from a passing docker and lit the cheroot. It was pure tobacco leaf and he thought he had burned his throat out with the first inhalation, while his head swam and he coughed violently. He stubbed the cheroot out against the crane and put it in his pocket as a souvenir.

In this great basin, where there were only three ships, all the light of day appeared to be concentrated, and in the intense path of the sun floating seagulls vanished as if they were burned away, like the phoenix-bird consumed by its own fire, and Regan blessed his luck for coming upon this ship in such glad weather.

The steamship was unloading a cargo of Canadian wheat, through an elevator projecting from her hold on to the warehouse roof. He went and leant against the sliding door of the shed and watched the wheat pour an aureate stream to the ground in a rising, golden hill. Then he saw a big, red-headed man descending the gangway of the wheat-boat. It was Big Willie McBride, the stevedore, who lived in his neighbourhood and picked up a living as a street bookmaker when there was no work at the docks.

'Hi, young Regan, come 'ere!' he called. 'D'ye want a job?' he asked as Regan came over. 'It's light work, shovellin' wheat for a couple o' days, an' worth thirty bob tae ye?'

What luck! Regan smiled eagerly.

'You bet, Mac! Glad to get anything! I'm skinned!'

MacBride took him aboard the steamship and sent him down the hold, where he was handed a light, flat-bedded wooden shovel and joined nine other men, five of whom fed the endless belt of the conveyor with wheat while four others poured it into huge sacks which were tied, roped together in fours and hoisted above by a steam-winch on deck.

Regan set-to shovelling the grain into the cups on the revolving belt. It was stifling down here; very soon he breathed with great difficulty, and his head was throbbing painfully when the ganger shouted, 'Come on, boays! Up on deck for yer blow!' They climbed up and were replaced by ten others. They could only work in shifts of half an hour, with fifteen minute spells on deck, as the wheat-dust clogged their throats and nostrils, turning to paste in the moisture of breath.

At every turn on deck, Regan leant on the stern-rail and gazed down on the *France*. One time, in the evening, the other men joined him, curious at his quietness, and Paddy, a six-foot, handsome young Irishman in dirty flannels and a blue guernsey said loudly, 'Take a good look at the old hooker, me buckos, for she'll mebbe never come up the Clyde again!'

Someone said, 'Aye, it's three years sin' she was last here. D'ye ye ken her, Paddy?'

Paddy replied, 'Dew Oi know her? Shure I sailed wid that same win'-jammer three years ago. Her skipper was a darlin' sailor an' a dirthy slave-driver. A big, yella-haired Dane, he was, wid a wallop on him like a steam-hammer. Shure Oi seen 'im knock a dago clean across the deck wid a little flick uv the back uv his han'! She was a hell-ship, I'm tellin' ye, an' her grub wasn't fit for pigs, so Oi left her at Ryo de Janeeraw an' sailed home to Belfast in a cattle-boat!'

Regan, listening to him, knew proudly that he would have sailed with her had he got the chance, no matter how hard might be the life she gave him.

After midnight, when they all sat up on deck, gratefully breathing the sweet air, Regan blessed the *France* for his luck. Her holystoned decks and every detail of her shone clear in the glow of the moon, as he whispered down, 'Thanks, lovely ship, for getting me this day's work!'

Behind him, Paddy, who was tipsy, produced a bottle of whisky and sat swigging and humming by himself. Someone said, 'Give us a song, Paddy!' The Irishman stood up proudly, swaying, and passed the bottle round. 'Shure, Oi'll give ye'se a song!' he shouted. 'Oi'll lift yer hearts to the mouths of ye! Sing up, ye sods! Sing up! They all laughed and joined him, singing:

> Oh, whisky is the life of man
> Whisky, Johnny!
> Oh, whisky murdered my old man,
> So it's whisky for my Johnny!

Regan turned and joined them. 'Shut up, everybody!' he cried, 'let Paddy sing by himself! Give us a solo, Paddy. Do you know 'Shenandoah'?'

He realised that the Irishman had a fine voice, but he was spoiling it with the drink. He wanted to hear a song that would honour the sailing ship, a sad old song of the sea. Paddy stared at him in drunken amazement and cried thickly, 'Dew Oi know 'Shenandoah'? Will ye'se listen to him? Dew Oi know 'Shenandoah'? Shure Oi lisped it at me ole man's knee!' He began singing. The lovely old shanty gripped him, and he sang it seriously, with romantic sweetness:

> Oh Shenandoah, I long to see you,
> Away, you rolling river!
> Away! We're bound away,
> Across the wide Missouri!

Someone produced a mouth-organ and played it softly and well, and it sparkled in the moonlight.

> Tis ten long years since I last saw thee,
> Away, you rolling river!...

179

From the ship across the basin a cook cast a pail of slop-water over the side. It flashed an instant tongue of silver and vanished in the dappled iridescence below, and the cook let the bucket dangle while he listened to the song quavering tenderly about the harbour. Regan was deeply moved. Ay, this was the song for a sailing ship! 'Shenandoah'. It was a poem in a name, and it sang of simple men who had travelled far, who carried pictures of relatives or sweethearts and were always promising to write home and always failing, men who had died abroad and never saw their homes again—the forgotten legions of wanderers in the long history of the sea. Ach, he must escape from the prison of the slums!

> Oh, Shenandoah, I love your daughter,
> Away, you rolling river!...

The big form of MacBride suddenly loomed before them, and his mighty roar burst amid them like a thunderclap. 'Heh! Whit's this? A bloody tea-party? Get doon below, ye shower o' bastards! Yer spell's up ten meenits ago! Jump to it, ye lousy bunch o' scimshankers!'

They all scuttled down the hold, except Regan and Paddy, who, gleefully swinging his bottle, lurched into the stevedore, and the two big men faced each other. Highlander and Irishman, they were of a size and breadth, and they measured each other's splendid build with admiring, mocking eyes. Paddy offered MacBride the bottle and the stevedore thrust it away. 'Tae hell wi' yer whisky, man! Ah've goat tae get the wheat oot o' this ship. Ah'll hiv a dram wi' ye efter that's done, no' before!'

In spite of the hatred of violence in himself, Regan sat watching, thrilled, expecting a fight.

Paddy suddenly vented a great laugh and stumbled down the hold, shouting, 'Ach, we're buddies, Mac!'

MacBride shouted after him, 'Sure, we're buddies, but you buckle into that wheat, sod ye!'

Then he turned. 'Whit's the matter wi' you, Regan?'

Regan jumped up out of his trance. 'Okay, Mac! I thought there was going to be a scrap!'

MacBride laughed good-naturedly. 'Ach, Ah wouldnae scrap wi' Paddy. He's okay! Noo beat it doon below.'

All night the wheat hissed down the elevator chute and the steam-winch rattled, hoisting up the sacks. Then the flanges of the bulkheads showed clear and the many tons of wheat sifted surely down till the floor of the hold was visible. Late in the next afternoon the elevator stopped, the last few hundredweights of wheat were hoisted up in sacks and run down the gangplank in trucks on to the dock, and the whole gang left the wheat-boat to be paid off in the warehouse.

'It's me for the boozer an' a bloody guid wet!' Regan heard some of them say as they went away with their money. For two days' and a nights' work he had earned over thirty shillings. He thrust it into his pocket and went and sat on the wheel of the crane. He was very tired, his head ached, and he coughed up wheat-dust from his throat, while he gazed longingly at the sailing ship till dusk descended. He had decided what he would do. He would give his mother half of his earnings, buy himself a second-hand pair of strong boots and tramp to London with his few shillings. But not before he had watched the *France* sailing down the Clyde. When he bade her farewell he would never return. She would speed to the ocean, he would take to the road, and with every mile that he walked his thoughts would follow her.

After supper he picked up the newspaper which his father had just laid down and his eye fell on the 'List of Sailings'. Only a dozen ships were listed, but with excitement he read that the *France* was sailing next day on the afternoon tide. He threw the paper aside and hunched by the fire, staring at the invisible, voyaging with a sailing ship, till his mother, fretted by his immobility, said, 'Whit are ye starin' at, Johnny? Ye look daft, glarin' like that! Ye should go oot tae the pictures or doon tae the chapel for an hoor. Ye hivnae been tae Mass since ye came hame fae London.' She was always ashamed to mention the word 'prison'. He rose and thrust past her.

'Ach, I'm tired!' he said and went into the parlour, undressed and lay down, wakeful a long while, thinking of the *France*.

At her hour of departure next day he was by her side, waiting while ropes were cast aboard her from the pilot-tug, watching every pause and turn she made in the great basin till her prow pointed away from the city. At last she set out, very slowly, in the wake of the tug, with that tall blond man prominent on her deck, shouting instructions, the man who had given him the cheroot. Regan took that out and looked at it, and the keepsake seemed to bind him to her more as he followed along the dockside till his way was barred. Then he hurried out to the road and jumped on a tram and rode till he came to another free part of the river, and stood on the shore waiting till she came up.

This way, riding on trams and buses, he followed her slow progress, while his heart grew sadder with every mile that she sailed beyond Glasgow. The flood was opening wider for her, the shores receding; she was leaving the grand little river, with its long and plucky history of shipmaking, maybe forever. He recalled the Irishman's words. He would never see her again!

At the end he took a bus out to Dumbarton and stood on the shore nearby the great Rock. He saw the tug leave her and turn towards home with a hoot of farewell from its siren, like the cry of a timid friend deserting a gay adventurer. Then, like a gallant gesture, she unfurled all her sails and made her terrible beauty for his eyes.

She was lovelier far than he had seen her as yet as she came slowly on like a floating bird unfolding its wings for flight. She had a dream-like loveliness, and as she came opposite where he stood alone, he impulsively tore off his cap and waved it, then threw it on the ground and stood with his head proudly up, ennobled by her grace.

Sunset met her like a song of praise and his heart went after her as she rippled past. Ach, if only he could have served her on her last few voyages, before she was dismasted and broken up! She dipped slowly into the dying sun and the waters fanned out from her bows like flowing blood. Then the sun went down and her beauty was buried in the darkness.

'Goodbye, lovely ship!' He called after her. 'Goodbye! Goodbye, *France* !'

So ecstatic was his concentration upon that vanishing ship that he felt her decks quiver under his feet, saw her high spars tremble and heard the flap of her sails as he gazed with uplifted head. He was sailing on, away from unemployment and slums and wretchedness, far from the ignorance and misunderstanding of his parents, to the infinite nobility of the sea! His eyes were moist, his hands in his pockets painfully clenched, his limbs shook like a saint's in the ardour of prayer. And for a long time he stood there bareheaded, unaware that darkness, with small rain and a cold wind, had enveloped his transported body.

SEALSKIN TROUSERS

I am not mad. It is necessary to realise that, to accept it as a fact about which there can be no dispute. I have been seriously ill for some weeks, but that was the result of shock. A double or conjoint shock: for as well as the obvious concussion of a brutal event, there was the more dreadful necessity of recognising the material evidence of a happening so monstrously implausible that even my friends here, who in general are quite extraordinarily kind and understanding, will not believe in the occurrence, though they cannot deny it or otherwise explain–I mean explain away—the clear and simple testimony of what was left.

I, of course, realised very quickly what had happened, and since then I have more than once remembered that poor Coleridge teased his unquiet mind, quite unnecessarily in his case, with just such a possibility; or impossibility, as the world would call it. 'If a man pass through Paradise in a dream,' he wrote, 'and have a flower presented to him as a pledge that his soul had really been there, and if he found that flower in his hand when he awoke—Ay, and what then?'

But what if he had dreamt of Hell and wakened with his hand burnt by the fire? Or of Chaos, and seen another face stare at him from the looking-glass? Coleridge does not push the question far. He was too timid. But I accepted the evidence, and while I was ill I thought seriously about the whole proceeding, in detail and in sequence of detail. I thought, indeed, about little else. To begin with, I admit, I was badly shaken, but gradually my mind cleared and my vision improved, and because I was patient and persevering—that needed discipline—I can now say that I know what happened. I have indeed, by a conscious intellectual effort, *seen and heard* what happened. This is how it began...

How very unpleasant! She thought.

She had come down the great natural steps on the seacliff to the ledge that narrowly gave access, round the angle of it, to the western face which today was sheltered from the breeze and warmed by the afternoon sun. At the beginning of the week she and her fiancé, Charles Sellin, had found their way to an almost hidden shelf, a deep veranda almost sixty feet above the white-veined water. It was rather bigger than a billiard-table and nearly as private as an abandoned lighthouse. Twice they had spent some blissful hours there. She has a good head for heights, and Sellin was indifferent to scenery. There had been nothing vulgar, no physical contact, in their bliss together on this oceanic gazebo, for on each occasion she had been reading Héalion's *Studies in Biology* and he Lenin's *What is to be Done?*

Their relations were already marital, not because their mutual passion could brook no pause, but rather out of fear lest their friends might despise them for chastity and so conjecture some oddity or impotence in their nature. Their behaviour, however, was very decently circumspect, and they already conducted themselves, in public and out-of-doors, as if they had been married for several years. They did not regard the seclusion of the cliffs as an opportunity for secret embracing, but were content that the sun should warm and colour their skin; and let their anxious minds be soothed by the surge and cavernous colloquies of the sea. Now, while Charles was writing letters in the little fishing hotel a mile away, she had come back to their sandstone ledge, and Charles would join her in an hour or two. She was still reading *Studies in Biology.*

But their gazebo, she perceived, was already occupied, and occupied by a person of the most embarrassing appearance. He was quite unlike Charles. He was not only naked, but obviously robust, brown-hued, and extremely hairy. He sat on the very edge of the rock, dangling his legs over the sea, and down his spine ran a ridge of hair like the dark stripe on a donkey's back, and on his shoulder-blades grew patches of hair like the wings of a bird. Unable in her disappointment to be sensible and leave at once, she lingered for a moment and saw to her relief that he was not quite naked. He wore trousers of a dark brown colour, very low at the waist, but sufficient to cover his haunches. Even so, even with that protection for her modesty, she could not stay and read biology in his company

To show her annoyance, and let him become aware of it, she made a little impatient sound; and turning to go, looked back to see if he had heard.

He swung himself round and glared at her, more angry on the instant than she had been. He had thick eyebrows, large dark eyes, a broad snub nose, a big mouth.

'You're Roger Fairfield!' she exclaimed in surprise.

He stood up and looked at her intently. 'How do you know?' he asked.

'Because I remember you,' she answered, but then felt a little confused, for what she principally remembered was the brief notoriety he had acquired, in his final year at Edinburgh University, by swimming on a rough autumn day from North Berwick to the Bass Rock to win a bet of five pounds.

The story had gone briskly round the town for a week, and everybody knew that he and some friends had been lunching, too well for caution, before the bet was made. His friends, however, grew quickly sober when he took to the water, and in a great fright informed the police, who called out the lifeboat. But they searched in vain, for the sea was running high, until in calm water under the shelter of the Bass they saw his head, dark on the water, and pulled him on board. He seemed none the worse for his adventure, but the police charged him with disorderly behaviour and he was fined two pounds for swimming without a regulation costume.

'We met twice,' she said, 'once at a dance and once in Mackie's when we had coffee together. About a year ago. There were several of us there, and we knew the man you came in with. I remember you perfectly.'

He stared the harder, his eyes narrowing, a vertical wrinkle dividing his forehead.

'I'm a little short-sighted too,' she said with a nervous laugh.

'My sight's very good,' he answered, 'but I find it difficult to recognise people. Human beings are so much alike.'

'That's one of the rudest remarks I've ever heard!'

'Surely not?'

'Well, one does like to be remembered. It isn't pleasant to be told that one's a nonentity.'

He made an impatient gesture. 'That isn't what I meant, and I do recognise you now. I remember your voice. You have a distinctive

voice and a pleasant one. F sharp in the octave below middle C is
your note.'

'Is that the only way in which you can distinguish people?'

'It's as good as any other.'

'But you don't remember my name?'

'No,' he said.

'I'm Elizabeth Barford.'

He bowed and said, 'Well. It was a dull party, wasn't it? The
occasion, I mean, when we drank coffee together.'

'I don't agree with you. I thought it was very amusing, and we
all enjoyed ourselves. Do you remember Charles Sellin?'

'No.'

'Oh, you're hopeless,' she exclaimed. 'What is the good of
meeting people if you're going to forget all about them?'

'I don't know,' he said. 'Let us sit down, and you can tell me.'

He sat again on the edge of the rock, his legs dangling, and
looking over his shoulder at her said, 'Tell me; what is the good of
meeting people?'

She hesitated, and answered, 'I like to make friends. That's quite
natural, isn't it?–But I came here to read.'

'Do you read standing?'

'Of course not,' she said, and smoothing her skirt tidily over her
knees, sat down beside him. 'What a wonderful place this is for a
holiday. Have you been here before?'

'Yes, I know it well.'

'Charles and I came a week ago. Charles Sellin, I mean, whom
you don't remember. We're going to be married, you know. In
about a year, we hope.'

'Why did you come here?'

'We wanted to be quiet, and in these islands one is fairly secure
against interruption. We're both working quite hard.'

'Working!' he mocked. 'Don't waste time, waste your life
instead.'

'Most of us have to work, whether we like it or not.'

He took the book from her lap, and opening it read idly a few lines, turned a dozen pages and read with a yawn another paragraph.

'Your friends in Edinburgh,' she said, 'were better-off than ours. Charles and I, and all the people we know, have got to make our living.'

'Why?' he asked.

'Because if we don't we shall starve,' she snapped.

'And if you avoid starvation—what then?'

'It's possible to hope,' she said stiffly, 'that we shall be of some use in the world.'

'Do you agree with this?' he asked, smothering a second yawn, and read from the book:

The physical factor in a germ-cell is beyond our analysis, or assessment, but can we deny subjectivity to the primordial initiatives? It is easier, perhaps, to assume that mind comes late in development, but the assumption must not be established on the grounds that we can certainly deny self-expression to the cell. It is common knowledge that the mind may influence the body greatly and in little unseen ways; but how it is done, we do not know. Psychobiology is still in its infancy

'It's fascinating, isn't it?' she said.

'How do you propose,' he asked, 'to be of use to the world?'

'Well, the world needs people who have been educated— educated to think—and one does hope to have a little influence in some way.

'Is a little influence going to make any difference? Don't you think that what the world needs is to develop a new sort of mind? It needs a new primordial directive, or quite a lot of them, perhaps. But psychobiology is still in its infancy, and you don't know how such changes will come about, do you? And you can't foresee when you *will* know, can you?'

'No, of course not. But science is advancing so quickly—'

'In fifty thousand years?' he interrupted. 'Do you think you will know by then?'

'It's difficult to say,' she answered seriously, and was gathering her thoughts for a careful reply when he again interrupted, rudely, she thought, and quite irrelevantly. His attention had strayed from her and her book to the sea beneath, and he was looking down as though searching for something. 'Do you swim?' he asked.

'Rather well,' she said.

'I went in just before high water, when the weed down there was all brushed in the opposite direction. You never get bored by the sea, do you?'

'I've never seen enough of it,' she said. 'I want to live on an island, a little island, and hear it all around me.'

'That's very sensible of you,' he answered with more warmth in his voice. 'That's uncommonly sensible for a girl like you.'

'What sort of girl do you think I am?' she demanded, vexation in her accent, but he ignored her and pointed his brown arm to the horizon. 'The colour has thickened within the last few minutes. The sea was quite pale on the skyline, and now it's a belt of indigo. And the writing has changed. The lines of foam on the water, I mean. Look at that! There's a submerged rock out there, and always, about half an hour after the ebb has started to run, but more clearly when there's an off-shore wind, you can see those two little whirlpools and the circle of white round them. You see the figure they make? It's like this, isn't it?'

With a splinter of stone he drew a diagram on the rock.

'Do you know what it is?' he asked. 'It's the figure the Chinese call the T'ai Chi. They say it represents the origin of all created things. And it's the sign manual of the sea.'

'But those lines of foam must run into every conceivable shape,' she protested.

'Oh, they do. They do indeed. But it isn't often you can read them. There he is!' he exclaimed, leaning forward and staring into the water sixty feet below. 'That's him, the old villian!'

From his sitting position, pressing hard down with his hands and thrusting against the face of the rock with his heels, he hurled himself into space, and straightening in mid-air broke the smooth green surface of the water with no more splash than a harpoon would have made. A solitary razorbill, sunning himself on a shelf below, fled hurriedly out to sea, and half a dozen white birds, startled by the sudden movement, rose in the air crying 'Kittiwake! Kittiwake!'

Elizabeth screamed loudly, scrambled to her feet with clumsy speed, then knelt again on the edge of the rock and peered down. In the slowly heaving clear water she could see a pale shape moving, now striped by the dark weed that grew in tangles under the flat foot of the rock, now lost in the shadowy deepness where the tangles were rooted. In a minute or two his head rose from the sea, he shook bright drops from his hair, and looked up at her, laughing. Firmly grasped in his right hand, while he trod water, he held up an enormous blue-black lobster for her admiration. Then he threw it on to the flat rock beside him, and swiftly climbing out of the sea, caught it again and held it, cautious of its bite, till he found a bit of string in his trouser pocket. He shouted to her, 'I'll tie its claws, and you can take it home for your supper!'

She had not thought it possible to climb the sheer face of the cliff, but from its forefoot he mounted by steps and handholds invisible from above, and pitching the tied lobster on to the floor of the gazebo, came nimbly over the edge.

'That's a bigger one than you've ever seen in your life before,' he boasted. 'He weighs fourteen pounds, I'm certain of it. Fourteen pounds at least. Look at the size of his right claw! He could crack a coconut with that. He tried to crack my ankle when I was swimming an hour ago, and got into his hole before I could catch him. But I've caught him now, the brute. He's had more than twenty years of crime, that black boy. He's twenty-four or twenty-five by the look of him. He's older than you, do you realise that? Unless you're a lot older than you look. How old are you?'

But Elizabeth took no interest in the lobster. She had retreated until she stood with her back to the rock, pressed hard against it, the palms of her hands fumbling on the stone as if feeling for a secret lock or bolt that might give her entrance into it. Her face was white, her lips pale and tremulous.

He looked round at her, when she made no answer, and asked what the matter was.

Her voice was faint and frightened. 'Who are you?' she whispered, and the whisper broke into a stammer. 'What are you?'

His expression changed and his face, with the waterdrops on it, grew hard as a rock shining undersea. 'It's only a few minutes,' he said, 'since you addressed me as Roger Fairfield, didn't you?'

'But a name's not everything. It doesn't tell you enough.'

'What more do you want to know?'

Her voice was so strained and thin that her words were like the shadow of words, or words shivering in the cold: 'To jump like that, into the sea—it wasn't human!'

The coldness of his face wrinkled to a frown. 'That's a curious remark to make.'

'You would have killed yourself if—if—'

He took a seaward step again, looked down at the calm green depths below, and said, 'You're exaggerating, aren't you? It's not much more than fifty feet, sixty perhaps, and the water's deep—Here, come back! Why are you running away?'

'Let me go!' she cried. 'I don't want to stay here. I—I'm frightened.'

'That's unfortunate. I hadn't expected this to happen.'

'Please let me go!'

'I don't think I shall. Not until you've told me what you're frightened of.'

'Why,' she stammered, 'why do you wear fur trousers?'

He laughed, and still laughing caught her round the waist and pulled her towards the edge of the rock. 'Don't be alarmed,' he said. 'I'm not going to throw you over. But if you insist on a conversation about trousers, I think we should sit down again. Look at the smoothness of the water, and its colour, and the light in the depths of it: have you ever seen anything lovelier? Look at the sky: that's calm enough, isn't it? Look at that fulmar sailing past: he's not worrying, so why should you?'

She leaned away from him, all her weight against the hand that held her waist, but his arm was strong and he seemed unaware of any strain on it. Nor did he pay attention to the distress she was in—she was sobbing dryly, like a child who has cried too long—but continued talking in a light and pleasant conversational tone until the muscles of her body tired and relaxed, and she sat within his enclosing arm, making no more effort to escape, but timorously conscious of his hand upon her side so close beneath her breast.

'I needn't tell you,' he said, 'the conventional reasons for wearing trousers. There are people, I know, who sneer at all conventions, and some conventions deserve their sneering. But not the trouser convention. No, indeed! So we can admit the necessity of the garment, and pass to consideration of the material. Well, I like sitting on rocks, for one thing, and for such a hobby this is the best stuff in the world. It's very durable, yet soft and comfortable. I can slip into the sea for half an hour without doing it any harm, and when I come out to sun myself on the rock again, it doesn't feel cold and clammy. Nor does it fade in the sun or shrink with the wet. Oh, there are plenty of reasons for having one's trousers made of stuff like this.'

'And there's a reason,' she said, 'that you haven't told me.'

'Are you quite sure of that?'

She was calmer now, and her breathing was controlled. But her face was still white, and her lips were softly nervous when she asked him, 'Are you going to kill me?'

'Kill you? Good heavens, no! Why should I do that?'

'For fear of my telling other people.'

'And what precisely would you tell them?'

'You know.'

'You jump to conclusions far too quickly, that's your trouble. Well, it's a pity for your sake, and a nuisance for me. I don't think I can let you take that lobster home for your supper after all. I don't, in fact, think you will go home for your supper.'

Her eyes grew dark again with fear, her mouth opened, but before she could speak he pulled her to him and closed it, not asking leave, with a roughly occludent kiss.

'That was to prevent you from screaming. I hate to hear people scream,' he told her, smiling as he spoke. 'But this'—he kissed her again, now gently and in a more protracted embrace—'that was because I wanted to.'

'You mustn't!' she cried.

'But I have,' he said.

'I don't understand myself! I can't understand what has happened.'

'Very little yet,' he murmured.

'Something terrible has happened!'

'A kiss? Am I so repulsive?'

'I don't mean that. I mean something inside me. I'm not—at least I think I'm not—I'm not frightened now!'

'You have no reason to be.'

'I have every reason in the world. But I'm not! I'm not frightened—but I want to cry.'

'Then cry,' he said soothingly, and made her pillow her cheek against his breast. 'But you can't cry comfortably with that ludicrous contraption on your nose.'

He took from her the horn-rimmed spectacles she wore, and threw them into the sea.

'Oh!' she exclaimed. 'My glasses!—Oh, why did you do that? Now I can't see. I can't see at all without my glasses!'

'It's all right,' he assured her. 'You really won't need them. The refraction,' he added vaguely, 'will be quite different.'

As if this small but unexpected act of violence had brought to the boiling point her desire for tears, they bubbled over, and because she threw her arms about him in a sort of fond despair, and snuggled close, sobbing vigorously still, he felt the warm drops trickle down his skin, and from his skin she drew into her eyes the saltness of the sea, which made her weep the more. He stroked her hair with a strong but soothing hand, and when she grew calm and lay still in his arms, her emotion spent, he sang quietly to a little enchanting tune a song that began:

> I am a man upon the land,
> I am a selkie in the sea,
> And when I'm far from every strand
> My home it is on Sule Skerry.

After the first verse or two she freed herself from his embrace, and sitting up listened gravely to the song. Then she asked him, 'Shall I ever understand?'

'It's not a unique occurrence,' he told her. 'It has happened quite often before, as I suppose you know. In Cornwall and Brittany and among the Western Isles of Scotland; that's where people have always been interested in seals, and understood them a little, and where seals from time to time have taken human shape. The one thing that's unique in our case, in my metamorphosis, is that I am the only seal-man who has ever become a Master of Arts of Edinburgh University. Or, I believe, of any university. I am the unique example of a sophisticated seal-man.'

'I must look a perfect fright,' she said. 'It was silly of me to cry. Are my eyes very red?'

'The lids are a little pink—not unattractively so—but your eyes are as dark and lovely as a mountain pool in October, on a sunny day in October. They're much improved since I threw your spectacles away.'

'I needed them, you know. I feel quite stupid without them. But tell me why you came to the University—and how? How could you do it?'

'My dear girl—what is your name, by the way? I've quite forgotten.'

'Elizabeth!' she said angrily.

'I'm so glad, it's my favourite human name. But you don't really want to listen to a lecture on psychobiology?'

'I want to now *how*. You must tell me!'

'Well, you remember, don't you, what your book says about the primordial initiatives. But it needs a footnote there to explain that they're not exhausted till quite late in life. The germ-cells, as you know, are always renewing themselves, and they keep their initiatives though they nearly always follow the chosen pattern except in the case of certain illnesses, or under special direction. The direction of the mind, that is. And the glands have got a lot to do in a full metamorphosis, the renal first and then the pituitary, as you would expect. It isn't approved of–making the change, I mean–but every now and then one of us does it, just for a frolic in the general way, but in my case there was a special reason.'

'Tell me,' she said again.

'It's too long a story.'

'I want to know.'

'There's been a good deal of unrest, you see, among my people in the last few years: doubt, dissatisfaction with our leaders, and scepticism about traditional beliefs–all that sort of thing. We've had a lot of discussion under the surface of the sea about the nature of man, for instance. We had always been taught to believe certain things about him, and recent events didn't seem to bear out what our teachers told us. Some of our younger people got dissatisfied, so I volunteered to go ashore and investigate. I'm still considering the report I shall have to make, and that's why I'm living, at present, a double life. I come ashore to think, and go back to the sea to rest.'

'And what do you think of us?' she asked.

'You're interesting. Very interesting indeed. There are going to be some curious mutations among you before long. Within three or four thousand years, perhaps.'

He stooped and rubbed a little smear of blood from his shin. 'I scratched it on a limpet,' he said. 'The limpets, you know, are the same today as they were four thousand years ago. But human beings aren't nearly so stable.'

'Is that your main impression, that humanity's unstable?'

'That's part of it. But from our point of view there's something much more upsetting. Our people, you see, are quite simple creatures, and because we have relatively few beliefs, we're very much attached to them. Our life is a life of sensation–not entirely, but largely–and we ought to be extremely happy. We were, so long as we were satisfied with sensation and a short undisputed creed. We have some advantages over human beings, you know. Human beings have to carry their own weight about, and they don't know how blissful it is to be unconscious of weight: to be wave-borne, to float on the idle sea, to leap without effort in a curling wave, and look up at the dazzle of the sky through a smother of white water, or dive so easily to the calmness far below and take a haddock from the weed-beds in a sudden rush of appetite. Talking of haddocks,' he said, 'it's getting late. It's nearly time for fish. And I must give you some instruction before we go. The preliminary phase takes a little while, about five minutes for you, I should think, and then you'll be another creature.'

She gasped, as though already she felt the water's chill, and whispered, 'Not yet! Not yet, please.'

He took her in his arms, and expertly, with a strong caressing hand, stroked her hair, stroked the roundness of her head and the back of her neck and her shoulders, feeling her muscles moving to his touch, and down the hollow of her back to her waist and hips. The head again, neck, shoulders, and spine. Again and again. Strongly and firmly his hand gave her calmness, and presently she whispered, 'You're sending me to sleep.'

'My God!' he exclaimed, 'you mustn't do that! Stand up, stand up, Elizabeth!'

'Yes,' she said, obeying him. 'Yes, Roger. Why did you call yourself Roger? Roger Fairfield?'

'I found the name in a drowned sailor's pay-book. What does that matter now? Look at me, Elizabeth!' She looked at him, and smiled. His voice changed, and he said happily, 'You'll be the prettiest seal between Shetland and the Scillies. Now listen. Listen carefully.'

He held her lightly and whispered in her ear. Then kissed her on the lips and cheek, and bending her head back, on the throat. He looked, and saw the colour come deeply into her face.

'Good,' he said. 'That's the first stage. The adrenalin's flowing nicely now. You know about the pituitary, don't you? That makes it easy then. There are two parts in the pituitary gland, the anterior and posterior lobes, and both must act together. It's not difficult, and I'll tell you how.'

Then he whispered again, most urgently, and watched her closely.

In a little while he said, 'And now you can take it easy. Let's sit down and wait till you're ready. The actual change won't come till we go down.'

'But it's working,' she said, quietly and happily. 'I can feel it working.'

'Of course it is.'

She laughed triumphantly, and took his hand.

'We've got nearly five minutes to wait,' he said.

'What will it be like? What shall I feel, Roger?'

'The water moving against your side, the sea caressing you and holding you.'

'Shall I be sorry for what I've left behind?'

'No, I don't think so.'

'You didn't like us, then? Tell me what you discovered in the world.'

'Quite simply,' he said, 'that we had been deceived.'

'But I don't know what your belief had been.'

'Haven't I told you? Well, we in our innocence respected you because you could work, and were willing to work. That seemed to us truly heroic. We don't work at all, you see, and you'll be much happier when you come to us. We who live in the sea don't struggle to keep our heads above water.'

'All my friends worked hard,' she said. 'I never knew anyone who was idle. We had to work, and most of us worked for a good purpose; or so we thought. But you didn't think so?'

'Our teachers had told us,' he said, 'that men endured the burden of human toil to create a surplus of wealth that would give them leisure from the daily task of breadwinning. And in their hard-won leisure, our teachers said, men cultivated wisdom and charity and the fine arts; and became aware of God. But that's not a true description of the world, is it?'

'No,' she said, 'that's not the truth.'

'No,' he repeated, 'our teachers were wrong, and we've been deceived.'

'Men are always being deceived, but they get accustomed to learning the facts too late. They grow accustomed to deceit itself.'

'You are braver than we, perhaps. My people will not like to be told the truth.'

'I shall be with you,' she said, and took his hand. But still he stared gloomily at the moving sea.

The minutes passed, and presently she stood up and with quick fingers put off her clothes. 'It's time,' she said.

He looked at her, and his gloom vanished like the shadow of a cloud that the wind has hurried on, and exultation followed like sunlight spilling from the burning edge of a cloud. 'I wanted to punish them,' he cried, 'for robbing me of my faith, and now, by God, I'm punishing them hard. I'm robbing their treasury now, the inner vault of all their treasury! I hadn't guessed you were so beautiful! The waves when you swim will catch a burnish from you, the sand will shine like silver when you lie down to sleep, and if you can teach the red sea-ware to blush so well, I shan't miss the roses of the world.'

'Hurry,' she said.

He, laughing softly, loosened the leather thong that tied his trousers, stepped out of them, and lifted her in his arms.

'Are you ready?' he asked.

She put her arms round his neck and softly kissed his cheek. Then with a great shout he leapt from the rock, from the little veranda, into the green silk calm of the water far below...

I heard the splash of their descent—I am quite sure I heard the splash—as I came round the corner of the cliff by the ledge that leads to the little rock veranda, our gazebo, as we called it, but the first thing I noticed, that really attracted my attention, was an enormous blue-black lobster, its huge claws tied with string, that was moving in a rather ludicrous fashion towards the edge. I think it fell over just before I left, but I wouldn't swear to that. Then I saw her book, the *Studies in Biology*, and her clothes. Her white linen frock with the brown collar and the brown belt, some other garments, and her shoes were all there. And beside them, lying across her shoes, was a pair of sealskin trousers.

I realised immediately, or almost immediately, what had happened. Or so it seems to me now. And if, as I firmly believe, my apprehension was instantaneous, the faculty of intuition is clearly more important than I had previously supposed. I have, of course, as I said before, given the matter a great deal of thought during my recent illness, but the impression remains that I understood what had happened in a flash, to use a common but illuminating phrase. And no one, need I say, has been able to refute my intuition. No one, that is, has found an alternative explanation for the presence, beside Elizabeth's frock, of a pair of sealskin trousers.

I remember also my physical distress at the discovery. My breath, for several minutes I think, came into and went out of my lungs like the hot wind of a dust-storm in the desert. It parched my mouth and grated in my throat. It was, I recall, quite a torment to breathe. But I had to, of course.

Nor did I lose control of myself in spite of the agony, both mental and physical, that I was suffering. I didn't lose control till they began to mock me. Yes, they did, I assure you of that. I heard his voice quite clearly, and honesty compels me to admit that it was singularly sweet and the tune was the most haunting I have ever heard. They were about forty yards away, two seals swimming together, and the evening light was so clear and taut that his voice might have been the vibration of an invisible bow across its coloured bands. He was singing the song that Elizabeth and I had discovered in an album of Scottish music in the little fishing hotel where we had been living:

> I am a man upon the land
> I am a selkie in the sea,
> And when I'm far from any strand
> I am at home on Sule Skerry!

But his purpose, you see, was mockery. They were happy, together in the vast simplicity of the ocean, and I, abandoned to the terror of life alone, life among human beings, was lost and full of panic. It was then I began to scream. I could hear myself screaming, it was quite horrible. But I couldn't stop. I had to go on screaming...

Neil Paterson

A LADY CAPTAIN

For four years the *Christian Dee*, refitted, carried slate from the Welsh quarries to the west coast of South America: to Pisagua, Iquique, Tocopilla and Antofagasta, where she loaded the incongruous product of the bleak and sterile Chilean desert: nitrate, nitrate enough to fertilise all the gardens of Wales.

The logs of these years in the west coast, or W.C. trade as they called it, make fascinating reading, and the detailed, day by day account of the long passages round the Horn leaves us with a vivid impression of the problems and hazards that beset the seaman in sail: williwaws, the fierce, heavy squalls of the Straits of

Magellan; the vicious easterlies off the Horn, that graveyard of fine ships; the sudden west-coast trembler; the terremoto, which flushes the sea into a seething cauldron, hot to touch; the tidal wave, which may lift a ship anchored in twenty fathoms and hurl her half a mile inshore; the physical strain of three–aye, five months of four hours on and four hours off; the cramped living conditions; the indiscipline (usually in the vicinity of the Line) with the resulting floggings and bad blood; the food–the black bread, the salt junk and harness beef, the rotting potatoes; the diseases– scurvy, yellow and breakbone fever, smallpox, pellagra, beriberi.

It was not much of a life, one would think, for even the rough, tough, sea-dog of the day. Yet Christian, a slip of a girl, exulted in it.

At first she occupied herself mainly with navigation. It has been said that navigators are born, not made, and this is largely true, for, though any man can learn to take and read his observation and work his sum from formulae, it is not one man in a thousand who is correct to a hair's breadth, and not one man in ten thousand who is always correct. But Christian was, and Dai soon stopped laughing at her parlour trick with the sextant. He no longer found it funny. He found it humiliating, and it was a long time before he got used to the uncomfortable idea of his wife's ascendancy. His chagrin was eventually replaced, however, by a genuine pride, for in the summer of 1858 we find him writing in his log: 'Mistress Evans fixed the longitude by a snap of Procyon which emerged briefly from a cloud bank and was not visible for more than three seconds. She has undoubtedly a genius for precise navigation and mathematical calculation, and has devised a method of minimising error in a position due to error in the observed altitude which, when published, should be of value to all mariners and will bring credit to our name.'

Having mastered navigation, Christian turned her attention to the art of sailing, and here too she built on a flair, for right at the outset she had the 'feel of the ship'–that instinctive timing which is the hallmark of the artist in sail, and the lack of which has cost many a master his spars. On the second trip to the W.C.S.A. her writing appears with unfailing regularity in the scrap log, and from the rotation of hands–the mate's, then the second mate's, then Christian's–it becomes clear that even at this early stage of her life afloat she had assumed the responsibility of taking a watch at sea.

At the end of the outward passage the second mate deserted. He may have resented Christian's new status. Second mates are notoriously touchy. On the other hand, as by all accounts he was not much of a seaman, and as it had been a grilling voyage, he may merely have decided for a quieter life. In any case he deserted the ship at Iquique.

He was not missed. One of the forr'd hands took over his duties aloft and Christian became second mate of the *Christian Dee*, a berth which she filled admirably and which she held until the time of Dai's death.

This melancholy event took place off the Falkland Islands, suddenly, on the 18th of September, 1858. 'Dai had,' Christian writes, 'for some time been suffering from abdominal pains and after breakfast on the morning of the 18th retired to his bunk with a severe stomach-ache which he attributed to the bad beef. I was standing the forenoon watch and shortly after six bells Mr Griffiths (the mate) sent for me, saying that the Captain was calling out and in great pain. I straightaway went below, but as I entered he was seized with a convulsion of such proportions that it hurled him clean off the bunk on to the deck. While we were raising him his poor body arched like a bow, and when we laid him on his bunk we saw that he had departed.'

No sailing ship in the vicinity of the Horn would tempt Providence with so potent a Jonah as a corpse, and that same evening the body was consigned–not without some difficulty–to the deep. It was blowing half a gale, and Christian, finding that her voice would not carry above the skirl of the wind in the ratlines, handed over the Bible to the mate. Twice, at the appropriate stage in the service, the remains, in their weighted shroud, were launched overboard, twice to return as the ship heeled over in a squall so that the corpse, slithering about on the deck, had to be recovered like a hat on a windy day. It seemed foolish to read the service yet a third time and, as if by common consent, all hands fastened on the unfortunate body and, somewhat out of temper, vigorously dispatched it.

Christian thus became the owner and assumed command of the *Christian Dee*. She was twenty-seven years of age, and had been five years and four days at sea.

* * * * *

Iquique, the main nitrate port, was a notorious eyesore, so ugly that in 1868 even a long-suffering God could bear the sight no longer and sent an earthquake to obliterate it. It was a town of wooden shacks clamped against nature on a slag hill, threatened by sand and sea alike, ankle-deep in bilious yellow guano dust, infested with flies, and under siege from clinkstone and soda sulphate that fell in a continuous bombardment from the bleak and arid pampas above. There was no fresh water, no tree, no blade of grass within a hundred miles. There was no harbour, no bay even. The ships lay in an open roadstead with a surf-beat shore, and all loading was done by lighters from a dilapidated landing-stage.

This was the *Christian Dee*'s destination, and it was here, off Iquique, that Mistress Evans threw her main yards aback and dropped her first anchor since taking over the ship. Immediately the vessel had her chain the touts and boarding-house runners came alongside and, emboldened by the news of the captain's death, boarded her and even swarmed up the rigging to project their high-powered sales-talk at the men still working aloft.

These pimps were dangerous men, and their talk ran to a pattern. 'Get wise,' they said. 'You're being victimised. Now I can get you a berth in a decent ship, big money, a shore job with a woman thrown in, a smart lawyer to sue your skipper, a profitable little business.' They had propositions by the score. Englishmen were at a premium in these parts, and there was always a fat commission for a tout with an Englishman to sell.

Christian heard the commotion and came on deck. 'Get off my ship!' she said.

They ignored her.

'Thomas,' she said to one of the seamen, 'fetch me a musket.' With the weapon in her hands she addressed the nearest runner, a swarthy gentleman who was sowing disaffection in the mizzen-mast.

'You,' she said. 'Lay down out of there!'

He paid no attention.

'This is your last chance. Lay down and get off my ship!'

'Oh, go to bed with a guano bird,' he said over his shoulder, and resumed his hawking.

Christian raised her musket, took careful aim, and fired. The bullet shattered his arm, and his friends, rising like crows at the report, flocked over the side and were gone in a matter of seconds.

'I do not regret the incident,' Christian writes, 'as it was greatly applauded by the crew, some of whom had previously become so restive that I had feared it might be necessary to order a flogging, a measure which I may now postpone, having shown them plainly that I am master and will brook no insubordination.'

The nitrate works sympathised with her in her tragic bereavement, and the manager of the *Oficina* himself came off in a boat to offer condolences and, behind her back, a shore billet to the carpenter.

Christian gave him short shrift. She was as suspicious as only a widow can be, and she had discovered that her cargo was underweight. She was in no mood to listen even to reasonable excuses, and she was impervious to Latin-American charm. Granted he had filled the hold, but did he really think she was as green as the stuff he had packed there! Green. Yes, green as a young tree, and liable on that account to ten per cent shrinkage on the passage home. She would stand no criticism of her dunnaging or stowaging. She demanded that he remove the entire cargo and reload with nitrate, repeat *nitrate*.

The manager could not agree to this. She already had first-quality nitrate. He could not possibly reload. He was sorry but adamant.

'It is deeply regretted, señora.'

'It will be much more deeply regretted,' Christian said.

That afternoon her boat's crew rowed her to the other ships in the anchorage—a barque, two schooners and a brig—all Welsh, all nitrate ships. She spoke to their captains and found them sympathetic to her cause—it is doubtful if she would have found them in the slightest degree sympathetic if she had not been an attractive widow—and a common course of action was decided upon.

The following morning a message was received from the *Oficina*, deploring the incredible error and informing Mistress Evans that a special cargo, selected by the management in person and offered at a reduced rate, was ready for loading at her convenience.

In reply Christian despatched a curt note demanding a loading party (an unheard-of luxury) *immediately*. Twenty Chilean rotos were sent out with the lighters and, the manager of the *Oficina* himself supervising, the loading was effected in record time. The widow was mollified. 'Feeling,' she somewhat naïvely comments, 'that in the end I had not been unduly imposed upon.'

The *Christian Dee*'s last night in Iquique was marked by an incident which, with variations, was to recur several times in Christian's life afloat. She was, it must be remembered, a young and presentable woman, described in Mr J.D. Munro's book, *Clipper Captains*, as 'a singularly attractive girl, with a proud head and sensuous carriage,' and even had she been as plain and short-sighted as her sisters she would still, ship-borne, have been the object of desire. She was a woman, and that was enough.

Clifford Griffiths, mate of the *Christian Dee*, was a sober, inoffensive fellow, but the night the loading was completed he fell in with the master and mate of the *Gwinneth Jones*, who were known drinking men. He accompanied them to 'One-thumbed Pete's,' where he was prevailed upon to toast his late captain in a *treepa* of *aquardiente*. The *treepa* emptied, a *chaouch* of fiery *anisardo* was produced to wish Dai God-speed through the celestial shoals, and, by the time this was consumed, along with a few *piscos* for luck, Mr Griffiths was in a ripe condition, ready for anything.

What actually happened is not clear. Mr Griffiths was persuaded—with difficulty, for he was a large and powerful man—to return on board, and was bundled into his cabin. Ten minutes later there was a great commotion and the fo'c'sle hands heard Mistress Evans calling out. When they went aft they found her at the foot of the gangway, in night attire and fluttering about in some agitation.

She kept clapping her hands for help. 'Steward, steward, come quickly!' she was calling. 'There's been a dreadful accident. Mr Griffiths has hurt himself.'

The mate was found lying across the doorway of her cabin, a lump the size of a duck's egg on his forehead.

Little was made of the incident on board, but several months later tongues began to wag when Clancy Vaughan, a sea-lawyer if ever man was, went aft in a mutinous spirit 'to git justice, see if I don't' and was served with the same sort of accident, Mistress Evans summoning assistance by clapping her hands and calling excitedly: 'Steward, steward, come quickly! Clancy Vaughan has hurt himself.'

The following year, a Swede, a great lady's man on his own showing, was signed on at Antofagasta. The crew made no attempt to restrain him when he decided on a midnight sortie to the captain's quarters, and he too met with an accident which resulted in his being carried up the gangway feet first. These accidents were all characterised by head injuries and by the manner in which they were announced, Mistress Evans on each occasion dickering about in a very feminine and helpless fashion, clapping her hands for attention and calling: 'Steward, steward, come quickly! There's been a dreadful accident. So-and-so has hurt himself.'

The order of the words never varied. It was simply the captain's formula, and was respected as such.

Christian herself, as one might expect, has little to say of these misadventures. In a letter to her sister Janet, the first page of which, unfortunately, is missing, she writes, however:

'I sent for him the next day' (Mr Griffiths obviously) 'and, as he had no recollection of the matter, gave him an account of it. The poor fellow was greatly distressed and put about and had some fear, I think, that I might reduce him and send him forr'd to the fo'c'sle. While he was in this frame of mind I took the opportunity of informing him of my decision to make young James Jones, the liveliest hand of the larboard watch, my second mate.

'Feeling the need for frank conversation, I told him, thus increasing his discomfiture as you may imagine, that I had for some time past noted that he regarded me with admiration and that he had, on occasion, been prone to deal harshly with this or that young seaman whom I had favoured with a smile. I explained–and you will have no difficulty in believing it, dear Janet–that such smiles were administered not as a woman but as a superior, and were as much a part of my office as orders to the helmsman. I assured him that, although it had not pleased God that I should return his feelings, I had nevertheless a high regard for his qualities, and I pointed out that he already shared an intimacy with me greater than that enjoyed by any other man. I counselled him, therefore, to be content with his lot, and this he declared himself ready to be with so many sincere professions of his respect and loyalty that I am satisfied the matter has been well resolved.

'I fear, Janet, that you may conceive me to have been forward in this, but I would earnestly beg of you to remember that in this life to which I have been called it is not possible, or indeed advisable, always to conform to the ladylike conventions in which we were reared. I have another confession to make, but I will not have it to be sinful, for, as the good Lord had seen fit that I should usurp the functions of my deeply lamented husband, it cannot be unseemly that in the execution of his duty I should appropriate certain insignia of his authority. In any case–and I implore you not to be shocked–I am wearing trousers. I know that Dai would not have countenanced this during his lifetime, but I am confident that he will now have a fuller understanding of the problems that beset a sailor in skirts, and the inconveniences, nay hazards, of petticoats at sea.'

At this time of the year–autumn–no voyage round the Horn was ever without incident, and the *Christian Dee*, running before a northerly with shortened sail and two men at the wheel, struck a full gale in latitude 50° South and had to be hove to. For forty-eight hours it blew like scissors and thumb-screws and she would not carry canvas. No sooner was a sail set than it was rent from clew to earing. The mizzen topsail was reduced to ribbons. Stays, shrouds, and halyards parted like cotton. The fore topmast staysail and the main foresail, in shreds, flayed and scourged the air like cats-o'-nine-tails, and the main royal, working loose of its gaskets, streamed out to leeward like a weighted pennant, whipping the mast into a fearful curve as though it had been as slender and as supple as a dowsing rod. The apprentice, a second cousin of the mate, leeched himself on to the rigging to secure the royal, but was so lashed about the face and arms that he could not hold on, and, blinded, was hurled with such violence to the deck that his leg was broken and his ribs stove in. The chicken-coop, with its precious cargo of poultry, carried away, and the sea that took it was so solid that no one even saw it go. Two new spencers were bent on to the fore and main spencer gaffs and the ship rode to these scraps of sail, taking it green, now standing up on her stern, now lying over almost on her beam ends, tossing and pitching fit to shake the sticks out of her.

Christian did not leave the deck. Muffled in streaming oilskins, protected only by a weather cloth triced up to give a lee, she stood the gale out, nursing the ship's head up to the seas, issuing her orders by megaphone and leaving the binnacle only to lurch to the companionway to consult the barometer, calculate drift, and drink an occasional cup of hot coffee.

On the third day the wind eased somewhat, and, as the glass was rising, she squared away under a little canvas which she was quick to increase, inch by inch, as the opportunity offered. For weeks, after the Cape was rounded, the log shows a hard beat to windward under reefed topsails and fore topmast staysail, then in 25° south, after a spell of variable winds, they picked up the southeast trades, and from then on, apart from a five-day calm in the Doldrums, it was plain sailing with Christian crowding on canvas in accordance with a new sail-plan which entailed a greater press of sail than the old ship had ever known, and under which she bowled along right merrily, rattling out her line like a steamer's. The tide was on the turn as she brought Hartland Point abeam, and she raced up the Bristol Channel on the flood.

While the ship was unloading in Barry Docks, Christian, sitting by her open port, overheard a conversation between the carpenter and the gaffer stevedore.

'A woman for Old Man!' the gaffer said. 'Holy God, you should be all right.'

'I dunno,' the carpenter said. 'She's skeely, man. I tell you, she's a hard case.'

Christian knew then that she had made the grade. Overcome, she hid her hot face in her hands. She even confesses to have wept a little. I doubt if any fashionable beauty ever heard a compliment that pleased her half so well.

George Mackay Brown

_____

THE FERRYMAN

A t noon on Martinmas day, disinherited, I left Mirdale–my
brother's wife sending her spiteful mirth after me across
three fields, and the old man cold with spite in his grave–
and turned my steps in the direction of the Hall. The factor could
offer me one job only, to row the boat *Lupin* between the island
and the town with any passengers who might wish to cross.

At that time of year, the threshold of winter, Hoy Sound is often
stormy, crammed with wave and squall, and a tide runs broken
and abrupt from the Atlantic into Scapa Flow and back again,
twice a day.

_____

I agreed to take charge of the boat until such time as Joe the ferryman recovered from his broken leg.

The next morning I waited at the rock smoking, before anybody came. A man walked along the beach with his face muffled and ordered me to take him across. I looked into the suffering eyes of Josie of Taing.

'I have the toothache in my jaw,' he said, 'and no man in this island can pull the rotten tooth out. My teeth are too deep in my skull. But they say the blacksmith in Stromness has fingers like nut-crackers.'

I rowed Josie across for sixpence.

At the pier of Stromness were three girls with a basket of herring who wanted to sell their fish in the island.

They were helping each other aboard the *Lupin*, chattering like starlings, when a dark hooded man walked down the slip and said: 'Behold, is this the ferry to the wicked Godforsaken island across the firth?'

When the three girls saw the black Bible under his arm they scrambled back on to the pier; for it is and always has been a thing of small luck to travel on the sea with a preaching man.

The preacher did not open his mouth all the way across. He sat in the stern and read his Bible. I didn't care for the look of the man. He didn't offer to pay his fare, and to tell the truth I was afraid to ask him. Still thumbing his Bible he stepped ashore and went swaying up the beach over the slippery stones. 'May your preaching prosper,' I shouted after him. 'It's a wicked island you've come to, and be sure to visit the croft of Mirdale. The worst woman in Orkney lives there.'

I sat on the thwart till noon smoking my pipe and nodding, and then didn't the two hawkers who have been scrounging and threatening and stealing their way through Hoy and Flotta and Graemsay since the middle of October come up to me as silent as otters. 'Take us to Stromness,' said the man.

'Sixpence each,' I said.

'We're poor wandering people,' said the woman. 'I have the black cough in my throat this week past.'

'A shilling for the two,' I said, 'if that sounds any better.'

'You have an unlucky look about you,' said the man. 'It isn't likely that you'll see age.'

'Half a florin,' I said, 'and that's as low as I'll come.'

All the way across they sat in the bow muttering to each other, and every now and then sending a black look across at me.

At last they stood on the steps at Stromness pier, and the hawker woman turned to skirl at me as sharp as a gull. 'May your boards fall asunder in the middle of Hoy Sound, and may the mouth of the shark be under you that day!'

The three herring girls ran down the pier out of the pub, red in the face with porter. They scrambled on board the *Lupin* with shrieks and grey flurries of skirt. Their names were Margaret, Annie and Seenie. They laughed most of the way across the Sound. Seenie took a half-bottle of rum from her skirt pocket and we all began to drink, the flask going from mouth to mouth. Margaret was sick in the middle of the Sound. The other three of us finished the rum. Seenie threw the empty half-bottle into the tide-race. I did not charge a fare. They gave me a bunch of herring for nothing.

I sat on the beach of the island smoking, my arms so stiff with rowing I could hardly lift my pipe to my teeth. It had been a fine blue day, but now the wind turned into the east and blew grey gurls over the Sound.

At ten past three there was a plaintive outcry mixed with cursing and swearing from the road above, and then appeared Mansie of Cott dragging a grey ewe over the tangle.

'I'm taking her,' he said, 'to the butcher in Stromness, and God help me, I'm loath to part with her. She's been a good ewe and dropped a dozen fine lambs, but Jessie-Bella wants a new coat and hat for the kirk on Sabbath. Truth to tell, I would rather the ewe was safe in her field and it was Jessie-Bella I was taking to the butcher in Stromness.'

I took sixpence for Mansie's fare and threepence for the sheep.

I had hardly pushed the sharny backside of the beast off the boat when who set his boot on the rocking thwart but the Stromness police sergeant, Long Rob.

'Turn your boat round quickly, my man,' said Long Rob. 'The Law's required this day in the island.' He had a blue paper, a summons, sticking out of his pocket.

By now the wind was racketing round the corners of the houses and tearing the gulls out of their clean circles.

'Is it the black preacher you're after?' I said.

'It is not,' said Long Rob.

'It wouldn't be the woman of Mirdale you're going to arrest?' I cried in sudden wild hope.

'It's Tom of Braewick,' said he, 'that must face the sheriff on Tuesday first for having no license for his motor-bike.'

'That'll be sixpence for your fare,' I said, and I wish I had never spoken, for I had to sign my name on a form in two places—a difficult thing for me at any time—stating that I had duly received the above-mentioned sum; and the boat jumping and stotting all over the Sound with the rising rage of the sea.

By the time I set the sergeant ashore in the island the sky was as purple as squashed grapes. I began to pull the *Lupin* up over the wet stones.

Only a fool, I thought to myself, will want to travel on a night like this! The thought had hardly shaped itself in my mind when six men came out of the gloom with a coffin on their shoulders. 'This is Williamina of Bewsley,' said Frank the undertaker. 'She's to be buried in Stromness, where she came from, tomorrow morning. If you ask me she's been on this island fifty years too long.' With that he put a sixpence on the lid of the coffin.

So I ferried Williamina of Bewsley across the waters of death. It was a black passage. Six other men were waiting at Stromness for the coffin. They lifted it without a word on to their shoulders and walked solemnly up the pier, the street lights falling dreich on to them till they turned up the close to the house where the dead woman had been born seventy years before.

Spray was flying across the harbour like smoke. I tied up the *Lupin* at the pier and slept that night on a truss of straw in the cattle shed.

I dreamt of the cornfields of Mirdale.

BUNG

In bright, blown-up raincoats they bobbed slowly along like bunches of balloons tied to a ragman's cart. Women and kids coming to watch the launching. By the yard gate men stood waiting for them: workers in faded blue or brown overalls, fishing in pockets for a half-smoked cigarette.

John Laurie, sulky-faced under the pushed-back welder's goggles, could see a bloated bit of green that was his wife, Katy, bending to jerk the child Ian's clothes to rights.

For a moment the two heads were together, insolently alike, with eyes liked plumped-up raisins in the smooth warm faces. There was nothing of John in the boy, he sometimes half-wondered if...Ah, no good thinking like that two years after he'd married her because Ian was on the way. He glanced inside at the shed where Ginger Bain and the rest of the scrap-metal ring were standing in a corner, nervously flicking fag-ash behind them as they plotted their latest scheme from nicking brass from the yard in a big way. Ginger and Katy had once been pretty thick, but Ginger wasn't the marrying kind. The kid had ginger hair, but so had Katy–a crimpy auburn that sparkled and crackled if a man ran his work-horned fingers through it.

As she crossed the street, a gust hurled grit and dirty paper in Katy's face. John could sense her muttering through the plastic shield of her dentures, 'Shut up, Ian. What a climate, we can't be away too soon.'

Above him, as he stepped out to meet her, a Union Jack and a red-and-gold house flag snapped and snorted at each other. He dived to pick up Ian, grasping him by the thickly-clad waist to swing him high and clear of his mother, At once her attack began, 'You could have stayed at your work another quar'ran hour, you're only flingin' away dough!'

A lorry, backing into the yard, was silenced by the din inside–but not Katy. Men waiting to take children off the hands of their wind-ravaged mothers, could still respond to the rough comedienne's voice, which gave her words a blatant fearlessness and would make strangers grin indulgently at what she said.

He muttered, 'You needny worry. When did you ever get less than your pound o' flesh?'

What in heaven's name did she do with it, the unopened pay-packet handed to her every week? He never was away from work, except once when he'd had to go and see about that bit of skin trouble, brought on by her rotten cooking, beans and chips instead of the good grilled steak his mother had always given him. Tenderly exploring his chin with a blackened finger, he wished Katy would let him grow a beard. She was dead against it, remembering that at one time he had experimented with facial ornaments—handle-bars, beards, exaggerated side-burns—to attract certain girls who were said to be sporting.

Katy herself had been one of them...working at the time in a department store, conning women into buying clothes that made them look like frowsy tarts, and herself borrowing the clothes to wear with dazzling effects in the evenings. Till she was found out and sacked.

As he tried to settle the child more comfortably on his shoulders, she narked on as if he had not spoken, '*And* I'll bet you forgot to post the form about goin' to Australia. Nothin' gets done unless I do it myself...*Don't, Ian!*' She gave the child's leg a stinging slap for trying to kick the wind-bellied front of her coat.

His automatic howl was cut short by the appearance of Thomson, the yard foreman. Wearing a grey, well-pressed suit for the occasion, he shot out on to the pavement, as if catapulted from the ways where the ship, *National Progress*, clung ready for launching. Before you could hear him, you knew he was muttering, 'Where the hell have they got to?'

'Hear anything?' he roared to Paddy McGuire, the gateman. Slowly the old man cupped his hand to his ear whose drum had been mangled by years of boiler-shop din.

Thomson fiddled violently with his watch-strap, then turned to look inside the yard again—as if the minute his back was turned the ship would probably ramstam into the river on her own. Then he was out again—glaring along the street—pushing back the natty tweed hat as if it had been his usual squashed homburg. (It was not so many years since Thomson had discarded the black, reinforced bowler, traditional foreman's protection against bolts and rivets dropped 'accidentally' from a height).

Fathers of families, lingering by the gate, nipped out their cigarettes to become workmen again, hands forward, listening. Children were shushed. Against the yard noises, against the wind and the thunder of main road traffic fifty yards away, everybody listened. 'Is it too quiet for you, Mister, will I drop a pin?' said Katy, but softly, listening too.

Her husband moved back against the wall. 'They're comin'!' Then to Ian, squirming above his head, 'Here's the band, son.'

Thomson waited only long enough to make sure the small group of pipers and drummers was heading for the yard. Maybe he'd hoped for some hitch like the lack of a band to give him an excuse to approach the directors again about postponement. They must have insisted on the launching—Thomson would know it was daft to let her go today, a big empty hulk with no sense in her to tack and manoeuvre with a gale.

Ah, she had to go now, for the band was here. They were not a stylish turn-out, but a scratch bunch of local men who had learned piping or drumming in boys organisations or the Orange Lodge, and now hired themselves out for football matches and launchings. The wind sported among their thick kilts and even tried to snatch the mace which the pipe-major tossed bravely as he entered the yard. There was a cheer from some of the men as he grabbed and caught it, less bravely.

'Well held, son!'

'That's a rare job, I wonder what bung they have to pay *him*.'

'It's nothin' to what some folk'll do for love!' roared Paddy the gateman with a wink at John Laurie. Paddy was Katy's uncle, and she turned with a grin and a casual 'H'llo, auld yin!'

A grey-painted bow, with the name, *National Progress*, in gleaming white letters, dominated the yard. On either side the iron uprights, bare now of staging planks, swayed in the wind, while underneath her the shipwrights hammered away one by one the huge wooden supports, which they might almost have left for the wind to winkle out. Job No.798 she had been, from the day the number was first pencilled on a blueprint by the foreman pattern-maker till it was stamped on the last small prefabricated metal part imported into the yard. Two berths away lay No.799, a few months off completion, with a prickle of staging planks on her stern. Between the two, No.800, with only her keel laid, made a fine platform for watching No.798 take the water.

Men glance at the two unfinished shells, estimating how much work was in them for this or that trade. The speeches at the celebration luncheon were quoted in the afternoon papers, which had been given advance copies.

'D'ye see what the chairman's been sayin'?'

'Aye–There may have to be sacrifices all round–All roundabout himsel', he means. Sacrifices in every home on Clydeside, but none for him and his pals!'

'Ach, they canny make work.'

'They canny make ships, you mean. We're the mugs that do that.'

Clouds hurtled over the sky, dropping a few fat samples of their load on waiting ships and people, then moving restlessly on. As restlessly as Katy, darting about with Ian by the hand, looking for a vantage point but choosing none.

'That's a nice boat you've got, son.' Paddy the gateman chatted kindly to his great-nephew, Ian. 'You should get the lady to launch it too.'

'Lady launch my boatie too!' the child cried excitedly, waving the toy sailboat he had insisted on bringing. 'Lady launch my boatie too!' he crowed, so that people standing near them laughed nearly as proudly as if he had been one of their own.

A man came up behind Katy, Ginger Bain putting his arm round her waist, his dirty hand crumpling the stiff PVC coat with casual insolence.

'Hello, Katy, long time no' see. 'Ve you come to see the launchin'?'

(Did he think maybe she'd come to get down to it with a rivetting hammer?)

She answered with husky affability: 'Ach, Ian's daft about ships. Not that a tanker's much–just a big petrol can gettin' heaved into the water on its backside.'

'It makes a change for the kids.' Ginger was very civil now, treating her as a respectable matron only good for looking after another man's brats. Then deliberately he turned his back on her and sidled towards John, the ferret face full of imitation joviality.

'Is this your kid then, Johnny? Fine wee chap. Takes plenty dough to keep 'em goin' these days, eh, Johnny?...Now, me and the boys was just talkin'. We were hopin' you'd change your mind about comin' in wi' us. If it's only a matter o' steppin' up the bung, Johnny—just say what you want an' we'll see what we can do...'

John looked at him distastefully. The ring was dead keen to get him, a welder working for long spells near the keel of the ship where all the dirt and refuse gathered. He could hide stuff among the rubbish till they were ready to take it away. And his wife's uncle was a gateman who might be persuaded, for family reasons, to turn a blind eye on what was being carried out.

John had always steered clear of big theft, thinking you were bound to cop it sooner or later. It must be big stuff they were after this time—probably brass portholes by the dozen, since nothing smaller would pay enough. They'd give him his whack for a week or two, but then his share would be cut, and if he tried to break with them the pressure would go on. Only last year Bill Carey, one of his mates, had got a prison sentence because he'd been made a scapegoat for the ring.

John shook his head. 'It wouldn't be worth while for all the time I'll be here. Katy wants to emigrate to Australia...'

Suddenly they were everywhere, overalled men who knew they had to stop work now if they were to see the launching. On the ship herself riggers lined the deck-rails, and on the roofs of sheds or underneath them other men stood close-packed as for a cup-tie football match. Every now and then a single ironic cheer went up; for the band, changing position, for someone in the official launching party being photographed by a pressman. For Katy Laurie, diving and swearing after Ian who, while John was talking to Ginger Bain, had run dangerously near the prow of No.800.

'Some folk's no' fit to be in charge o' a mongrel pup, let alone a kid!' Lugging and shaking Ian, she strutted away on steel club heels that John had not seen before. Another new pair–she must spend a fortune in shoe-shops. Or...there was that place in Copeland Road where they had shoes on display on the rack outside. Katy was a compulsive picker up of ashtrays and glasses in pubs, toilet rolls from lavatories. 'Ach, they owe us a bit o' bung for the prices they charge!' she would grin with those ugly false teeth. All the beauty had gone out of her smile when she had to have her own quartz-pebble teeth hauled out because they went rotten after Ian was born.

Catching sight of Ginger Bain still hovering near, she stopped in her tracks and began shamelessly to make up to him. 'Just like old times, i'n't it Ginger? D'you mind what the old bitch said when she saw the van waitin' outside?'

As they went off together, John suddenly knew that her dismissal from the shop had not been on account of borrowing clothes to wear in the evenings. She and Ginger had been in cahoots, she slipping out bundles of garments to a waiting van and telling her boss they had been shoplifted.

'That one needs her backside warmed, and if her mother was livin' she'd get it.' Paddy McGuire, Katy's uncle, was looking at her and Ginger.

John shot him a look, but had an urge to confide in the old man. 'She wants to go to Australia,' he said.

'Ach!' Paddy spat, grinding his spittle with his boot. 'I remember a green frock she once wanted when she was just a lassie–nylon wi' a bunchy skirt. It was in a shop window in the Govan Road and she thought if only she could get wearin' it at the school dance she'd be queen o' the Clyde.'

'Likely she wasn't far wrong.'

'She never had half the looks o' her mother, nor the contented nature. Her brother Mike bought her the frock, but she never wore it because she discovered that the other lassies were goin' to the dance in sweaters and jeans. Now it's Australia. Her brother's in Melbourne, doin' well for himsel'. He spoiled her rotten when she was wee, so now she thinks everything would be hunky-dory if she was there too. As if every thousand miles she travelled was a bit o' bung she was payin' for life to give her the best o' everything.'

Bung, the shipyard term for bribery or graft. You slipped the craneman a bit of bung, a packet of fags for lifting a hunk of prefabricated shell into position so that you needn't stand idle waiting for him. Or you gave the foreman a bottle of whisky or a few quid (if he was known to be the kind who'd take it) so he'd put you on jobs where there was most money to be made on piecework, or when times were bad, as they were now on Clydeside, he wouldn't list your name among the men to be sacked.

Bung...some folk thought there was nothing it couldn't do if you offered enough of the right kind.

'Johnny!' suddenly Ginger Bain was back beside him, grinning like a mangy cat that had just swallowed a bird of paradise. 'Johnny, I've got her talked out of it for you. She says she's no' carin' aboot goin' to Australia, providin' she gets a bit more dough to make ends meet. So gettin' back to that wee bit of business we were discussin', Johnny.'

'*Ach-aw!*' A low growl went round the yard as men realised the ship was 'coming alive',trying to creep down the ways on her own. Thomson, the foreman was hopping about, muttering, 'For Christ's sake hold on to her!', his talk profane because the shipwrights' foreman would expect it, but subdued in deference to the platform party. They were now reshuffling for the launching, the official kicking of *National Progress* out of the yard with a broken bottle at her head.

A shout from Thomson was the signal for it to begin, for the bottle to be flung, the last stay to be knocked out, the *National Progress* to start moving. Eyes and cameras took her to themselves in a series of nose-to-tail impressions chasing each other with growing rapidity. Everything moved to receive the ship, turbulent water, hovering tugs, draggled sky...and wind.

Now she was cleaving the water...and a scream cleaved the air. The familiar outraged protest of Ian Laurie being prevented from doing what he thought was right and just to himself.

Unnoticed by either parent, he had snaked to the very front of the people on No.800. He laid down his boat, the better to clap and jump to the music of the band as the ship went down the ways. As Paddy had prophesied, there was a second launching, for the wash from the ship flooded the new keel; and swept away his boat.

Ian tried to snatch it back, and was himself snatched by his great-uncle Paddy who, unlike the child's parents, had seen what he was up to. Struggling in mid-air, Ian screamed against the injustice of a world where boats were launched and taken away from you.

It was different with the *National Progress*. Before tugs could control her the wind rushed in, forcing her sideways, slowly, back to the land. With a splintering crack of staging-planks, her stern rammed the stern of the partly finished No.799.

And John Laurie rammed his wife.

Triumphantly, even as the tugs got busy charging and leaping and putting out smoke, he roared at her: 'Of all the bloody rotten mothers. He could easily have been drowned—I suppose that would suit you fine—save you the bother o' lookin' after him. You might as well know it now, you're goin' to Australia, whether you like it or not. I've made up my mind.'

'*You've* made up *your* mind.'

'And you're goin' nowhere near Melbourne, you're goin' to the outback where there's nothin' but sheep and you'll have to pay attention to the kid.' She'd have to be nice to her man too. There'd be no competition but kangaroos and Aborigines.

She laughed in his face and strutted away, still yapping at Ian. 'Shut up, you'll get another boat the very same. Oh, all right, you'll get one o' the big clockwork ones that go round and round the pond,' as if she was already confident of having extra money between her fingers. A few yards away Ginger and the rest of the ring stood grinning, confident too.

Other men, moving slowly back to work, looked at the damaged ship, already on her way down-river for fitting out. 'That'll be a bit o' overtime for somebody, goin' to Greenock to sort her plates.'

Paddy McGuire, staring at the wind-scoured empty berth, said, 'You miss a ship when she's awa'. She kept the draught oot o' the yard.'

'There's others comin' on.' John waved towards the growing No.799 and the embryo No.800.

'And after that?' Paddy as a young man had lived through the hungry thirties, when this and other yards had been a forest of rotting cranes and empty uprights.

They were hard times coming again. You couldn't lift a paper or switch on the telly without getting more bad news. Maybe he'd better take a chance with Ginger and the rest, John thought, for the sake of having a few quid behind him when the crash came.

As if he read the thought, Ginger moved in close to John. 'Look at Thomson messin' his pants for what he'll say to the directors about the bad launchin'.'

'What's he worryin' aboot?' Paddy McGuire, time-pitted hook by which the ring must hang or fall, looked John in the eye. Then he roared above the growing sounds of work re-starting, 'Even the director's ken the wind's like a guid gateman—it'll no' tak' a bung frae anybody!'

THE WOMAN
AND THE WAVES

I woke up crying with the seagulls, but my mother rose and left
me in the dark. She came back cold and wet, telling me to rise,
for my father had gone to sea and there was much to do
before he returned.

My father was known as Venus Peter, after the name of his boat.
He was a kind man and smelled of salt and sunlight. He carried
the sea in his eyes.

When I was older my brother and I helped get my father ready
for the sea. While he was still asleep I ran with Alan to the braes
for armfuls of grass. In the summertime we ran back to the house

with them beneath a roof blue with birdsong. In winter the long grasses were like spears of ice and we pulled them with hands that were on fire, our frosted fingers clutching like lobsters.

Mother laid the grasses in layers between the lines that she coiled into the big baskets, separating them so that they would go down smoothly from my father's hands. Later we learned to shell the mussels ourselves so that we could help with the baiting of the lines.

There were many hooks on a line, a thousand on the biggest one. It had to go down fifty fathoms, my father said, among the mermaids.

'Bait each one carefully, lass,' he told me, 'putting the hard part on last of all. Do it like that all the way down to the last hook. You never know, there might be a big one waiting at the bottom.'

'A big mermaid?' I asked.

'What would I want with a mermaid?' he laughed. 'A cold bosom and no bum to spank.'

'That's enough of that talk,' my grandfather growled from the corner.

My father's blue eyes clouded over and he shook his head.

Grandfather was like an old twist of tobacco with no more softness or fragrance left in him. All day long he sat lip-deep in the black silence of his bible, from which he seldom emerged, except to mend the creels for an hour or two. But he never helped us in the mornings.

'My work,' he said, 'is to carry out God's will.'

So Alan and I buried the mussel shells in the earth at our back door, and carried the lines in the scull between us, down to the boat. My mother was thin-breasted, but when she reached the boat she lifted my father to the side, wearing all his heavy gear, so that his feet would be kept dry.

'A fisherman can't go to sea with wet feet,' she said. 'If your feet are cold the rest of you is the same.'

Then she would hurry home, wet-legged herself to the hips, and dry herself in front of the fire. There was no breakfast to be had though, until grandfather had read to us out of the big bible that he carried over and laid on the table like a black marble slab.

They that go down to the sea in ships, that do business in
great waters;
These see the works of the Lord, and his wonders in the deep.'
For he commandeth and raiseth the stormy wind which
lifteth up the waves thereof.
They mount up to the heaven, they go down again to the
depths: their soul is melted because of trouble.
They reel to and fro, and stagger like a drunken man, and are
at their wit's end.'

My heart bobbed like a cork in my chest as I thought of my father with nothing but a few planks of wood between him and the billowing sea. His longest line reached fifty fathoms under.

'Hush man,' said my mother, 'don't tempt providence.'

A squall rose between the old man's eyes, but he returned to the passage he was reading from, his voice rising in hoarse triumph.

'Then they cry unto the Lord in their trouble, and he bringeth
them out of their distresses.
He maketh the storm a calm, so that the waves thereof are
still.
Then they are glad because they be quiet; so he bringeth
them unto their desired haven.'

We ate in silence after that.

Father shot his lines in the early morning.

While he was away I went down with my mother to the mill stream to gather more mussels. During the winter haddock-fishing we tore them from their tough threads with shredded fingers. My hands went white beneath the freezing water but came out glowing like a peat fire.

One winter mother grew big-bellied.

Like a still sail, she had a fluttering one morning, then day by day she slowly billowed and filled. The sickness, she said, was not a sweet sickness. It was a sourness, not a burgeoning. But the gathering went on for her, with everything else. Mussel bait was scarce and a cartload cost twenty shillings.

When her time came we were among the mussel beds one sore morning. There was a spitting of rain and a bitter breeze was ruffling the rock pools. As if a fishknife had gone through her she folded up with a shriek. Then she unfurled herself on the edge of the sea and gave birth.

I scooped the bait to one side, so as not to lose it, and placed the blue bundle, dripping red, into the scull, covering it with one of mother's ripped petticoats. I was six years old and I had a sister.

I lifted up the big basket. The thin cry that came from it was lost among the hunger of the seagulls. The mouth was a tiny red wound. I carried it home, mother walking by my side as if through heavy seas. By the time we reached home my sister had wept briefly at being born and turned again to the darkness.

Grandfather said that there should be a proper funeral but instead my father paid the sexton a shilling when he came home and went with him to the graveyard after dark.

They put her into the ground without a name. There had been no time. The only baptism she had received was the salt spray that the wind had whipped off the sea in the bleak hour of her birth.

'In any case,' said my father, 'what's the point of a name when you've never done anything?'

Grandfather said that her life would be hidden with God.

After that she was never spoken of again.

For two years, maybe three, I went to school.

The dominie's dark, clouded face came between me and the sunlight.

'What is the chief end of man?'

'The chief end of man is to glorify God and to enjoy Him for ever.'

'Sir.'

Alan left school when he was nine. I stayed till I was ten. When he was fourteen Alan went with father, and later that year they left the Firth of Forth with the fleet, to cast their nets on the Lammas sea.

I watched them leave from the braes.

The harbour was a swaying forest of masts that suddenly uprooted and began to stream out towards the sun. The oars dripped silver, the sails' red cheeks puffed and blew, and the dark fins of the Fifies strung themselves out, hung from the skyline like flags. They were bound for Yarmouth and the lure of the herring.

For eight weeks they were gone from home, their hands hauling on hundreds of miles of nets, landing thousands of cran of living silver. They worked in sunsets and dawns and rising moons, and when they slept at all, they said, they were shooting and hauling in their dreams.

When they came home their teeth flashed as they laid gold sovereigns on the table, Every season my father brought me back presents of glass and china. The plates were always ribbed and fluted, like the sand when the tide has gone out. Shepherd lads kissed milkmaids in a leafy world that was rich with blue and bordered by gold. I was to put these away, piece by piece, my father said, beneath the bed, to save up for my wedding.

By the time I was sixteen I had a complete set.

One season, while the men were away, grandfather turned ill.

He lost his appetite and sat for long hours staring out of the deep windows towards the harbour. The sun filtered dimly through the thick, green glass, bathing his white-bearded face, turning it the colour of the sea, so that he was like a ruined old ship in a bottle.

He seemed to soften as he failed. Some of the warmth of his younger days, that my father had told me of, crept back into him as he slept, and when he awoke, he looked at me with a kindness in his face I had never known. He laid his knotted old bark of a hand on me and smiled.

'How are you feeling today, Grandad?' I asked.

His eyes were drawn again to the windows, as if there were some secret behind them.

'Ah, lass, I'm not long for this earth, I doubt.'

But by the time father and Alan came back from Yarmouth, the old man was anchored to a bed of pain which made him lose all knowledge of us. The thing that spiked him to the bed tore screams from him in the night, and what little food he swallowed was thrust back from him in a black tide of sickness. By day he lay in a trembling sweat, his lips quivering, his eyeballs burning, the ball of his nostrils twitching.

In his dreams he raved from scripture, shouting on God for deliverance.

'O my God, I cry in the daytime but thou hearest not.

I am poured out like water, and all my bones are out of joint; my heart is like wax; it is melted in the midst of my bowels.

Be not thou far from me, O Lord. O my strength, haste thee to help me.'

But he lay for another fortnight after that, burning in a fire that nothing would quench.

I rose to his screams one night. My father was already by his side.

'Father! Father!' he shouted, gripping the flapping hand.

The screaming went on.

I stood in the doorway for a moment, watching him as he blotted himself against the wall in the misery of his helplessness. When he turned round his face was twisted like the devil's. I went to him silently and we stood there, two shadows watching the shadow death do its work on my grandfather.

In the morning the shadow had passed. Grandfather's white beard jutted towards the ceiling. His twisted arms hung out over the bed. They were as thin as ropes, as dry as corks.

'Well,' said my mother, 'he went ready to meet his maker.'

My father said nothing. He raised his arm and slammed his

clenched fist down on grandfather's great bible. Then without a word he suddenly picked it up and walked out of the house with it under his arm. No one dared to follow him. When he came back the bible was missing but the hurt was still in his face.

'I threw it into the harbour,' he said simply.

My mother put her hand to her face.

'He read that thing as if it were a tombstone!' shouted my father. 'And what did it bring him? An animal dies with more dignity than my father died with. It goes dumbly, expecting no mercy.'

That was the longest speech I ever heard him make.

Late that afternoon the elders came to our door in a black vengeful gathering. The chief elder carried grandfather's sodden bible in his arms.

'May you think black burning shame of yourself!' he roared.

'That was an act of dreadful blasphemy. But no more than is to be expected from a man who has never been seen in the kirk for a twelvemonth. The session summons you to answer for it, and offers you your chance to repent.'

Father flashed his anger at them.

'I'll offer you a chance to leave my house without my foot in your holy behind,' he said to the chief elder. 'And don't darken my door again with your kirk faces. The old man did all the preaching that was needed for his family.'

Late that night I heard my father praying.

That winter the *Venus* went down, and only one of her crew came ashore, Adam Reid of Pittenweem.

I no longer had a father.

The elders gloated and hung out his death like a banner from the church walls. For his sins he had been plunged into a watery grave along with all those who had the misfortune to follow him. Only one had been spared as a living witness to God's terrible retribution.

Adam Reid told us what happened.

The *Venus*, he said, had been fishing off Kingsbarns, not far from home, when the wind had suddenly backed and blackened into a gale. They were caught so quickly that they had no time to alter sail, and almost at once the waves became their graveyard.

Adam remembered my father's last words.

The seas came over the gunwhale, he said, like snow-covered mountains, and the men were up to their waists in a welter of water. Then he saw my father clasping his arms round Alan's white face. He heard him shouting his final sentence before the wind carried it off and the sea entered their mouths.

'Don't be frightened, Alan, your father's going with you!'

Then they were buried beneath the waves that became blue again almost as quickly as they had blackened. Even as he sank some floats were wrapped about Adam Reid's neck, and he rose to clutch at a spar and so reach the shore.

I went down with my mother, now so suddenly a widow, to Anstruther harbour, where we found a farm cart standing waiting to carry any recovered corpses home. A black-shawled old woman was cradling the head of her son in her arms, her voice keening like a seagull on the wind.

We waited and waited.

The tide sighed and stretched and the great brown tangles lifted and turned, then disappeared. But no corpses came to give us that coldest of comforts.

When night came we put our arms together, mother and I, and walked wearily home.

Then we sat down and looked at one another across the table.

The sea had turned over once and I had lost my father and brother. It was so simple. Yet it was the hardest thing in the world to alter, and to bear.

For two years the tides came and went for us without a purpose.

No folk of our own fared forth on their darkness; no men came back to us on their floods, laden with the sea's bright bounty. We worked for other men, strangers, gathering mussels from the Eden, near St Andrews, mending the torn nets in the months after the herring season.

Time for us was as dry as our needles of bone that flickered in our vacant fingers. Our movements were without music, joyless as the listless seaweeds waving in the surge. The sea became a weariness.

In the winter of my nineteenth year another weariness entered my mother, a weariness that fed on her blood and drew out her life in the long-drawn darkness of an unheard sigh.

Her passage from life to death was almost imperceptible, like the turning of the tide. One quiet whisper, and she had turned from me, slipped into that invisible strand that always separates the sea and sky.

Her last words to me were that I should waste no time in marrying but be wed as quickly as I could.

I chose John Boyter, a Kingsbarns fisherman who held a cord on my mother's coffin. He asked me for my hand as soon as she was buried.

Our banns were cried at Kingsbarns and the wedding flag was hoisted on his boat the *Olive*. We were married at the manse three Fridays after that. There was a wild surge of drinking and dancing in the big barn.

After midnight the tide of revelry ebbed away, leaving the drinkers cast upon the shores of sleep. The dancers' feet faltered and stilled. We slipped into our new house like two ghosts.

I saw my pieces of china all laid out for me in the corner cupboard, the ones that my father had bought for me, piece by slow piece, at Yarmouth and Lowestoft, by the strength of his hands and the salt strain of his labours on the sea.

The bridal bed had been made up by a woman with milk in her breasts. It lay in the recess like a white calm snowdrift that the slightest touch would sully.

I laid myself down in its coolness and gave up my maidenhead with no mystery. There was neither beauty nor pain. It was as simple as shelling a mussel.

When it was over I lay in the long darkness thinking of my father, still tossing somewhere on the cold green bed of the ocean bottom, hidden by the tumbling coverlets of waves that worried him in whispers. And Alan, bone of his bone, was he still locked in his father's last embrace? Where were they? Without knowing why, I wept in the secret darkness, and for the first time in my life I wondered what my life was.

John took the morning tide on the Monday.

They were fishing for cod that spring, with the great lines and I never saw him for two weeks. When he returned, dead on his feet, he slept for two days and nights in the box bed, hardly stirring when I moved in beside him.

On the Monday the *Olive* went to the other side of the May to look for ling. It was John's turn to stay ashore and take partan bait. He had a bannock and a herring for breakfast and he gave me a cold little kiss with a shyness in it. Then he took out his creels to Caiplie.

When I answered the knock at my door my arms were floury to the elbows. I knew the man standing there. It was Thomas Mathers, a St Monans fisherman. I also knew the look he wore on his face. I had seen it many times before, on the faces of mothers, wives and sisters. It was woven out of the waves.

'I wasn't far from him,' he said. 'I saw it happen.'

Looking over his shoulder I saw a horse and cart, and a man standing by. I knew what thing they had brought me.

'What was it that happened?' my mouth asked him.

'He was shooting his very last creel,' Thomas Mathers said, 'when I saw him pitched overboard by an invisible hand. I got alongside of him as fast as I could, but by that time there was nothing to be done. It was a bonny morning too—a flat calm on the water. I could see him lying there on the bottom just twelve feet below me, with the creel on top of him.

When I got him up I could see what had happened. The messenger rope had twined itself round one of the buttons of his jacket–you oughtn't to wear sea-waistcoats to the creels–and he was dragged over the side by the weight of the pot. It kept him pinned down there till he was drowned.

'I'm very sorry, Mrs Boyter. There was just nothing I could have done in time. It was just one of those things.'

I went outside, stopped a moment before lifting the heavy wetness of the tarpaulin. His eyes were closed and his expression was white. But the tiredness had gone out of his face. I felt a deep sorrow–he was only eighteen. I reached out my hand and touched his cheek. When I drew my hand away, a tiny particle of flour stayed there, from the bread I had been baking for his tea. When I saw this the tears were suddenly torn from me and Thomas Mathers came to comfort me. But it was not John Boyter I was crying for. It was all men with the sea in their mouths, and all the women who lost them to the waves.

Was this my husband? That tiny dusting of flour was all he had of me. His breath had barely brushed against mine.

My fragrance remained shut up.

It was Davy Keay who made me open like a flower.

I remembered his coal-black curls and his white flashing teeth from school. But after three years on my father's boat he had left Fife and gone with the Dundee whaling vessels. I could still see him saying his goodbye to Alan.

'I'm bound for Orkney,' he said, 'and the Davis Straits.'

Then he had pulled my hair and laughed.

I had eaten the bitter bread of widowhood for two years when Davy Keay came back one autumn and saw me sitting among the herring nets. He sat down on the black bundles beside me and put his head on one side.

'How much do you earn for that, my bonny lass?' he asked me.

'Sixpence a day,' I said, 'if I work all day at it.'

'That's a long day and a slow sixpence,' he said. 'Why do you do it?'

'I've little choice,' I told him simply.

'I'll give you a choice,' he said. 'Are there men around here too blind to offer you one?'

I looked at him.

He dipped into his deep blue pockets and brought out a handful of foreign gold. The coins burned in his palm like the suns of strange countries. He had been among mermaids and monks and winters and whales such as I had scarcely dreamed of. I had never seen further than the lights of the Lothians across the Forth, like fallen stars at midnight. Now this man was telling me of the secrets that lay behind the horizon's brow, and I was telling him that I would marry him,

We flowed into one another with long fulfilment, he into the quiet harbour of my arms, I into the running tide of his strange coming, a mingling of milk and honey, of sweetness and salt. Above us the stars blew their silver trumpets and no one heard them on the earth except ourselves.

Davy said he would do one last season at the whales, enough to earn the gold for a boat of his own. Then he would come back for good, to hug the waters of home, he said—and me.

All the way up to Dundee the bare brown fields were stirring in their sleep, under the covering of the sun. The day was golden blue when I watched him board the *Thomas* with James Bowman of Arncroach who had travelled up with us. The two of them shouted and waved to me from the topsail yard as the ship bore out to sea.

I waited a year and a half.

But I never saw Davy again and the *Thomas* never came back to port.

I was down among the mussel beds one fine harvest morning when a hand touched my shoulder. I glanced up. It looked like the ghost of James Bowman. His paleness took the sun out of the morning. But neither he nor I moved while he told me what there was to tell.

This is what he had to say.

'There was only once between Stromness and Baffin's Bay that we heard the old cry, 'All hands shorten sail!' The Atlantic was like a mirror. It was an easy run.

And we took whales like herring. I've never seen anything like it–we thought ourselves as rich as kings. The oil shone in the hold and the whalebone was stacked like ivory.

We were hardly into September when the winter came in.

It was just like a great white hand that suddenly clenched one day, and there we were in its fist. We asked the captain to steer for the south but it was no good. The ice had shackled us in. The bergs were like white fortresses barring our way.

Then the cold really clamped down on us.

The whole ship was just like an iceberg itself, hewn in the rough shape of a vessel. The water casks were lumps of ice, even our bunks were solid ice, and when we rose in the mornings we had to tear our heads away–the very hairs were frozen onto the pillows.

The only fires we knew were the fevers that made us rage, and the vermin that ate like flames into our flesh. There was scurvy and asthma–some of the men just stopped breathing. It was like breathing crushed ice into your lungs, and some of us simply couldn't take any more.

God and I alone know what else there was. Some men's gums became so black that their teeth just fell out. One man died of a wound he'd had ten years ago. It just broke out afresh and wouldn't heal. Our oldest harpooner had had a fractured leg in his twenties. It had been knitted for over forty years but it had to be reset. Others just died of cold, and a terrible death that was. There were some of the men suffered convulsions so bad that their knees and chins were locked together when they died and their frozen bodies were as round as mill-wheels.

As often as six times a day the white funeral processions could be seen staggering with their strangely shaped burdens to the nearest hole in the ice. That's how Davy was buried, Mrs Keay. I thought you would like to know that I helped to bury him myself. He died one night in his sleep and he thought he was with you all the time. Believe me, it was a merciful death.

It was on Christmas Day that the ship was lost.

All round us there was the howling of the wind and the grinding of the icebergs. Then there was a terrible screeching sound. I thought it was some terrible monster at first but everybody ran to the side shouting that the ship was stove in. The timbers were splintering under the squeeze of the ice.

Those that could move jumped onto the blocks that were killing us, and they became our last hope. A few of us that could still walk started the long trek to where we hoped there might be some other ships of the fleet.

I don't know, but I don't think anyone made it to a ship but myself. I stayed alive two days and nights out on the ice in time to reach the *Norfolk* before she got clear and bore away for home. That was in the middle of February. The fleet had been shut in for over five months.

When I got back to Anster I was reduced from twelve stones to seven. You can see what I am like. But at least I made it home. I'm sorry for all the rest of the crews, and especially about Davy, Mrs Keay. He was my best friend on board and you were all he thought about out there. He thought about you all the time.'

And for many years after that, all I thought about was the lad that had waved to me from the topsail yard, though in my dreams about that stilled young heart, lying so many frozen fathoms deep in the Polar seas, the iceberg the only monument that lay upon his grave. And my heart would grow cold for sorrow.

When I was thirty years old I married an Anstruther skipper called William Brown. He was ten years my senior and a good man, an elder of the kirk. In his house the pages of the bible turned like the quiet waters, He had his own boat. It was called the H*elen*.

To William Brown I bore six children and of these five died in infancy.

We called our first child Helen, after the name of William's boat. Hers was a frail little vessel. She sickened from the day she was born, and died aged three months.

Three years later we had a son. He was named William, after his father. But he never lived to sail with him. He had just taken his first step at fourteen months when he caught a cold which put him to bed the very day after he had learned to walk. He never got up to walk again. The cold worsened and he coughed his way into an early grave.

Two months before William died, Catherine and Elizabeth came together, two buds on the same stalk. When Catherine was one year old consumption planted its bright red roses on her cheeks and its lilies on her brow. She withered and drooped and we lost her to the earth.

She had been dead two years when Elizabeth had a sister. Grace was just one year and a half when she died. The invisible flames that burned in her head spread unseen to Elizabeth. The sexton had barely replaced the scarred turf on the little one's grave when he had to wound the earth again, for her sister.

William bought a stone and had it erected in the kirkyard, to mark their graves. It had all their names and dates carved on it, and at the bottom a little verse which William had written himself. It read:

> These lovely buds so young and fair
> Called hence by early doom
> Just come to show how sweet those flowers
> In Paradise would bloom.

I never though to lay any more children in the kirkyard after that.

Six months later David was born, and he grew strong. But he breasted the years only to sink with his father. He was a lad of twenty by then, and William's hair was like the foam on the sea.

This was how it happened.

It was a fine March morning when the two of them left the house for the last time, and there was nothing in the eye of the weather to warn me that a squall was coming. I just sat down in my chair in one suffocating moment. The salt sea was streaming through my veins and my hair lifted. Quickly I left the house and walked down to the harbour.

Even then all was well in the world of men.

A breathless silence. And the wide spirallings of seagulls were the only movements on the face of things. Boat and bird wove their woof against the warp of sea and sky, spinning the white wool of surf and cloud.

Then the clouds began to darken.

Suddenly Spring shook the sea's carillon of bells until they were jangled and harsh and out of tune. Rain flicked its wet stinging whiplashes about my face. The wind ripped open the sea, which bled in a white welter, tore the gulls out of their calm orbits and sent them wheeling and heeling off into space. The boats began to turn for home.

One by one they were whipped to the shore.

We stood and watched them, hooded and drawn, a black huddle of seabirds motionless on the rocks. And as each boat came in several figures detached themselves from the group and ran to meet the men, skirts flapping wildly in the wind, shawls fluttering from their heads.

Soon I was left alone, with the single handful of women who were waiting for the *Helen*. We waited and waited, while the sea stampeded like a mad white bull, plunging and roaring.

Then we saw her, and the shout went up.

But even as we shouted we saw the white forest that was flowering round her stem. Over the gunwhales it grew, and over the dark figures huddled on board.

Then there was nothing.

The white forest had withered and the figures were somewhere beneath its ruin, tight in the clutch of those unseen roots that wind to the sea's bottom. A long cry went up from the shore.

It was the oldest cry in the world.

The bodies were long in coming to the shore.

When the men called me down to the rocks I knew that it would be for David. I came as they were lifting him from the boat to the pier. The sea slurped out of his pockets and ran from his hair. As they laid him at my feet and I looked at his body dripping there on the stones, I felt a strange peace wash over me. What was there to grieve about? He was one last child to put to his bed. My husband's body was never recovered.

Over my head I pulled the black shawl of years.

But for ten seasons after that, I went with the fisher girls on the path of the herring.

For seven summers I worked in Lerwick, and for three in Stornoway. Then I came down to the Isle of Man. By the end of every autumn I had reached Yarmouth, where my father had fished years and years ago.

That was ten years of cut hands and freezing feet, the gutting troughs by day and a hard cold bed by night. The young girls beside me lay and dreamed of their fisher lads, and marriages in the morning. I reached out my arms to the darkness. There was hunger in my belly and rain in my hair. But I did not know what else to do.

At the end of the tenth season I was seventy.

By then I was nearly blind, and my hands were so crippled I was cutting them oftener than the fish.

I turned again in age to the rocks of my childhood.

I am now a very old woman, knowing only white hairs and a dark roof.

The ashes are quiet in my black grate. The hearth, once the heart of my house, lies withered on its stalk. It no longer warms me with its red beating. The seagulls have deserted my cold chimney.

But that was long ago.

Sometimes I can earn a painful penny mending nets. At other times I gather limpets. If I cannot sell them for fishbait I eat them myself. One lonely meal is as good as another when you reach my age.

Some summers I walk to the silent green breaker of the graveyard. Winter turns it to a white frozen wave. But I am still waiting for the winter that will take me there, to lie beside my children.

Why am I so old?

At nights I dream of those other folk of mine that lie hidden in the sea. There are whelks on their hands and seaweeds in their hair. And the cold green fingers of the waves strum over their bones.

Or I hirple down to the pier and look over the harbour wall. I stand there for hours sometimes, thinking of their bonny heads still tossing with the turning tangles, out there somewhere. Sometimes I see them.

All I have loved is turned to coral and to kirkyard clay. Ah, the weariness of time and sea! They have taken from me everything I had, and left me an old empty shell. And yet, time and the sea are all I have ever known.

Death, as I approach it, is the wash of the waves inside my skull.

NAVIGATOR

The Cutty Sark shut at three and we moved on.

Once I've paid up my house, I said, you'll not catch me offshore. I'll jack that in and never go near the fucking sea.

It wouldn't be so bad if you could move around a bit, said Finn. Follow the fucking sun, ken. It's just being stuck in the one place that's the bastard.

I started to cross the road, then walked on. Ach, it's just the seaman's mission. I thought it was a bar.

I'm going to get myself a boat, said Finn. One with a bed and a wee cooker and everything. That's the fucking ticket. Then head off into the wild blue yonder; point the nose of the thing for the equator and cheerio!

Where the fuck's that pub from last time? I said. What's it called? The Schooner...

Finn pushed open a shop door. Quick, in here...

I followed him. There were ropes and buoys on the floor, lifejackets and flares and compasses on shelves, and maps of the sea on the walls.

I want some of those, said Finn.

Charts? said the guy behind the counter.

Aye.

Where of?

The Sargasso Sea, said Finn. Zanzibar, North-west Iceland, Honolulu, the Great Barrier Reef, Van Dieman's Land, the Amazon Basin, Timbuktu, Montego Bay...

We only stock British coastal charts, said the guy.

What!

The guy shrugged. Sorry.

Shit...Finn leant his hands on the counter, his head hanging down. He seemed to be away to burst out greeting.

I gave him a clap on the shoulder. Never mind, I said, then turned to the shopkeeper. Could you tell us how to get to the Schooner Bar? I said.

ACKNOWLEDGEMENTS

Thanks to many people who helped me in various ways while I was compiling this anthology:
to David Bruce, John Burns, Willie Donaldson, Douglas Dunn, Bill Findlay, Hamish Henderson, Robert Alan Jamieson, Dougie Lindsay, Iain MacAlister, Alan Riach, Iain Crichton Smith, Gavin Wallace for suggestions about possible material to include or about where to look for material;
to Cate Trend for helping me with the difficult decisions and for putting up with my distractedness and books and photocopies all over the floor for ages;
to Marion Sinclair and Jeannie Scott for all the things that publishers do.

Needless to say, none of them are in any way responsible for whatever shortcomings the book might have.

The stories came from the following books. The editor and publisher gratefully acknowledge the permission of the copyright holders listed to reprint copyright material.

BLAKE, George; *Rest and be Thankful*, Porpoise Press, 1934.
By permission of Faber and Faber Ltd.

BONE, David W.; *The Brassbounder*, Duckworth & Co Ltd, 1910.
By permission of Duckworth & Co Ltd.

BOSWELL, James; *Journal of a Tour of the Hebrides*, London, 1786.

BROWN, George Mackay; *A Calendar of Love*, Hogarth Press, 1967. By permission of John Murray Ltd.

BUCHAN, John; *The Watcher by the Threshold*, Blackwood, 1902.

CUNNINGHAME GRAHAM, R.B.; *Rodeo*, Heinemann, 1936.

DRUMMOND,Cherry; *The Remarkable Life of Victoria Drummond: Marine Engineer*, Institute of Marine Engineers, 1994.
By permission of the Institute of Marine Engineers.

GAITENS, Edward; *Growing Up and Other Stories,* Jonathan Cape, 1942. Unable to locate copyright holder.

GALT, John; *The Provost,* Blackwood, 1822.

GUNN, Neil M.; *Highland Pack,* Faber, 1949. By permission of Chambers Harrap Ltd.

HAMILTON, Margaret; *The Other Voice: Scottish Writing Since 1808,* Polygon, 1987.

HAY, John MacDougall; *Gillespie,* Constable, 1914.

MUNRO, Neil; *Para Handy and Other Tales,* Blackwood, 1931.

LINKLATER, Eric; *The New Penguin Book of Scottish Short Stories,* 1983. By permission of the Peters, Fraser & Dunlop Group Ltd.

McLEAN, Duncan; *Looking for the Spark: Scottish Short Stories 1994,* Harper Collins, 1994. By permission of the author.

PATERSON, Neil; *The China Run,* Hodder & Stoughton, 1948. By permission of Mrs Rose Paterson.

ROBERTSON, R. MacDonald; *Selected Highland Folk Tales,* Oliver & Boyd, 1961. By permission of House of Lochar.

RUSH, Christopher; *Peace Comes Dropping Slow,* Ramsay Head Press, 1983. By permission of the author.

SCOTT, Michael; *Tom Cringle's Log,* Blackwood, 1833.

SCOTT, Walter; *The Antiquary,* Constable, 1816.

SMOLLETT, Tobias; *Roderick Random,* London, 1748.

STEVENSON, R. L.; *Across the Plains,* Scribners, (New York), 1892.